WITHDRAWN

The Girl
Who Would
Speak for
the Dead

The Girl
Who Would
Speak for
the Dead

PAUL ELWORK

AMY EINHORN BOOKS
Published by G. P. Putnam's Sons
a member of Penguin Group (USA) Inc.
New York

æ

AMY EINHORN BOOKS
Published by G. P. Putnam's Sons
Publishers Since 1838
Published by the Penguin Group
Penguin Group (USA) Inc., 375 Hudson Street, New York, New York 10014,
USA • Penguin Group (Canada), 90 Eglinton Avenue East, Suite 700, Toronto,
Ontario M4P 2Y3, Canada (a division of Pearson Penguin Canada Inc.) • Penguin
Books Ltd, 80 Strand, London WC2R 0RL, England • Penguin Ireland,
25 St Stephen's Green, Dublin 2, Ireland (a division of Penguin Books Ltd) • Penguin Group
(Australia), 250 Camberwell Road, Camberwell, Victoria 3124, Australia
(a division of Pearson Australia Group Pty Ltd) • Penguin Books India Pvt Ltd,
11 Community Centre, Panchsheel Park, New Delhi–110 017, India • Penguin Group
(NZ), 67 Apollo Drive, Rosedale, North Shore 0632, New Zealand (a division of
Pearson New Zealand Ltd) • Penguin Books (South Africa) (Pty) Ltd,
24 Sturdee Avenue, Rosebank, Johannesburg 2196, South Africa

Penguin Books Ltd, Registered Offices: 80 Strand, London WC2R 0RL, England

This novel is an expanded version of *The Tea House*, originally
published in 2007 by Casperian Books LLC, Sacramento, California.

Library of Congress Cataloging-in-Publication Data

Elwork, Paul.
The girl who would speak for the dead / Paul Elwork.
p.   cm.
Expanded version of The tea house.
ISBN 978-0-399-15717-2
1. Brothers and sisters—Fiction.   2. Twins—Fiction.   3. Spiritualism—Fiction.   4. Family
secrets—Fiction.   5. Nineteen twenties—Fiction.   I. Elwork, Paul. Tea house.   II. Title.
PS3605.L85G57   2011   2010044996
813'.6—dc22

Printed in the United States of America
1   3   5   7   9   10   8   6   4   2

Book design by Meighan Cavanaugh

For my sons,

Elias and Gabriel

AUTHOR'S NOTE

Anyone familiar with the birth of the Spiritualist movement in the mid–nineteenth century will recognize the story of the Fox sisters as the inspiration of this novel. And anyone who recognizes the Fox sisters floating behind the narrative will also see the flaw in the novel's attempt to mimic historical reality (such as it is)—namely, that the occult-minded people in this book, who would certainly be familiar with the sisters from upstate New York, treat the Stewart twins as a new and exciting phenomenon. For this indiscretion, I ask the reader's forgiveness and a suspension of disbelief. History suggested the novel's basis and theme; its specific events and characters are the responsibility of my own imagination.

In that far off sweet forever,
Just beyond the shining river,
When they ring the golden bells for you and me.

DANIEL DE MARBELLE

Did you ever think as the hearse rolls by
That some of these days you must surely die?

WORLD WAR I HEARSE SONG

PART ONE

1.

June 1925

THE GIRL WHO WOULD SPEAK FOR THE DEAD STOOD ALONE on the cobblestone drive after the rain.

Body poised, she balanced on one broad stone, her arms to either side, her bare toes clutching the cool, pitted surface. The polished stones all around her glowed in the soft daylight. She gathered herself together and continued jumping from one cobblestone to another, moving toward the little redbrick house just off the curve of the drive; moving away from the towering white house and its black-framed windows behind her. The girl, slight and short, had a spring in her arms and legs that made her appear a few years younger than her age. Landing on each stone, she felt her toes slip and her heels slide before catching and holding. As she regained her balance, the girl grinned and waved her arms. She bent at the knees, hunched her shoulders, and launched herself again. When she landed on the next stone, she had to quickly crouch to keep herself from being carried off her perch.

The girl had been thirteen years old for three days. Her brother had turned thirteen with her, but having already developed a certain cynicism toward birthdays, he did not share her enthusiasm. This difference was not the only one between them. They looked more like cousins than twins, or even brother and sister.

On the morning of her birthday, the twenty-third of June, the girl had gone to the sunporch where her mother always drank coffee. Her mother sat at the breakfast table with Mary, the last of the live-in help at the Ravenwood mansion. Her mother's long dark hair, wound up in a loose bun, looked about to spill down her long neck. In her thin pale fingers, the girl's mother cradled her cup against her chest, as if huddled around its warmth. Mary was in her fifties and had a round face the color of polished chestnut. When Mary asked a question, her even tone gave the girl the impression that the question had been asked not once but twice—the second time, slowly, in a somewhat louder voice.

Mary noticed the girl's entrance first. "Look who went to bed a little girl and woke up a young woman."

The girl's mother turned from the window and the Delaware River beyond. "Good morning, Emily," she said. "Happy birthday."

"Thank you, Mama."

"Sit down with us, Em," Mary said.

"But get yourself a cup first," Emily's mother said.

"A cup?" Emily asked. "Of coffee?"

"There's no tea in the kitchen," Mary said, her eyes gleaming through the steam rising from her cup. Up until that morning, any interest Emily showed in her mother's coffee had been met with a careless and absolute refusal. "Everything in its time," her mother liked to say.

When Emily returned with her coffee and took the seat beside her mother, Mary said, "Cream and sugar?"

"Yes, please." Emily did not know how she liked her coffee, or if she liked it at all, but both Mary and her mother took cream and sugar.

"Two spoonfuls?" Mary asked, opening the sugar dish.

"Yes, please."

Emily lifted the cup to her lips.

"Careful," her mother said. "Hot." She watched Emily with a languid intensity that sometimes made strangers nervous. Even her neighbors didn't know what to make of the young widow in the big house on the river, mistress of the estate that had known such great social events in the past, so quiet now and for some time. Mary had been part of staging many of those old celebrations, knew what was expected and admired, and had long ago given up on encouraging Emily's mother to open up the doors at Ravenwood for more than just the odd, occasional guest.

"Here's to a long life, Emily Stewart," Mary said.

Emily's mother lifted her own cup, and the three of them sipped their coffee. Emily's eyes widened as the flavor of the beans, sugar, and cream washed over her tongue in bittersweet softness.

"It's a great pleasure of life, Em," Mrs. Stewart said, "to sit here and drink coffee." She took a sip from her cup and her gaze dislocated itself from Emily's eyes. "Go tell your brother to lift his gloomy head and come get his cup."

Now, three days later on the cobblestones after the rain, Emily leaped to an odd, protruding stone along the side of the drive, almost falling in the little stream of water hurrying down the concrete gutter toward the gate. Emily turned on her toes and jumped back up the drive, taking a zigzagging course from stone to stone: *I may fall, I may fall, I may fall.* The fresh smell after the rain somehow made Emily think of her father reading some book or other on the porch, his features mildly concentrating on the words within. Emily had only been six years old when her father left for France and the War, only to become a stone among rows of stones when returned home. The Japanese dogwood trees he'd planted along a short path from the house to the river stood for him at the estate, particularly in the glowing spring when they burst with soft red flowers. His books, lined up on the shelves in the library, seemed to belong to the same world he had. The marble sundial and birdbath he'd placed out on the open lawn, ringed by trees at a distance on all sides, looking dutiful in its lonely glory when empty or filled with rain, and somehow ridiculous when birds flapped and splashed in its bowl. He had requested a verse from Omar Khayyám on the rim: *The Bird of Time has but a little way to flutter—and the bird is on the wing.*

Emily's memories of him resembled snapshots taken on a sunny afternoon (a look, a pose, a gesture), but these snapshots were slow in fading away—they drifted up into focus when something like the smell of rain or light on a windowsill stirred them. She thought of him often but hardly spoke of him. She felt sure the same was true for her mother and Michael, sometimes when all three sat in a room without speaking, sharing the quiet of his great absence.

Emily stepped off the drive and went toward the river until the trees shrouded the house from her. She stood on the bank and wiggled her toes in the wet grass, watching the geese circling each other in the current. She moved a small muscle in the place where her foot met her ankle, and the muscle touched a tendon, and the tendon a small bone, and a dull crack arose around her. Her foot never appeared to move. She could almost see the sharp, sudden noise float up over her head, something like a feather, if feathers were only so many scattered reverberations. She had discovered this ability only a week before while lying in bed and had fascinated herself with the trick since, studying its tones and sensations. Emily found that if she concentrated, she could make the cracks from her ankle a little louder, slightly clearer, more insistent. She reserved the trick for her times alone on the riverbank, for her quiet moments in bed or the bathtub, for her isolated hours in the little redbrick house—the former garden house, made a playhouse during Mrs. Stewart's childhood. The little house that Mary had begun to call the tea house when Mrs. Stewart took her dolls and toy cups there, years before. Sun-drenched images for Emily, believable and somehow difficult to grasp, fragments of other people's lives.

Each day she thought of sharing the trick with Michael, and each time thought, *Not yet.* Such a strange thing seemed connected to all the mystery in the world, to unknowable secrets. Emily breathed the cool river wind and worked the muscles in her ankle, making a series of cracks, trying to create a rhythm. She squeezed her eyes closed and listened to the sounds spring from her and dissipate in the air all around—arresting and somehow mystical, then gone as if each one had never been.

2.

MICHAEL

THE FOLLOWING AFTERNOON, EMILY'S BROTHER SAT IN THE shadow of an oak tree beside the river, his skinny legs stretched out in the grass before him. His gray eyes looked out at the water, and small locks of light brown hair blew across his pale forehead.

Emily approached her brother, watching to see if he noticed her. This was an old game of theirs. The game had no name, but a good one might have been Hello, Unsuspecting Stranger, something their mother sometimes said when catching them unaware.

"Michael?" Emily said, arriving at his side.

"Yes, Em?" Michael said, as if he had been expecting her for some time.

"Alone again, I see."

"You caught me."

Before his tenth birthday, Michael had discovered that he could not tolerate most people well, and had already developed the habit of speaking in condescending tones. He tended toward a suspicious, dismal nature, but he smiled when others laughed at his clever remarks. He had a fascination for details that emerged unpredictably and fastened itself from one thing to another. Michael had pored over the histories of world exploration, memorizing the perils the conquistadors faced at sea and in landing their vessels, but seemed to lose interest when Cortes and Pizarro brought their soldiers on shore to claim the jungle. He had carried a copy of H. G. Wells's *The Time Machine* around like a biblical scholar and seemed to think that such a journey was worth facing a few subterranean cannibals—until forgetting the book out in the rain on the riverbank. He had tossed aside the history of locomotive power for the succinct and prolonged ticks on a telegraph line that spelled out Morse code, without a backward glance.

"What are you doing, Michael?"

"Thinking."

She sat down in the grass beside him.

"You'll get grass stains on your skirt," he said.

The sun was beginning to set. The insects had started their slow evening incantations. On the river, a pink ribbon from the horizon rippled and spread against the current, borrowing some of the failing light streaming from the sky behind them.

"What are you thinking about with your big brain, Michael?" Emily asked.

"I was thinking about heaven." He paused. "Suppose, just for a moment, that there is no heaven. Suppose that heaven is a place people made up."

"Of course there's a heaven," Emily said.

"I know . . . but suppose just for a moment that there *isn't*. Have you ever tried that?"

The thought had crossed her mind, once or twice. "No," she said. "What got you thinking of all this?"

"Good question," he said. "Do you want to know what else I was thinking? I was thinking about death. About me dying, you know, us dying."

"You are the only thirteen-year-old boy who sits around thinking about death, Michael," she said. It seemed to her something their mother might say.

"What if heaven is just a place people made up?" He paused. "What if Daddy . . . what if he's just—"

"He is in heaven," she said.

"Don't get mad, Em."

"I'm not mad," she said. "Just don't talk like that. I don't want to hear any more."

"But if nobody died there would be no need for heaven, Em. I mean, for people to talk about heaven."

"That's what you think?" Emily said.

"I think so. Only dead people need heaven."

"What do you think Mama would say about all this?"

Michael half shrugged. His relationship with their mother had always seemed strange to Emily. In the evenings, sometimes, Michael and his mother had discussions in the parlor about the neighborhood or school, and when Emily caught some of these conversations it seemed to her that they talked like an old married couple. Michael often got up from his chair and put himself at a distance from others in the room, standing by a window or examining things on a shelf. At these moments, Emily was sure that if Michael could vanish at will and be suddenly far away, then watching him squint at a familiar vase might be the last thing she'd see him do before he disappeared into a life neither of them could imagine, some place where the quiet order of every day didn't seem so preordained, some place with things at stake that he hadn't even begun to take seriously. Their mother was never quick to draw Michael back from these sudden, remote breaks.

Michael knew that Emily would never betray their discussion to their mother. "All right," he said. "You asked what I was thinking."

"So now you don't believe in heaven, Michael? Is that it?" She felt as if she had been duped into a conversation about her father lying in a box underground.

"I didn't say that, Em." He lazily folded his hands on his chest. "I was just thinking. Maybe it was something I ate."

Emily rose, turned, and went back toward the house. The deepening sunset caught in high corners of the mansion's third-floor windows and on the still upper branches of the trees. Twilight already crowded the redbrick house down the drive, lending a blue tint to its green shutters and a misty cast over its roof and steeple.

3.

GOBLİNS

EMILY STROLLED ALONG THE STREET OUTSIDE THE GATE IN the bright sunshine. It was Wednesday afternoon. The narrow road outside the estate and the perpendicular streets connected to it made a dusty, bare, cross-cut rectangle lined with trees—a drowsy and secluded resort town of the last century that suggested nothing of the larger paved roads and sidewalks nearby. Other old summer estates, hotels, and a former casino in the neighborhood stood hardly changed from a time when wealthy families came here to escape the city heat and bustle, before automobiles shrank the distance to the New Jersey shore. Now the residents stayed year-round and most of the summer tourists fled farther from the city. The place had an abandoned, off-season feel even in late June.

Emily and Michael had been sent on a break by their tutor— Mr. Holt—whom their mother hired to keep them involved in studies on Wednesdays during summer vacation. Mr. Holt relished these twenty-minute breaks, and all breaks, by smoking a cigarette or two, sometimes humming or whistling a tune to himself.

Emily made her way to the far end of the estate and passed through the west gate, following the winding path over the rolling lawn and through clusters of trees along the fence, beside the river, and in irregular bursts across Ravenwood. She saw the groundhog that roamed the estate emerge from a hole tucked in the thick and wildly outgrown roots of a maple tree. She sometimes glimpsed it through a window or at a farther distance, waddling comfortably in its suspicions and nervous as a squirrel at the smallest change. The groundhog shook off its subterranean thoughts and looked ready to venture across the grounds, until it caught sight of Emily, more than a hundred feet away, and slipped back into its hole—a vanishing blur, certain above all else that extreme caution was the only available option. Emily wished the groundhog luck on its next attempt.

She reached the river to find Michael sitting under his accustomed tree. She sat beside him. "We should have a dog," she said.

"Mama doesn't like dogs."

"Don't you like dogs?"

"That is not the question."

"How can someone not like dogs?"

"I like dogs fine," he said. "Mama doesn't."

Somewhere on the other side of the house, Mr. Holt whistled a short and sweet pastoral strain, like the song of a strange bird with a long memory.

"Do you believe in ghosts?" Michael asked.

She considered. It seemed to Emily that she would be expected to say no, perhaps adding that ghosts were for little children to believe in. "Sometimes."

"At night?"

"Yes."

"It's easy to believe in ghosts at night," Michael said. "Of course there aren't supposed to be ghosts, or bogeymen, or goblins, or any of that, are there? Not really—only in stories. But if you look out of the window at night, there are goblins out in the trees, lots of them, and you can almost hear them."

They looked out over the river, almost listening to the goblins.

"I think about ghosts sometimes," Michael said. "Lots of times."

"You *are* a ghost," Emily said.

"I think about them," he said, ignoring her remark, "and sometimes I believe in them. I was thinking that this place is perfect for ghosts."

Emily had always thought the mansion ideal for all kinds of night creatures. She recalled the old family pictures on the walls and shelves inside; she thought of her great-aunt Regina, who had died by the river at the age of sixteen, who was remembered for having spells and falling down staircases. In one photograph taken in the sunporch, Regina looked almost puzzled and barely interested, and yet her dark eyes and uncertain mouth seemed to tell of things she couldn't know on that day in the sunporch, things to come, as faces in old photos often do. Their grandparents, their great-grandparents, had all died here. Their mother's older brother, Michael, who had simply disappeared out of the family history one day years before—their lost uncle, whom Mrs. Stewart had offered her son as a namesake and never spoke of. Their father.

Emily said, "I thought you didn't believe that dead people—"

"Never mind that. I'm just talking. Can't you just see them out by the river? Out in the trees?"

"In the house," she said, her mind passing out of the shadow of the mansion and moving toward the old garden house. "The tea house."

"I had a dream last night," Michael said. "About a ghost. I wake up in the house, and I'm sitting in the living room. And there's lots of moonlight coming through the windows. I'm there alone, and then I'm floating around the room—everything is so quiet, and I know you and Mama aren't there, Mary isn't there, but Daddy is there. I didn't actually see him, but I knew he was there. It was as if he were the walls and floors and moonlight all at once, and I was floating around on his voice."

"Do you remember his voice?" She sometimes believed that her father's voice was clear in her memory, but at other moments felt a dread that her memory only fashioned odd fragments together over time into some new voice that wasn't her father's at all.

"No," he said. "I don't think so. But in the dream it was his voice. You know?"

"Yes. What did he say?"

"I can't remember. But it was something about everything."

Mr. Holt's whistle approached from up the riverbank. Soon he would step out onto the porch. The twins made no effort to return to their studies, though they both knew he would come to collect them in a few moments. The fragile, lilting tune moved away, around the corner of the house and out of hearing.

That night, Emily dreamed she stood outside the house in bright moonlight. She walked down the drive, past the tea house and into the shadows among the trees, expecting to hear something slow and haunting, something the boughs of the trees might sway to, something like music.

In the darkness she could hear a company of goblins laughing and calling to each other, goblins made up of moonbeams and rotting leaves. She saw them jumping among the branches and darkened trunks all around her. It was a celebration—they were expecting her. But she was afraid. The goblins moved too quickly to be seen straight on; she could only sense their forms out of the corners of her eyes. The goblins sang a song that was not quite words but still somehow contained her name. The goblins sang, *"Em-i-ly . . . Em-i-ly . . . Em-i-leeeeeeeeeeeee . . ."*

4.

THE GHOST OF REGINA WARD

A DUSTY SILVER PATCH OF MOONLIGHT LAY ACROSS EMILY'S bed when she opened her eyes. The clock on the stairwell landing ticked heavily in the stillness of the house. Her awakening mind followed the sound downstairs, where she found the moonlight making the seams in the floorboards black and bottomless; making the doorways yawning caverns and the staircases irregular, treacherous, and secretive; making the andirons in the fireplace appear as pointed, barely concealed teeth. On the wall, the dim photographs of the family—of the generations of Ravenwood—hung as faint suggestions of personality in the depths of picture frames. She lay in bed and blinked at the ceiling.

Getting up, Emily walked on bare feet out into the hall. She cocked her head and listened again, concentrating on the dream she had awakened from, of goblins in the trees—the dream already beginning to dissolve as she stood in the dark hall. On the stairs, the clock ticked.

A half-formed thought of the safety of her bedsheets held Emily in the doorway, and was joined by another to remind her that in the forests of her sleep, goblins danced. And so because she did not want to reenter a forest full of dancing goblins, and because the clock ticked so loudly, and because she was not quite far enough removed from sleep to make any decisions better than a drifting sort of acquiescence, Emily did not return to bed. But the goblins in the forest had already made the night theirs, and Emily's wakefulness lingered close to dreaming.

She turned toward the top of the stairs, and in the hallway of her own imagining (very similar to the hallway that stretched before her) she saw the ascending figure of a girl in a white nightgown like her own, a girl a few years older, whose hair caught the moonlight and shone in a luminous mass around the absence of a face. Emily recognized the faceless girl—she saw in the unseen face the girl from the photograph taken on the sunporch. *Regina.* A pleasurable chill crawled over her scalp and along her legs. The girl at the stairs took a step forward, her delicate foot silent on the hardwood floor.

Emily turned from the girl and looked down the hall away from the stairs at the open door to Michael's room. She watched Regina approach her from behind in her mind's eye, watched the girl move with the same intent observation and pass into her, changing her flesh into something translucent, the memory of flesh. Emily moved toward Michael's room, her fear of the shadows and the dead gone, as she had become the ghost and ruled the night. She entered Michael's room on weightless feet and crossed to the windows on the other side of his bed. The woods appeared beautiful and dark and welcoming from this height. In the groves beyond the footpaths, the goblins would be preparing to receive their queen.

As she turned to her sleeping brother, Emily felt a strange pity for this defenseless mortal creature. She slipped into the corner by the windows and curled up, arms folded over her knees, knees to her chest. Her passing whims had coalesced into an inspiration. After a moment, a soft cracking noise like knuckles rapping on the air rattled the quiet. Sets of two and three sounds followed—tentative, almost random. A series of single, double, and triple knocks echoed in the dark bedroom like short and certain sentences.

A creak came from Michael's bed, then a brief rustle.

Emily wondered if he could see her and waited. He made no sound; he did not lie back down. Another knock rose from the shadows, and he cocked his head to one side. Again Emily fought the urge to laugh. She released a few more measured knocks. The air shook with the deliberate presence of the sounds—they rebounded from the walls and gathered just above the bed, just above his head. His vulnerable form, rigid and stricken, crouched alone in the dark. But not *really* alone, and he knew it.

A single knock, speculative, provoking, as full of purpose and meaning as any of the patterned breaks had been. And from the corner, a small, furtive creak.

Michael's head turned toward the sound. The light from the window illuminated a path on the floor and made the darkness of Emily's spot in the corner darker by contrast. Emily had reached out along the floor to steady herself (she had shifted her balance during the last set and released the quick, low groan of the floor-boards) and her fingers encountered a small rubber ball in the dark beside her. Michael, she knew, had rediscovered the ball, an old toy of his, a few months before; for a time, he had bounced it while walking around the estate and across the school courtyard. Before long, he had forgotten the ball again, abandoning it in the corner.

Emily laughed in silence, her body shaking with delight. She created six more knocks and, as the last one faded, rolled the little rubber ball out into the path of light on the floor.

Her brother drew a quick breath.

Emily said, "Michael." Her voice, sweet and simple in her dark corner, seemed unearthly even to her. She stood up in the moonlight and took two steps toward his bed. She made no threatening gestures, only stood there. In the moment after she revealed herself to him, he hunched farther over in his bed and said, "Oh God."

She laughed and began to move to the door.

"It's you," Michael said.

She went out into the hall, leaving him alone to laugh without breath.

She stuck her head back into the room. *"Boo."*

5.

Spirit Knocking

Emily watched her brother across the breakfast table. Michael gazed back.

"How did you sleep, Michael?" she asked.

"Very well, *Em*. I did dream about this horrible girl." He grimaced. "Putrid and hateful; hair full of maggots. You'd like her."

She bared her teeth at him.

Mrs. Stewart got up from the table with her coffee cup and went into the kitchen. "Excuse me," she said as she turned from them. "If bloodshed is unavoidable, remember the mop is in the cellar."

After the door to the kitchen closed behind their mother, Michael said, "How did you do it?"

"Do what?"

"That *noise*. How did you make that *noise*?"

"It's just a little trick." She looked at the kitchen door a moment, then pulled her right foot from its slipper and placed her heel on the table. She wiggled her toes at Michael. He looked at her foot with annoyance and bewilderment. She produced a single knock, clear and sharp on the sunporch.

He leaned forward. "Do it again."

She made another knock, then two more. Nothing visibly moved in her ankle, even under his scrutiny. The sounds seemed to arise from the air around her.

"How are you doing that?"

She shrugged. "I just do it."

"How many can you do?"

"As many as I want, I think."

"How long have you been able to do this?"

"A couple of weeks," she said.

"And you just discovered it one day?"

"Yes." She could not conceal her pride—it burned behind her eyes, she knew, and the more fascinated Michael looked, the harder it was to conceal.

"I'll be damned," he said, looking down at his own ankles. "Of course this is a freakish thing."

Emily sniffed. "Anything's freakish if only one person can do it."

"Yes, that's what I meant," he said, ignoring her bluster.

The voices of their mother and Mary came from the kitchen, approaching the door to the sunporch.

"Now you've got your ghost," Emily said, pulling her foot off the table.

A Delaware Valley summer settled over the estate in a listless wet heat, weighing heavily on the eaves of the house and the trees. The

few weeks since the end of school had fallen into timeless indo-
lence except for the twins' lessons on Wednesdays. Even these
days had more of the habit than the sensation of school about
them, since Mr. Holt slipped his dry humor in everywhere, and
seemed to be winking when empires fell or Galileo plucked the
Earth from the center of the solar system and flung it among a
scatter of other satellites. The twins diverted themselves with
each other, with books, and with visits from other children in
the neighborhood in the long hours between meals that passed
without notice, swept up into the vast and mysterious dream of
previous hours, days, and weeks. Mrs. Stewart presided over the
mornings and appeared as dutifully as the twins at lunch and dinner, but she often disappeared upstairs to her room, where records
played softly or the radio murmured. Mary saw to everything else,
like a stage manager who knew it all depended on her.

Emily sat curled up on the porch swing, reading Dickens's
Great Expectations for the third time. At the bottom of the drive,
Michael came through the front gates with his friend Albert
Dunne, who lived in one of the large homes down the road.
Albert's older brother, Patrick, had been killed in the War. Albert's
parents, often home behind closed curtains, rarely appeared on the
street together. Albert's father, a portly man in a gray hat and
jacket, quickly offered a grin but had a face that promised deep
frowns. Albert was a year younger than the twins, slightly taller
than Michael, and had a nervous way of smiling, as if every time
he regretted it.

"Look, Albert," Emily heard Michael say as the boys drew
closer, "I'm telling you, it's true. I understand why you wouldn't
believe me—if you told me the same, I guess I wouldn't believe

you either." She perceived in Michael's tone that he said this last part for her benefit, so she would be sure to pay attention.

"Albert doesn't believe me about your talent, Em," Michael said as the boys reached the porch.

"Oh," she said. "Really?"

"Yes, and so I brought him here. He doesn't believe that there are ghosts at Ravenwood." *Paying attention?* his eyes asked Emily.

"Ah," she said. *This ought to be good.*

Just wait. "Or that you communicate with them. He doesn't believe they make that noise through you."

"You can see why not," she said.

"Yes, of course. Which is why we're here. I told Albert how the spirits seem to reach you only in the tea house, for some reason."

"Yes," she agreed. She flicked a glance at the little house, looking like another collaborator in the sun.

"And so I thought we could go there and show Albert," Michael said. "That is, if you feel up to it."

"Sure. Seems like a good day for it."

"They're not all good days for it, you know," Michael told Albert.

Albert looked from Michael to Emily, eyes full of doubt.

"All right," Emily said, laying her book aside and standing up. She stretched with great pleasure—she'd had enough reading, anyway. She led them down the cobblestone drive to the tea house. To her eyes, the stones beneath her feet had a secret glow not very unlike the gloss after the storm. She opened the door and stepped across the threshold into the stone coolness within. She went to the other side of the white table and sat, her back to the wall, and folded her hands on the tabletop. The table, floor, and walls had acquired a hum that Emily could feel in the very tips of her fingers and toes. She allowed a look of peaceful contemplation to settle over her face.

"Well?" Albert said.

"Not so fast, Al," Michael said. "Have patience."

Emily closed her eyes, thinking of how she should begin. If she could only know just what Michael had told Albert already.

"Who do you . . . talk to?" Albert asked Emily.

"There are lots of—" Michael began.

"Regina Ward," Emily said. She looked at her brother, whose expression warned her to be cautious. "There have been others, but mostly Regina Ward."

"Who is Regina Ward?" Albert asked.

"One of our great-aunts," Emily said. "She died in 1883 at the age of sixteen, not far from where we're sitting."

Emily watched the images and the date take hold of Albert. "What happened?" he asked, leaning forward.

"She fell down the riverbank, on the rocks," Michael said. "She hit her head and died. Our great-grandfather found her in the morning," he embellished, "on his morning walk."

"Her body," Emily added, "was twisted on the rocks, and her eyes were open."

Albert looked at the surface of the table for a long moment, the information working through the features of his face. "Is she here?"

The twins paused, watching each other without ever exchanging looks.

"Yes," Emily said. "She is right beside me." She felt a thrill like the sensation of the phantom girl passing into her in the hallway. "She has been here all along."

Albert's eyes darted to the air around Emily and squinted, as if expecting to see Regina there, perhaps bloody and twisted.

"Okay, Albert, are you ready to talk to Regina?" Michael asked.

"I don't know what to say," Albert said, his skin paler than it had been.

"Ask a question," Michael suggested. "Regina—hopefully— will answer it in that noise I told you about—how would you describe it, Em?"

"A knocking noise," she said. "You'll hear it—you tell us what kind of noise you would call it."

Michael said, "Just ask a question, a 'yes' or 'no' question, and your answer will either be one knock, 'no,' or two knocks, 'yes.'" Michael made eye contact with his sister long enough to make sure she understood. With a flicker of her lids, she told him he worried too much.

Michael and Emily waited. Finally, Albert said, "Did it hurt when you died?"

All three children sat very still, the twins holding their breath with Albert. One crisp and clear sound reverberated in the small room. The sound emanated around Emily and doubled back to them from the four white walls.

"She died instantly," Michael explained.

Albert cleared his throat. "How're you doing that?" he asked, his voice shaky. "Come on, now," he said. "Come on." He looked at Emily with wide, moist eyes.

Michael held his hands up. "Honest, Al, I'm not doing anything at all," he said. He stood up from the table. "I'll just go over here." Michael went into the corner nearest him, by one of the small windows, and stood in the flat sunlight. "Go ahead, Albert. Ask something else."

Emily pushed away from the table and raised her hands as Michael had. "Go ahead, Albert," she said.

Albert considered again. He creased his brow and covered his mouth with one hand, looking at the tabletop. He glanced over at Michael. Albert said, "Are there lots of dead people, where you are?"

The silence hung around them like a fourth, watchful presence. Slowly, even more deliberately, two more knocks filled the tiny house.

Albert said nothing. He looked from Michael to Emily, his eyes never quite resting on either of them.

"Go ahead, Al. Ask her," Michael said.

Albert asked Regina if she missed being alive, if things were really better in heaven, if she was happy. He came to the questions slowly, and the knocks in the air played out around them, and time slipped away. The knocks said that Regina did miss life, though heaven was after all a nicer place to be, and she was happy. Albert asked Regina if she was with her parents. She was, two knocks assured. He asked if she knew who would die next. One knock dispelled the notion. The sun moved a short way across the sky, and the shadows in the room shifted without the children ever noticing.

Michael stepped back toward the table. "You look tired, Em," he said.

Emily allowed her eyelids to droop and repressed the surprised look she had for Michael. "I am, a little."

"Let's not overdo it," Michael said. "We're still learning about this."

She touched her forehead instead of shrugging at him. "Each question does take its toll."

"Right. We should be careful before we try more." Michael turned to Albert. "Don't go running and telling everyone about this," he said. "We want to keep this as quiet as possible."

"Nobody else knows?" Albert said.

"Nobody else," Michael said. "That's why I brought you, because I knew you could be trusted with this sort of thing."

Emily knew her brother had chosen Albert Dunne for entirely different reasons, not the least of which being that Michael was Albert's only real friend.

"I don't even want to think of what might happen if adults got involved in this," Michael said. "Can you imagine?"

Albert made a noise to say that he could.

"And they couldn't ever understand all of this, how special this is. They would want to be *practical* about it."

"Yes," Albert said. "That's right."

"Of course. Or they would make Emily stop, or send her away—"

Emily glared at her brother.

"Anyway," Michael said, "just be careful, that's all. And we'll meet again soon. Maybe start a little club. Okay, Albert?"

Albert again gazed at the table, his eyes troubled and dreamy.

"Al?"

Albert regained himself. "Okay." He stood up, just precarious enough on his feet to rock a bit from toe to heel, causing his shoulders to wind up behind him.

"Remember," Michael said, "hush-hush, for now."

"Yes, all right," Albert said. He stood there a moment, turned on stiff legs, and walked out of the tea house and down the cobblestone drive to the gate.

Michael leaned in the doorway and watched Albert leave the estate. "Incredible," he whispered. He was more pleased than Emily had seen him in some time. "I wasn't sure it would work, even on Albert."

"We'll discuss things further?" Emily said.

"Sure. We can't just let this go, Em, this is too *big*. This is the most remarkable thing I've ever seen! He was completely taken in by it. Amazing."

She remembered how the knocks had sounded even to her own ears, and it occurred to her that she had made them more real in sharing them. She had made the sounds more real and lost the safety of the lonely knocks forever. "Fooling Albert Dunne is one thing," Emily said. "It might not always be so easy."

"You may be right. But what an experiment, Em." He collapsed into his chair.

Emily considered the possibility of a group of children looking at her as Albert had, feeling the presence of Regina Ward in the tea house as Albert had. And then there was the larger world, which came into her mind as a fierce and unblinking spotlight; and she could not say if the figure standing in the spotlight of the larger world—a figure that might be her, tiny and almost lost in its brightness—cared whether all the eyes out in the dark could tell a sound of this world or another apart, so long as they waited eagerly for more. "How many do you have in mind?" she asked.

"Oh, just a small group. Come on, let's enjoy this for a week, one week, Em. This is too much to pass over. You have a gift, a real gif—"

"All right," she said, looking steadily at him. "Just see that you don't get carried away."

"Yes, Em," he said, turning toward the door.

"And don't start thinking I'm Albert Dunne and you can run me in a circle. Michael?"

But he had already gone through the door and was on his way up the drive to the house, his strides bent to catch up with his thoughts.

On the same afternoon, Albert climbed the hall staircase in his family's house and stood outside the door of his father's study. He waited a moment, gazing at the dark-stained oak. From within the room, silence. Albert knew that his father sat in a chair, on the far side of the room, with a photograph album in his lap. Many of the pictures in the album were of Albert's brother Patrick. Mr. Dunne never spoke of Patrick. He never boasted of his bravery. He never wept. He would, from time to time, go into his study and close the door, and hours would pass. When he emerged, Mr. Dunne's eyes fell on everything and everyone without interest, except to show an insulted disappointment if any particular thing demanded his attention.

Albert knocked on the door and took a step back.

A shuffling came to Albert from inside the study. He pinned his heels to the floorboards beneath him. The door opened, and Mr. Dunne stood before Albert in his robe, an awful, collapsed look on his face.

"Father?"

Mr. Dunne released a slow breath. "Yes, Albert?"

"Do you—" Albert cleared his throat.

Mr. Dunne raised himself to his full height, his shoulders squared.

"Do you believe in ghosts?"

Mr. Dunne closed his eyes. "Why," he said, placing his words like slow footsteps, "have you disturbed me to ask me that?"

"I just thought—"

Mr. Dunne's eyes snapped open. "What in God's name would make you knock on this door and ask that question?"

"I know someone who talks to ghosts," Albert blurted. "I've seen it."

"Don't tell me stories, Albert. Just go outside for a while longer. I want peace in this room." Mr. Dunne closed the study door, leaving Albert to face the dark-stained wood and its reeling lines of grain.

August 18, 1872

SUNDAY EVENING

Elaine Ward watched her husband Robert cross the lawn from the house to the garden house—which would be called the tea house in years to come—in his quick, hobbling stride, striking his cane before him. She sat at a desk by the window, her pen floating above an unfinished letter to her mother to let her know when the family would be back from the summer house and in downtown Philadelphia again. Elaine might have put a great deal more detail in her letter, but instead directed her mind to write in an elegant and proud hand about things like carriage rides, guests from out of town, children swimming in the river, summer colds, and days and days of rain. She wrote about the rain pouring down on the house without mercy, how it sounded to be inside and hear the storm collapsing from above. A busy movement on the lawn had drawn her eye and there was Robert, mostly gray-haired now in his late forties, still somehow youthful for a man with a wrenching limp and a walking stick.

Robert stood outside the little redbrick house and spoke to

one of the gardeners there, an older man with almost no hair on his head and huge, freckled ears. The two of them spoke to one another but continually looked about them, pointing and gesturing, as she had so often seen men do. As if they would have liked to marshal the summer to a close in all of these gestures, as if they stood together and ordained it, casting their hands toward such things as the low-hanging trees along the river, the rose garden near the garden house, and the blight of bagworms on the cedars and spruce trees around the carriage house, unseen from where they stood and at the other end of the estate. At the end of the season Robert settled into a doomed efficiency, and seemed everywhere seeing to closing matters. He dreaded the end of summer, Elaine knew, but he would have no one else see to it. She had known him to be possessive of few things—an odd thing for a man of such financial success, she had always thought—but these few exceptions obsessed him, and one of them was this riverside paradise he had built five years before and brought her and their son Jonathan to from Virginia, the first house they had occupied in the North, the house where their daughter Regina was born.

Elaine looked at where Robert and the gardener stood talking, knowing that they stood several feet over a brick-lined tunnel running beneath them underground—marveled at it, having stood in the tunnel herself, felt the cold dampness from the bricks, watched the shadows bounce ahead of her, fleeing the light of her flickering gas lantern, fleeing as if for safety in the garden house, where the tunnel led. Knowing that of the two men talking below, only Robert knew of the tunnel running from the house to the garden house. Knowing that Robert believed she didn't know of it, how much he would need to believe it, standing there, the lord of the estate, his will expressed from one end of Ravenwood to the other. Robert not knowing that she had discovered the way into the tunnel and where it led. And why. This last part was the easiest—she had known it long before walking through the shadowy brick passage and feeling the cool embrace of the earth all around her.

Robert turned back toward the house, stopping midway across the lawn to smile at someone on the front porch. Elaine leaned back in her chair, to disappear into shadow and reflection from the view below. She could still see Robert's face, and from his eyes knew it was Adeline on the front porch, Addie the former slave of Robert's father's house, born three years after Robert and eighteen years before Elaine. Addie, the mistress of the kitchen and laundry, Robert's childhood friend. Elaine watched Addie walk out from under the porch overhang to Robert with her back straight, holding her plain skirts just above the grass and moving with unhurried steps, careful and certain. She stopped a few feet from Robert; Elaine saw Addie cock her head just a bit in saying something, and for the first time since Elaine had begun watching him, Robert looked up at the second-floor windows. Elaine watched his unseeing eyes skate over the dappled pane between them. She bent to her letter again. *Beautiful weather, lovely sunrises, children happy, perfect days, miss you so very much, love to you and Daddy, love to all.*

Robert entered the room a little while after and went to his own desk at the far end. He turned his back to Elaine and opened the drawer.

He has already checked downstairs, Elaine thought. She looked up at his back, at his bent head. "Have you seen my reading glasses?" Robert asked without turning, perhaps feeling her look on his shoulders and the nape of his neck.

Elaine had expected to feel satisfaction in this moment, even triumph, but instead she felt herself shrink up around her disappointment. "No," she said, a low note.

Robert closed the drawer and straightened. She saw the hesitation in his whole body, saw his head just begin to turn as he scanned the shelves on the wall. Then he moved toward the door, his cane beating a quick march.

"Robert," Elaine said, barely loud enough to hear. She drew a long iron key from the waistband of her skirt and held it up for him to see. On the end of the key, two molded hands held a heart under a crown.

He stood looking at the key. When his eyes shifted to her, she thought she saw relief there, and she blinked away the blur rising up over her eyes. "Why did you build this house, Robert? Why did you bring us here?"

"I did it for all of us," he said in a flat voice. She saw him level his shoulders and lift his chin. "You know that."

"No. I know why."

Robert only blinked hard at her.

"I know what goes on in the garden house."

Robert watched her for a long moment. "What goes on there, my dear?" he said, his eyes expressionless.

"And I want her to leave this place. Permanently." She set the key down on the table and began folding her letter as if he'd already gone.

"I'd like to know what you think is going on," Robert said. *Yes,* she thought, *he is actually insulted, outraged.*

Elaine put the letter in an envelope and turned back to Robert. "I know where you two go when you disappear from this house," she said. "I know how you are here and then suddenly gone, nowhere to be seen in the house, nowhere to be seen outside. I have always known, but now I truly know. And I want her away from here."

"Addie has been a part of this family for—"

"She is not part of my family." Elaine turned again to her desk and sealed the envelope. She dipped her pen and began writing her mother's address across the cream-colored paper.

"Are you going to tell me what you think you've seen?" Robert asked.

"I haven't seen anything." She set down her pen and looked up at him.

He took one step forward and thumped his cane on the floorboards. *He thinks I've only found the key,* she thought. A different kind of relief came into his eyes, a fearful and desperate kind. "Well, how can you accuse me—"

"Regina saw you together in the garden house." Elaine stood up, taking the key from the desktop.

"Regina . . ." Robert looked away from Elaine, through the window she had seen him through. "What did she see?" Now his voice was low and his face held a pale glow.

"Enough to mention it to me." Elaine crossed the room to Robert and held his eyes. "She is a little girl, Robert. She doesn't know what she saw. She doesn't understand why Papa hugs Miss Addie so in the garden house. She asked me why you would do that in such a dirty place."

Robert squeezed his eyes shut.

"I told her Papa loves his family, that's all," Elaine said. "But she isn't going to be a little girl forever. And you're lucky it wasn't Jonathan—he's eight years old now and knows more than you think. I don't believe there's a person in this house who knows as little as you would like them to know." She lifted one of Robert's limp hands and placed the key in it. "Two weeks, Robert. She isn't going back into the city with us." Elaine left the room and shut the door behind her, and the rattle of the door frame followed her to the stairs.

PART TWO

6.

OLD FRIENDS

MARY DROVE THE FAMILY'S SEDAN UP THE COBBLESTONE drive to the house. Mrs. Stewart sat in the front passenger seat and looked out at the river. The children sat in back, Michael leaning forward, engrossed in his folded hands; Emily gazed out the right window at the trees that gathered into woods as the estate rolled toward the west. The family was returning from Sunday services. *"Vanity of vanities; all is vanity,"* Reverend Atkins had read with regret. *"For all his days are sorrows, and his travail grief; yea, his heart taketh not rest in the night. This is also vanity."*

"Look at that," Mary said as the car climbed the drive. "We have a guest." Very few people had dropped by Ravenwood unannounced—or at all—in the seven years since Donald Stewart had left for the War. The estate had entered a kind of permanent calm, even before Donald walked out of the front door for the last time. It seemed more and more secluded even as the number of neighbors slowly grew over the years. Elaine Ward had held great affairs there, the century before, when the guests arrived in carriages with footmen and the horses' hooves raised the dust on the road outside the gates of Ravenwood. She would invite people from miles around and do her best to greet each one, sending Robert off on some task when he had taken too much drink and begun to playfully torment one of the guests. Robert and Elaine's son Jonathan had tried to maintain his mother's efforts to make the place a source of local pride, when he was a younger man, but his gatherings at the mansion dwindled and became sporadic with each passing decade. Naomi Stewart decreased the staff and tended to dwell toward the back of the house, as if the entry hall and rooms along the front façade were a kind of hollow, shuttered armor.

Mrs. Stewart touched her cheek and said, "Stan Loewry," as if just remembering a boiling kettle on the stove. Emily and Michael looked up at the house to see the figure of a man, tall and thin, standing on the porch and watching the car approach. Emily thought the man looked fearless at the top of the steps, his posture still but not rigid. The man wore a light sports jacket. His eyes rested familiarly on the car.

Mrs. Stewart got out of the car and embraced the stranger. Emily watched Mary's expression in the rearview mirror, saw her eyes narrow. Mary caught Emily's look and held it in the mirror. "Children," she said. "We have company—please make an effort to convince the gentleman that we are polite people."

"How many years has it been?" their mother was saying to the stranger. Both Emily and Michael could tell she was happy to see her visitor, but her speech seemed strained, too full of laughter.

"Twelve," the stranger said in a voice that carried something extra in its tone the twins could not quite place. If they had been older, they might have described the stranger's voice as vaguely European.

"Twelve years," their mother said.

"You haven't changed, Naomi," the man said.

"Still a pleasant liar," she said. She turned to the twins. "Emily, Michael, this is Mr. Loewry—he went to school with your father."

"Hello," Michael said. "Medical school?"

Mr. Loewry stepped forward and extended his hand, which Michael awkwardly accepted. "Hello, Michael. No, not medical school—we were at Princeton together." The invocation of the university rang in Emily's and Michael's ears like the mention of Camelot. Princeton was where many of their father's most interesting stories had taken place, or at least the ones their mother occasionally retold. Emily imagined that the Princeton stories her father hadn't told her mother were even better, and that everything worth losing or winning had been lost and won there.

"Hello," Emily said.

Mr. Loewry extended his sturdy, tanned hand again. No one had ever offered to shake hands with her before, though on occasion male guests had been courtly enough to kiss her hand. When she took his hand, Mr. Loewry gently squeezed hers. "Hello, Emily," he said. Before he released her hand, he added, "You two have changed a bit. The last time I saw you, you were less than a year old and crawling all over the porch. Now look at you: a young man and woman. I have been away a long time, I see."

Mr. Loewry turned to Mrs. Stewart. "I'm sorry I didn't make it back for the funeral. I didn't hear until a few months later."

"That's all right, Stan," she said. She lowered her eyes and brought them right back up, brighter. "Would you like a cool drink?"

"Yes, that would be perfect."

Emily and Michael followed Mr. Loewry and their mother up the steps and through the front door. They listened to Mr. Loewry speak in his strange voice, telling them about leaving Paris for London and London for Johannesburg and, finally, Johannesburg for the United States. "A long time," he said.

The twins, Mrs. Stewart, and Mr. Loewry sat around the table in the sunporch, where most conversations and meals took place. Mary insisted that Mrs. Stewart and the twins sit down with their guest. She brought them a pitcher of lemonade from the kitchen, poured each one a glass, then stood apart from the table and excused herself. Mary told Mr. Loewry he was looking well, and wished him a safe trip. She was as cordial as ever, as poised as ever, but the twins knew the tense set of her eyes.

Mr. Loewry made no sign of noticing, other than a soft understanding look. "Thank you, Miss Paterson. It's wonderful to see you again, too."

Neither of the twins had ever heard anyone call Mary anything other than Mary. They exchanged a glance.

"Mary, please sit down with us," Mrs. Stewart said.

"No, thank you," Mary said. "I have things that need doing."

"It's Sunday morning," Mrs. Stewart said. "What needs doing?"

"It's all right," Mr. Loewry said. "The whole place needn't grind to a halt for me."

After Mary had gone into the kitchen and up the back stairs,

Mrs. Stewart sat back and allowed Mr. Loewry to do most of the talking, watching him and the twins with amused eyes, making dry remarks here and there. She seemed to have come out of the nervous flutter Emily had noticed outside. Mr. Loewry, too, seemed more relaxed—Emily hadn't sensed any nerves from him on the front porch, but the contrast of his mood at the table suggested that he had felt less steady than he appeared when the car pulled up. And Mr. Loewry glowed under Mrs. Stewart's considering gaze, so unnerving to some. Through some suggestion of her presence, through the influence of her sly, benign remarks, Mrs. Stewart encouraged a conversation that went beyond polite questions directed at the children about hobbies and studies, that never bogged down in pleasantries about families and extended families. Mr. Loewry told stories of his travels, and Michael came out of his usual reserve and pelted Mr. Loewry with questions about how far he'd gone and what he'd done. Mr. Loewry had climbed mountains, crossed deserts, sailed in the shadows of glaciers. He had stood on savannahs at sunset and felt the rains come in giant, ancient forests. For Emily, Mr. Loewry's life was a glittering constellation of all the places he'd been. And he was an old friend of their father's.

"What was he like, in school?" Emily asked.

Mr. Loewry paused for an instant and looked at the twins' mother, who nodded.

"He was the smartest man I knew in school—the smartest I've ever known. And probably the kindest. He was a much better student than I was, and there's a very simple reason why—besides being so smart. He actually wanted to *be* something. So many of us hadn't even considered *becoming* something. We already had the world laid before us." Mr. Loewry looked at Emily; his eyes had been drifting away from the table. "Your father wasn't like that. He was always learning. He had a way of looking at you as if he could take you apart and reassemble you, without ever feeling superior. He looked at me, and he knew me, and he liked me anyway." He took a sip of his drink and shook his head in remembering. "I think he was probably too plain for most people, too honest I mean. He never seemed quite at home in the social world at Princeton. The world's biggest theater group, he called it, wearing masks of comedy and tragedy. They resented him for not engaging them in the ways they expected, for not playing the roles they played. He hadn't been bred to play those roles like a lot of us, for one thing—but I like to think he wouldn't even if he'd come into the world a Vanderbilt. I envied his detachment from all of that, I marveled at it."

In her mind, Emily could see him, her father, an ease in his motions and words, the great power of such control. It thrilled her to hear Mr. Loewry echo this image of Donald Stewart, one of the strongest lingering impressions she had of him.

"When I was still just getting to know your father, pretty late in the evening at one of these parties, I was arguing with someone— a young man named Edgar or Edward or something—that people only did things for their own gratification, even good deeds. He had been boasting about his family's charitable contributions, that's what it was. And I told him he liked filling bowls of soup because hungry children were so grateful, something like that. I made a joke about fishes and loaves. I told him that he and everyone like him only did such things so they could speak louder at the country club. I didn't like Edgar-Edward very much, did I mention that? I hardly knew him but I knew I didn't like him."

Mrs. Stewart chuckled and shook her head.

"So I told him there was no such thing as a good deed, only people dreaming about being heroes and saints. Your father stood by and watched it all. And after Edgar-Edward barked a bit and stormed off—red and barely able to keep from strangling me, I think—your father looked at me with his unassuming smile and said, 'You don't believe that.' I won't swear at your mother's table, but I insisted in a crude, late-hour party way that I absolutely believed it if I believed anything. 'No, you don't,' he said, 'you only wish you did.' And he walked off to put his empty glass on a table."

"He had an infuriating way of doing that," Mrs. Stewart said gently, "of getting the last word and then walking off as if nothing had happened."

Mrs. Stewart and Mr. Loewry shared a laugh about it.

Emily spoke up. "And did you? Believe it?"

"I believed in seeing that fellow turn red, I know that," Mr. Loewry said. He looked at Emily as if they had an understanding, as if they were the old friends at the table, and she felt her face turn warm and blinked, looking away toward the windows and the river.

"I've probably bored you two enough," Mr. Loewry said, "but I was thinking of a little trip I took with your father when we were at Princeton. It came to me as I drove here today, and I found myself unable to put it completely out of my thoughts since. Not much to it, really, but I've never forgotten it."

Mr. Loewry allowed a moment to test the willingness of everyone around the table, Emily knew. He looked in each of their eyes before going on.

"We went to all sorts of parties at Princeton, as I said, and I dragged your father around to a good many more than he would have attended on his own, I'm sure. He was a relief and a pleasure to me. So many people there would hear my father's name—or already knew it—and they would just perform. Of course there were always girls there—none so beautiful as your mother, but not bad, all the same."

Mrs. Stewart squinted at him, and Mr. Loewry pretended not to notice.

"I was always introducing your father to these girls, but the way they behaved put him off. Anyone who knew him knew you couldn't get far being phony around him. Naturally, the phonies didn't like him . . . but never mind that."

Emily caught a proud glint in Michael's eye. For a boy who thought manipulation was play and deception a game, Emily knew Michael's scorn for people who put on shows for form's sake alone.

"Anyway, I was always introducing him to girls at these parties, and finally he found one he actually liked himself at some cocktail mixer. She was pretty but not gorgeous; she had style but wasn't trained for the dress-ball circuit. And she was funny. Joanna, I think her name was. Well, Joanna wasn't from the area—her family was up in New England, north of Boston, and she was down here visiting some old family relations. I knew of her through a friend, just as I recognized most of the people there. Summer break had just started, and she showed up at one of these parties and turned your father's head."

The twins looked at their mother, who showed only soft amusement. Mr. Loewry had cleared the air of all possible offense in his innocent manner, in countless little gestures and inferences toward her.

"Your mother doesn't mind," Mr. Loewry told Emily and Michael, as if she couldn't hear him. "This was a schoolboy crush. Your father didn't even know what love was yet."

"Go ahead, Stan," she said, taking a sip of her drink. "I don't know how much longer these two can be polite."

"All right, all right. So he met Joanna at a party, spent a lot of time talking to her, and took me aside to tell me how struck with her he was. 'You know how to pick them, don't you?' I said. 'She's from Massachusetts, and she goes home tomorrow. Didn't you ask her where she's from?'"

"'We haven't just been making chitchat, Stan,' he said. Just like that. 'I barely got her name before finding out how fascinating she is.'"

"Your father hated small talk," Mrs. Stewart told the twins. "He called it the Great Empty Prattle."

"He was tough, sometimes," Mr. Loewry said. "But he was fun. I'm sure you two remember that?"

The twins nodded that they did.

"Well, he was so taken with this girl, I had to do something. I was going to catch her before the night was over and try to make further plans, but she was gone before I knew it. You see, she didn't seek me out to say good night like a lot of the other people there. That's why your father liked her."

"Mr. Loewry is saying that he was the richest man there, children," Mrs. Stewart said, in the same innocent tone as Mr. Loewry's.

"Naomi!" He actually sounded embarrassed. "I am not saying that, and anyway it's my father who was so rich—"

"It amounts to the same, and you're right. You were probably the richest one in that room of rich people, and Donald was probably one of the few people there who saw more than that when he looked at you. Except for Miss Pretty but Not Gorgeous, of course."

"Right. Except for her." He turned to the twins. "Your mother has never been overly impressed with me, either. Very irritating. Now, where was I . . . Oh, right. Joanna. So after she left, your father and I stayed up too late and had too much to drink, and I talked him into going on a little trip with me to see Joanna. If we left in a few days, we would catch her at home. Another friend of mine who knew her, he was also very taken with her—though he was probably a bit too dull to really appreciate her finer qualities as your father did—and he seemed to know her itinerary pretty well, from rooting around for information. Charles, his name was. Charlie. Did I say he was a friend? In respect to the memory of your father, I should admit I didn't much like Charlie. So I convinced your father to take this little trip with me, and I made the arrangements. Two days later, we took a train to New York and another one to Boston. And on this train to Boston, we met another girl."

Mr. Loewry turned to Emily. "This is the good part." He shot a look at Michael. "All the rest has been Great Empty Prattle."

Emily and Michael laughed and watched their mother, who made a show of being impervious to anything Mr. Loewry could ever say. Emily marveled at how Mr. Loewry made them all part of the story, somehow, invited them to travel in time with him rather than just listen, to take part in something that happened years and years before she and Michael were born. She wanted to be a part of it, and so did Michael, beaming along with her, and so did her mother, behind her invincible pretense.

"We hadn't been out of New York long when we went to the dining car for coffee and something to eat. We lived on coffee then. Not long after we'd made our order, a girl with bright blue eyes and brown hair up in a bun came in and sat down nearby. She hardly looked at anyone, and she went to the table fast, as if she didn't want to be noticed, and sat there like she'd be more comfortable under the table. I watched her out of the corner of my eye, and your father glanced up at her. When the server came over, she said hello in awkward English. German, I thought it sounded like. She was asking for soup—*zoopa,* that's how it sounds in German. The server should have known what she meant, but he kept asking her to repeat it. This was years before the War, but some people just don't like foreigners. I was about to say something, because I figured I knew what she wanted—and because she was so pretty and shy—but before I could say a word, your father turned around and started speaking to her in German. I guess someone from over there wouldn't be too impressed, but he sounded like the kaiser himself to me."

"His grandparents on his mother's side were German immigrants who never spoke English around the house, and he spent lots of time around them as a child," Mrs. Stewart said, something the twins had heard several times before.

"Right—so he stepped in and asked this shy little German girl what she wanted to eat. The gratitude and relief on her face almost outweighed her fright at dealing with a complete stranger. But your father had that way about him—he was tough-minded about a lot of things, but he had a way of putting people at ease. I always told him he'd be wonderful at running rackets, if he weren't so righteous all of the time."

Another sparkle of pride in Michael's eye.

"The waiter stood there looking kind of dumbfounded, and your father got it out of her that she wanted soup and water. I didn't understand it word for word, of course—I had to make do with what your father said to the waiter and to her, and with what he would tell me, during and after the conversation. They had some kind of vegetable soup, and your father asked her if she wanted more. I thought she looked like she could use more, myself. She turned bright red. I've never seen anyone blush so hard. Somehow your father got her to admit that she didn't have much money, and before I knew it, he had her join us for dinner. She kept saying, '*Nein, nein, nein,*' and blushing, but anyone could see she was just embarrassed. Your father talked to her a moment about what she wanted to eat, then waved the waiter back over and ordered her a full meal. Chicken with potatoes and gravy, a side of vegetables. He even got her to agree to an ice-cream dessert. While we were waiting, he introduced her to me. Susannah, her name was. He spoke with her a moment and said, 'Susannah is going to a nunnery in New York State, not far from the city.' 'How nice,' I said. 'A nunnery. You do know how to pick them.' He told her who I was, and she looked at me with her astonishing blue eyes and nodded politely. Your father kept up this soothing line of conversation, speaking gently to her and including me whenever he could. While we were waiting, I saw her hands begin to tremble, and suddenly she looked very pale. I thought she must be terribly hungry and raised my hand to ask the waiter what the delay was about, and she took your father's hands and spoke to him, low and fast. Big tears poured down her face. I remember sitting there, my hand raised like a fool, watching her tell your father something she could barely say. The waiter stopped midway across the floor and stood there staring until I told him never mind. Your father kept talking to her in that soothing voice, and he sounded like *her* father, and I doubt there was even five years' difference between them. He asked me to excuse them and led her on his arm from the dining car and back toward the passenger cabins. On his way back to the table, I heard him ask a porter to please deliver the food to our cabin. He said his wife wasn't feeling well and needed some quiet. Then he came back to the table and sat down. He sighed at me and ran a hand through his hair."

Emily could remember her father doing that, lost in a thought and running his hand through his thatch of blond hair. The light around him was either soft morning light or made so by memory.

"'Your wife?' I said. 'You get familiar fast.'

"'I offered to say so. She's terribly embarrassed,' he told me.

"'They know very well she isn't your wife. They saw her come in alone,' I said.

"'I know. But she's. so frightened. Her family put her on this train for New York by herself with hardly any money and she's humiliated.'"

"Why?" Michael asked. "What's so terrible about being alone?"

Mr. Loewry looked at Mrs. Stewart. "Oh, go ahead, Stan," she said. "They aren't babies."

Mr. Loewry sighed now. "She was pregnant, she told your father," he said. "Her family packed her up and sent her to this nunnery because she was pregnant. She was sure everyone knew, that they all looked at her and knew. She was hungry and sick at the same time. She was scared. So your father laid her down in our cabin and we sat in the dining car for hours, to allow her to sleep. When we did venture back to the room, your father said he would see how she was and then sleep in her seat in coach, but she was already gone. Her tray of food was gone, too. She left a note, a blessing in German, for your father. He folded it up and put it in his bag. And just like that, we never saw her again. I wonder where that girl is now. I wonder how it all worked out."

Mrs. Stewart leaned forward. "He was a good man."

"Yes, he was. Kind. That's what I've been babbling on about all this time."

"And Miss Pretty?" Mrs. Stewart said, as if she already knew and asked for the twins' benefit. "Did you ever see her?"

"Oh, her. No, we didn't. That damn fool Charlie had her schedule all wrong. She was probably trying to shake him off. All we found at her family's place was her family. It was right near Concord in Massachusetts, the house. But her parents seemed happy for visitors, anyway."

"And happy to meet Graham Loewry's son, I imagine," Mrs. Stewart threw in.

"Her father had us up in his drawing room in no time. He suddenly had a little boys' club in the house—I think Miss Pretty was one of his several daughters—and he broke out the brandy and cigars. So we sat up talking with him and ended up staying over. I don't even remember what time we finally got to bed. My God, that man could talk. His biggest regret seemed to be having been born too late to fight in the Civil War. And the next morning, your father woke up with this idea of going over to Concord to see a bunch of writers' graves there. This is exactly the kind of thing he would drag me into up there, of course. He wanted to see Hawthorne's grave, so I will never forget now driving out there in our host's carriage and standing in the cemetery in Concord. It was perfect. We couldn't have ordered a better morning—drizzly gray, with sun just starting to emerge from behind the clouds, the wind gusting, shadows moving all around. Hawthorne's grave at our feet, fading from years of wind and rain. 'There he is,' your father said, and 'Such a little stone.'"

Mr. Loewry had drifted away from his own story. His eyes wandered from the table, until he caught all three of them watching him. He laughed a bit at himself. "It is a pretty modest stone for the old man. You should see the boulder they have for Emerson. And now I've prattled on enough, I think. Thank you for your kindness."

The twins sat there, not knowing what to say. Just as he had built the story around them in his way and brought them into it, he gently took them out of the story and folded it up with one gesture. A hollow quiet hung in the room for a moment.

"Feel like some present-day sunshine, children?" Mrs. Stewart said. "I think Mr. Loewry and I will sit here mucking around in the past for a while."

Emily got up first, saying how nice it had been to meet Mr. Loewry. Michael remained at the table, watching Mr. Loewry. Finally he stood up and followed Emily out, pausing long enough to also say it had been a pleasure to meet Mr. Loewry. Michael did both with a dreamy sort of resignation, an automatic fulfillment of expectations. He had been so caught up in Mr. Loewry's words;

Emily thought it strange that he seemed reticent now, as if he had trusted the stories but not the man who told them.

"What time will we be having dinner?" Michael asked their mother.

"The usual time. Nothing ever changes around here, you know that. Mr. Loewry will be joining us, if he has time."

Mr. Loewry said it would be his privilege.

Emily went out on the front porch, and Michael followed her and immediately stepped down onto the drive, heading for his typical tree by the river. The wind had picked up since they had arrived home from church, and the tops of trees tossed about in a sleepy bluster. The shadows of the limbs and leaves shifted across the lawn and the drive, and Emily felt the whole estate was a graveyard in New England, years before, the old stones just at her feet.

7.

The Astonishing Emily

The portrait of Regina Ward, taken four months before her death: a thin face, large, bright eyes, slightly curved nose, small mouth. A choker encircling her long neck. A charm, lost in the yellowed photograph. Her hair falling in dark, loose curls on her shoulders. A lacy blouse. A shadow against the pale relief of her collarbone. Her pupils, sharp and bottomless, looking out of the photograph at Emily from across forty-two years, looking more like a poet or a young queen than a doomed teenage girl.

Emily found the portrait in the attic while searching for props with Michael to dress up their game. After their initial success with Albert Dunne, the twins had decided to develop their performance. Out of the anonymous days of summer, swept up together into the haze of a long, still afternoon, this new game arose and took hold of everything, like a storm that blusters up and refigures the light and air. Michael was adamant; the act would play to a larger audience. Emily could not forget the look on Albert

Dunne's face when he believed Regina had joined them in the tea house. Emily had been simply Michael's sister to Albert before, a presence at the mansion—suddenly he had looked at Emily as if he could barely believe he was in the same room with her. And though she may not have cared much to capture the attention of Albert, it was thrilling to see herself transformed in his eyes into something he'd never imagined, someone touched from far outside the everyday, someone walking out on the edge of things.

The attic seemed the best place to search, so full of old clothes and possessions, things people had lived in, held in their hands, saved for some unknown future. The other main storage in the mansion, the basement, was full of old furniture, paintings, and other housewares, all draped in white drop cloths and assembled together in blind humps. The basement itself had been made in the rathskeller style, per Robert Ward's specifications, and was a place of dark wooden panels and mantels, with four ornate benches, one on each wall, more like thrones to celebration in this dream of a Bavarian beer hall. On each bench, engravings of intertwining ivy vines and occasional carvings of birds and roses. In the center of all this, the quiet draped forms, an underground and forgotten city of mice and spiders.

As they dug through the first few dusty boxes in the attic, Michael asked, "Do you remember that magician at Aunt Becky's birthday party? The Amazing . . ." He fumbled to remember the name.

"The Astonishing Antoine."

"Right, *right*!" Michael said. "He had a big black trunk with his name on it in gold and red letters."

"And a cape with a purple lining."

Aunt Becky's forty-third birthday party, four years gone by. Aunt Becky was not an aunt by blood or marriage, but an old family friend who lived in Baltimore and collected Chinese vases. The Astonishing Antoine, a large man with a graying beard and a French accent obviously put on for comic effect, strode out to the center of the reception hall stage and bowed elegantly to Aunt Becky's guests. The magician tripped over his cape and muttered to himself in unintelligible, French-sounding gibberish that implied obscenity. Then he threw a temper tantrum over being unable to find a rabbit in his hat—whereupon the rabbit hopped onto the stage to the magician's left. When the magician noticed the rabbit behind him, he sat down on the stage and wept into an enormous red handkerchief. The laughter of the crowd nearly drowned out the sound of the man blowing his nose like a trumpet.

The guests' laughter had turned to gasps when the magician plucked oversized cards from the air, making an astonished face himself. After introducing a lovely redheaded female assistant, the Astonishing Antoine placed the girl in a long box and sawed it in half—all while the redhead smiled at the guests and wriggled her ankles. The crowd's applause shook the room. She accepted the affection gracefully before requesting that the magician make her whole again. This kicked off a farce in which he searched through a notebook for a way to reverse the trick, while the redhead appealed to the guests with pained grimaces and whimpering, her ankles—removed from her by a distance of a few yards—kicking in protest.

"And," Michael said in the attic, "do you remember how they clapped? And whistled? They loved it."

"Do you want a rabbit, Michael?" Emily asked.

"I'd rather have the redheaded assistant, thanks," Michael said.

"But she would be difficult to smuggle into the tea house. Even Mama would notice that, I suppose."

"I think so. Sorry."

"Oh, well. There's always the rabbit."

Michael found a box of hats, scarves, and vests. Then he opened a closet and uncovered, under the old coats hanging there, boxes of their father's books and papers. As Emily watched, Michael crouched down and pushed the boxes aside, peering around and behind them. The coats clustered around his head and shoulders; they shook and jostled as if they would at any moment drop from their hangers and consume him. Emily watched and imagined the sound of such a thing—so much slithering and dull thudding, the hungry clatter of buttons. Michael thrust the row of coats aside, his eyes still searching beyond the boxes at his feet. Within a foot of his head, a heavy white garment bag emerged from the wall of coats. A five-pointed gold star surrounded by green laurels hung outside the bag on a blue band covered in white stars. Emily released a breath. She did not need to lean in closer to know that a banner marked VALOR, clasped by an eagle, connected the star to the blue star field, or to see the profile of Minerva in a war helmet surrounded by the seal UNITED STATES OF AMERICA. She had seen the star years before. A soldier in a pressed and starched uniform had brought the star and a tri-folded flag to Ravenwood. Her mother had explained to the twins then and many times since that their father had died attending wounded men in an artillery barrage; he had come out from safe cover and saved the lives of three men, pulled bits of shrapnel from their bodies and stopped their bleeding; he had been with a fourth man, very nearly dead several yards away, when a shell exploded over their heads.

THE GIRL WHO WOULD SPEAK FOR THE DEAD

Michael looked up and found the garment bag angled toward him. His father's uniform, in the dust and mothballs.

The twins' mother had refused to leave their father buried in a field in France. She had insisted he be brought home and buried in the tuxedo he wore on their wedding day.

Michael pushed the boxes of papers back in their place, dragged the pushed-aside coats back to the center of the closet, and closed the door. He looked at Emily. She turned from him and went to explore the other side of the room.

In a cabinet under a dusty old gas lantern, in a patch of soft light by a dirty, narrow window, Emily discovered a stack of photograph albums: bound in soft leather, creaky, cracked here and there, crumbling along one spine and buckling into deep creases on another. She sat on the floor in front of the cabinet and paged through the albums, one by one. Almost all of the pictures had been taken before the turn of the century. The images, yellow and ancient to Emily, might as well have featured medieval knights and maidens. The album contained many pictures of her mother as a child. In one family portrait, Jonathan and Gwendolyn Ward, Emily's grandparents, stood dignified and well dressed with their three children. Emily's mother, perhaps two or three years old, her face chubby and serious, her dress cascading in frills. Emily's uncles Michael and McEntyre, several years older, looking uncomfortable in their suits and collars, like boys containing laughter in a choir photograph. Jonathan and Gwendolyn stood remote, like wax figures, a historical tableaux dressed up with living children. None of these people had seen an automobile when the picture was taken. An airplane would have been a miraculous machine like the ones in some of the novels Emily's brother read.

As Emily turned the pages, she occasionally found spaces where photographs had been removed. She brushed the empty spaces with her fingers, her eyes unfocused.

She took the stack of albums in both hands and crouched forward to place them back into the cabinet. As she set the stack inside, something bumped against the back of the cabinet and rasped along the smooth wooden base beneath. Emily removed the albums again, reached into the cabinet, and pulled out the photograph of a young woman she barely recognized as Regina Ward. Dark eyes caught her. She held the portrait up to the light. Its humanity stopped time for an instant—a pretty girl, dead many years.

"Michael!" she called.

The rustling and bumping across the room ceased. Michael's voice emerged from the maze of old things. "Yes?"

"Come look at this."

Michael led a short procession of children up the cobblestone drive. "Emily is expecting us in the tea house," he told them over his shoulder. "She has been preparing all morning and afternoon, so there'll be no delay." The group of children consisted of three girls and two boys, one being Albert Dunne. Emily and Michael had carefully selected this audience after lengthy discussions. The other boy was Ed Oakley, wearing freckles and tiny worried eyes. He seemed always in fear of not knowing something all of the other kids knew. The girls were Cindy Rose, Olivia Bell, and Catherine Pomeroy. Cindy's brown hair bounced fearlessly as she walked along. Cindy liked to believe in things as a test of personal courage. She had proclaimed a belief in Santa Claus over a year after her schoolmates had settled the matter and considered it dead, a worldliness they could share with the adults, a cause for knowing looks. Olivia, thin and waifish, watched the way ahead with unease. She rarely started conversations, but she listened with great appetite, her eyes growing larger and presuming nothing, ready for wonders. Catherine, following the other children in light, restrained strides, looking ready to sprint ahead, watched Michael lead the group, her eyes twinkling. Michael had suggested Cat Pomeroy as a show of confidence, Emily knew. Cat was quick to doubt and defiant. She teased Michael more than any of the boys she knew, and seemed determined to catch him without a fast answer or an indifferent shrug just once.

"All right," Michael said. "She shouldn't be alone by now." He let these words hang in the air behind him.

Emily sat at the table, her back to the wall, her hands folded before her. She regarded each child with serenity. She wore a soft yellow sundress; her dark hair framed her face. Above her hung the photograph of Regina Ward. The portrait's penetrating eyes gazed out at the five onlookers. Emily appeared as untouched by Cat's small giggle upon entering the tea house as the portrait of Regina on the wall above.

"Who's that?" Cindy asked.

"That is Regina," Michael said. He motioned toward the chairs around the table—the twins had slipped in a few extra chairs from unvisited and forgotten corners of the house. "Please, take your seats."

Emily closed her eyes and lowered her head.

"If this is your first time," Michael said, "I hope you'll be patient with us. Spirit knocking isn't an exact science."

Emily had named the game after the first successful test with Albert. The idea of spirits knocking from another world gave her a genuine chill and a grin. Once, she had thought of her father not knocking from another world and went into her room, where she burrowed under her sheets and cried until she could remember that this was a game, a silly game, and that one had nothing to do with the other. When she felt reminded, she went into the bathroom a short way down the hall from her room, splashed her face with cold water, and stood with her eyes closed, creating the sounds that knocked and rattled back from the tiles around her, suspending her in a mysterious well of sensation where she could no longer be just a girl.

"Albert," Michael said in the tea house, "would you like to begin?"

Albert cleared his throat. "All right."

Michael glanced at the others as they watched Albert.

Albert said, "Are you here, Regina?"

The children became still.

Albert had not been let in on the gag, as the twins had briefly considered. No amount of plotting or dusty things from the attic could beat Albert's earnest expectation in setting the mood.

A single knock rose above the table, then a second. The children did not move.

"Two means yes," Albert reminded them, his face pale.

Michael waited, hands folded. "Olivia?" he said.

Olivia blinked at Emily. She swallowed and took a breath.

Cat pushed her chair back.

Olivia watched Cat, only turning back to Emily when the group's refusal to forget her turn settled over her. "Are you in heaven?" she asked.

Cat ducked her head to watch beneath the table.

Two knocks, a short pause, and a single knock struck the air.

Cat sat up, her eyes lingering on Emily.

"Yes and no?" Ed asked.

"Yes and no," Michael repeated. "She is here, and she is not. She is in heaven, and she is here with us. Ed?"

Ed lowered his head. "Is my dog Archie in heaven?"

A single knock hung in the air. After a pause, a second knock followed. Ed's features brightened for an instant, then his troubled expression returned.

"Cat?" Michael said.

Cat had been watching Michael across the table, and had even stolen a glance under the table in his direction. She met Michael's gaze now, before turning to Emily. "Have you seen God, Regina?"

Quiet around the table. Then two knocks, as if from above— clear, crisp, close together.

Cat turned toward Michael. "And what is your question?"

"All right," Michael said. He looked at his sister. "Is there a hell, Regina?"

The children sat very still in the quiet. They strained their ears for any sound.

Emily looked evenly at her brother.

"No answer," Michael said. "Sometimes she does not answer. All right, let's have another round, then. Why don't you try asking her about the Devil, Albert?"

Albert winced, a twitch seizing his whole face that would have gotten a laugh around the table had the other children not been watching Emily, who showed no lingering response to the echoes only just faded around her in the little house, unmoved as a pail gathering rain.

8.

MAKE-BELİEVE

AFTER THE FIRST PERFORMANCE FOR A GROUP, THE WORD about spirit knocking started to move through the open spaces and sparsely populated streets on the outskirts of Philadelphia, fanning out from the river and the estate, out toward the nearby train station. The children passed it around in debate and fascination, accepting it without effort into a lore already full of magic, fluid and resilient even to jokes and doubts—fed by them, in fact—and they came in clusters to see if they could sit in a room with ghost knocks and come out unchanged. And though Emily didn't say so to Michael, and didn't even admit it to herself, she had begun to believe no one could.

A network of narrow corridors, opening here and there into intersections of doors concealing unused rooms where beds and chairs sat under white drop cloths, led to the library at Ravenwood.

Beyond a set of double doors, in the center of the library, stood a long table with thick, ornate legs ending in dragon claws. On the table stood a bronze statuette of Neptune, a foot and a half tall, with the usual Olympian physique, flowing beard, conch shell, and trident. Donald Stewart had bought this piece in Naples from a half-blind landowner. Bookshelves, nine feet tall and filled with books of all kinds, covered the walls on either side. In odd spaces between the books stood occasional figures: a knight in full armor bearing a crested shield; a bronze of Thomas Jefferson, standing between *The Adventures of Huckleberry Finn* and the collected plays of Sophocles, looking off into the distance; a porcelain image of the Hindu god Vishnu standing in long robes, his blue skin almost translucent, his four arms radiating from him in the traditional manner, and in his hands a discus, a conch shell (like Neptune's), a club, and a lotus flower. Emily's father had purchased this last piece only a few years before his death, having been drawn to the statue's resigned happiness and closed eyes. "Do you know what he called that?" Emily's mother had once asked, referring to the figure's expression. "Peace of mind."

The library—until now a retreat for Emily—had taken on a strange unfamiliarity since Mr. Loewry's visit. The shelves were stocked with many of her father's books; his small statuary stood silent all around. Now she had shaken hands with a stranger who had known her father well as a young man. Mr. Loewry possessed a store of memories—sharp and alive, she imagined—and she had never even heard the man's name before he had appeared on the porch. Mr. Loewry carried memories from lost years, shared by no one at Ravenwood.

Emily pulled out one of her father's favorite books, *The*

Encyclopaedia of Make-Believe. She thumbed through the pages and breathed deeply. The musty smell of the book took her to dry, forgotten footpaths in a forest. She came upon a drawing of a griffin, its eagle eyes cruel as it bared its talons. It stood upright on its lion hindquarters and, whipping its long tail, spread its great wings to either side. She passed over several familiar paintings of giants, elves, gremlins, goblins, and the misty isle of Avalon, where King Arthur's body was to have been carried in state on a spectral barge. The Greek goddess Persephone, maiden of fertility, queen of the underworld, stood in a spot of light, surrounded by blooming flowers and ripe, near-bursting fruit, her bare feet on the verge of a great, cavernous shadowland, thronging and indistinct, not so much a place of torment as one of forgetfulness.

She lingered on a full-page illustration of a group of gnomes dragging a cart through a small underground cavern, each of these small, strangely dressed creatures wearing expressions somehow related to Vishnu's peace-of-mind smile. In the text beside the illustration, Emily found that the word "gnome" came from a Greek word, *gignosko*, meaning "to understand." According to the book, gnomes maintained a complete harmony with the universe. She looked at the little bearded men hurrying through the cool, dark earth, under a lowering blue twilight, and floated on the associations of night and distance and magic.

Emily sat at the small white table in the tea house. The table had been moved from the middle of the room and placed so that Emily's chair was pressed into a corner. Regina's portrait hung on the wall above. A group of nine children—the largest crowd Emily had yet performed for—sat cross-legged on the floor in arranged rows. "Remember," Michael said, "we are not always successful in reaching Regina, but we usually do reach her, and the more Emily does it, the better she gets at it. Also, and this is very important, we need you to *want* Emily to reach Regina, and we need you to concentrate your thoughts toward contacting her." This short speech at the end of Michael's opening, in slight variations, was becoming an essential part of each spirit-knocking performance. "If everyone could just concentrate on Regina."

After a few moments, Emily opened her eyes, the signal that she was ready to begin. Dusk had begun to take hold of the mansion and the paths on the riverside. Emily lowered her eyes and looked into the faces of the children, a group of four boys and five girls. The faces of some—Albert, Cat, Ed, and Olivia—were familiar to Emily; some were seeing the performance for the first time. In the shifting candlelight, the spectators' eyes were dark, secret, and devouring.

"I will begin," Michael said. "Regina, are you with us?"

Emily exhaled and watched the children all hold their breath together as one.

By the third week of July, Emily and Michael had orchestrated twelve spirit-knocking performances. The twins used no props other than the portrait of Regina and a candle if a session was held at sunset or after. Emily usually wore white—she had a great many white dresses and summer outfits to choose from. Emily quickly mastered her peculiar talent and toyed with it, experimenting with the dramatic textures in varying the periods of silence around each knock. She improved on her rhythm, although given the simple code prescribed for communicating with Regina, this did not affect the presentation. Michael was careful in his scripting and delivery, never making large changes but always interested in sharpening a word or a phrase for maximum effect.

Their mother asked about the processions of children Emily and Michael brought to the tea house. She questioned the twins one night at dinner while the three of them waited for Mary to bring dessert from the kitchen.

"You two have always kept mostly to yourselves," she remarked. "And now you've become so popular I half think you're making moonshine out there."

"Best price in the neighborhood," Emily said.

"Don't worry," Michael said. "If they raid the place, you don't know a thing."

"Just remember that," Mrs. Stewart said, winking at Mary, who had just returned to the table, "when they come breaking down your door."

Michael kept a notebook of scribbled ideas for new ghosts to visit the tea house. He spent a great deal of time by the river with his notebook in his lap, gazing out across the water, waiting for the ghosts to appear before him. In this way, Michael dreamed up two Union soldiers who had dueled on the banks of the Delaware with pistols over a girl. The soldiers, both lieutenants who had gone to school together (grown up together, Michael hurriedly added), had drawn their pistols at sunrise and, in their passion, had not followed the traditional rules of pistol dueling Michael had discovered in an old encyclopedia, but instead fired at the same moment, both bullets finding the other's heart. Michael scrawled out the disjointed notes of his thoughts and took the notebook to Emily, who read the notes and added her own touches to fill in details: the girl had agreed to marry both soldiers, for fear of breaking their hearts; the soldiers had faced great danger in saving one another during battle; the girl had learned of the duel and came to stop it, arriving in time to hear the gunshots and see the soldiers fall.

Sitting by the river, Emily imagined a struggling artist desperately in love with a woman—a rich man's wife, Michael amended; no, his daughter—who did not care for the young artist (a sculptor—a painter) at all, and even despised him. After wandering through the streets of Philadelphia in despair on a gray morning in the spring of 1838, the poet had gone down to the docks on Delaware Avenue and thrown himself into the cold water. The poet did not fight the current, Emily added; he did not resist the water that engulfed him; he opened his mouth, took in water, and sank to the bottom.

Michael wrote in his notebook of an Indian killed by U.S. troops for scalping an officer—*a great and bloody warrior.*

Emily imagined an old man named Mr. Walters, who had spent the end of his days searching for his lost dog—a basset named Pal—and died without ever recovering his friend. In the notebook's enchanted night, Mr. Walters walked along the riverbank and whistled for his lost dog forty years after his own death.

A headmaster, burned to death in a fire set by the boys he had been assigned to watch over.

A farmer accidentally shot by his brother and hastily buried in the woods.

A nun who had fallen down a flight of stairs and cracked her skull.

Emily suggested that these fallen characters had all died in or near the old Delaware River, and that their spirits had been carried to the estate on the current to be washed up near the tea house on the tide following the moon's rise.

"Maybe the ghosts come here because of Regina," Michael mused.

"Or because they know they will be heard," Emily said. She watched Michael scribbling and nodding. "And remembered," she said.

9.

QUETZALCOATL

EMILY DREAMED A MEMORY OF THE NEW JERSEY SHORE
and a beach house belonging to an old school friend of her father's.
She dreamed it while awake, as she washed her face before the
tall mirror in the twins' bathroom. She saw her face in morning
shadows and an almost forgotten dawn returned to her. Her parents had spent a few weeks in this same beach house every year
from the time they were married. Emily, looking at her reflection, found herself sitting on the back porch of that house, taking in the seashore smells, feeling the incoming breeze and the
ocean's immense presence. Her father walked out onto the porch
in loose pajama pants and an undershirt. He walked to the end
of the porch, looked out at the waves, and took a deep breath. In
Emily's mind, her father stood there as a softly burning silhouette,
though in the weak light of that time of morning he could hardly
have cast a shadow.

"Em?" he said, without looking back. "What are you doing up?"

"I just woke up," she said. She started getting out of her chair, obeying his order to return to bed before he gave it.

"Wait a moment," he said. "As long as you're up, let's watch the sunrise."

They walked out onto the beach together, feeling the cool sand between their toes. The sky gained color quickly. Emily watched the clouds become clouds out of a painting, layered in deep reds and bright pinks. The water took on a preternatural luminance— a silver-pink glow hung in the tide, rolling and breaking and reforming. The sunrise made the ocean into a magical ocean, a place where mermaids, nixies, and giant sea serpents roamed, and where the world could be reinvented and reinvented again. In the bathroom at Ravenwood, Emily looked into the mirror and tried to stand on the cool sand with her father, tried to see the ocean as it had been, and knew her memories of the dream she believed to be a memory were fading pictures and sensations of something that had passed on.

Emily sat in the tea house drinking a glass of lemonade and gazing at the portrait of Regina Ward. The door to the tea house stood open. *Can you see me, Regina?* Emily wondered.

"The plumed serpent," a man's voice said from the doorway.

Almost jumping in her chair, Emily looked up to see Mr. Loewry leaning against the door frame. She glanced over his pressed slacks, his suspenders, his polished shoes and regained herself.

"Excuse me?" she said. Warmth flowed up into her cheeks. Her forehead tingled.

"The plumed serpent," Mr. Loewry repeated. "The Aztecs had

a god named Quetzalcoatl—he was a god of the winds, I think. In human form, he was a young man in a headdress that looked like a snake with lots of feathers, so he was also known as the Plumed Serpent." Mr. Loewry took a step into the tea house. "He had an enemy, another god with an unpronounceable name, and this enemy wanted to weaken Quetzalcoatl and cause him to doubt his godliness, I guess you would say. So this other god showed Quetzalcoatl a mirror, and Quetzalcoatl looked into it, and recognized his own humanity."

Emily half concealed the portrait under her arm.

"When I saw you sitting there looking at that photograph, you reminded me of old Quetzalcoatl and the mirror. Recognize anything in there?"

Emily could not imagine what to say.

"Your father told me that story, a long time ago," Mr. Loewry said. "I'm sure he meant to teach me some lesson or other about myself. I may have even learned a bit of it." Mr. Loewry sat at the table. "He was mad for mythology, your father."

"And you still remember that name?" Emily said.

Mr. Loewry laughed. "I bought a book with all these mythical stories in it while I was in Europe, a book your father had talked about. I read that story a few times. May I see your photograph?"

Emily handed the framed picture to him without hesitation. She gazed at her empty hand in faint wonder.

"She's very pretty," he said. "Striking. An unusual-looking girl."

"That's Regina Ward," Emily said. *I connect with her spirit, right here at this table,* she nearly said. "She's a relative of ours—she died out by the river."

"Ah," Mr. Loewry said. "Does she haunt the place?"

"I hope not."

"I wouldn't worry about ghosts," he said. "It's the live ones that you have to watch out for."

Mr. Loewry considered the portrait. Emily listened to the quiet.

"Why did you stay so long in Europe?" she asked. She had barely thought the question before it was in the air.

Mr. Loewry drew a breath. "I went to Europe because I was unhappy. And I came back for the same reason. Strange, isn't it?"

"Why were you unhappy?"

"Too much to get into, Emily. And too boring."

"And you never came back to visit my father."

"Your father and I had something of a falling-out."

"What about?"

"We argued about some things. I didn't go to Europe because of your father, anyway."

Mr. Loewry made a study of looking at the portrait, and Emily made one of not looking at him.

"Is Mama expecting you?"

"Yes," he said. He handed her the portrait and stood up. "I should go to the house. I could use an escort, if you're not too busy."

"Mr. Loewry," she said, "would you mind not mentioning that old picture to my mother? It's one she'd probably prefer we kept in the house. She's very particular about some things."

"Yes, she is."

"I'd rather she didn't know I had it in the tea house."

"All right. Just get it back where it belongs in one piece, Emily. And please, call me Stan. I feel like an old headmaster when you call me Mr. Loewry."

PAUL ELWORK

The front door of the house opened as they walked up the cobblestone drive. Mrs. Stewart stepped out onto the porch. Emily detected in her mother's stance an effort to appear nonchalant when she saw Mr. Loewry.

"Are you having lunch with us, Emily?" her mother said.

"Yes, if that's all right."

"It's perfect," Mr. Loewry said. "I don't often take my meals with two beautiful women."

"Flatterer," her mother said. "And anyway, I'm sure it's not true. That's the worst part." She turned to Emily. "Where is your brother?"

"I don't know. I haven't seen him."

"Probably out running Albert in circles, or sulking in a cemetery somewhere," her mother said, "looking for a grave to dig up."

10.

Ripples

In late July, Cat Pomeroy appeared outside Raven-wood, striding through the gate and advancing up the drive. Stopping at the head of the drive, she scanned the riverbank until her eyes fixed on Michael, sitting by the river under his favorite tree, his notebook in his lap, writing with a pencil. Cat came toward him, seeing that he perceived her well before she reached him. When she stood beside him, Michael glanced up at her and raised his eyebrows.

"Well?" she said.

"Well what?"

"Aren't you going to say something?"

"Hello, Cat."

"Hello, Michael. I told my grandmother about spirit knocking."

He closed his notebook.

"My grandmother tells stories—like how my great-grandfather's

ghost walked into her mother's room the night before my grandmother was born and sat down on a chair. Or how candles never
stayed lit in this one room of her aunt's house—the room where
her husband died of scarlet fever. She was telling me her stories
again—that last one, about the candles—and I asked her if she'd
ever seen a ghost. She told me that she was always seeing a man in
a gray coat outside her house at night when she was a little girl—
she was sure he was a ghost. So I asked her, 'Have you ever talked
to a ghost?' She looked at me kind of funny."

"And?" Michael tapped the cover of his notebook with his
pencil.

"I told her I knew someone who could talk with ghosts. I told
her about Emily."

Michael considered his pencil, suddenly still. "What did she say?"

"Nothing, for a minute. I thought I'd made a mistake in
telling—but after a minute she said she wanted to meet Emily."

"She believed you?"

"I think so. *Shouldn't* she believe me, Michael?" Cat's raised
eyebrows defied him to speak the truth.

Michael returned her gaze and held it. "Of course." His own
challenging look followed, slow and friendly. "But just like that?"

"She seemed sort of happy about the whole thing. I told her I
would have to arrange it with you."

"I'll have to talk with Emily, of course."

"Of course," she said. A sly gleam, almost a taunt.

"Come back to the house in two hours, Cat, and I'll have an
answer. I imagine something can be arranged."

She hurried down the cobblestone drive and through the
gate. Michael watched her stop to look back at him through the

fence. Emily might not like the idea of including an adult in their game—but what was one old lady? An old lady who liked to tell ghost stories. And besides, the routine was in danger of becoming stale.

He reopened his book and added a new note, which he underlined: *Scarlet fever.*

Cindy Rose had also spoken to her mother of the tea house. "They're real," she insisted. "I was there."

"Aren't you scared, Cindy?"

"Scared?"

"Ghosts are scary, even for pretend—"

"Pretend?—no—"

"But fun . . . a fun game . . ."

"Yes—but—"

"Thank Mrs. Stewart for letting you play there, Cindy."

Cindy would flap her arms stiffly at her sides. "We never *see* Mrs. Stewart—"

"I don't see much of Mrs. Stewart, so you thank her for me—"

"But—"

"Thank her nicely for me, Cindy."

Emily, sitting in the tea house again, with the portrait of Regina in her lap. She sat at an angle toward the open door, so that she would notice anyone coming from the house down the drive. She tried to keep her concentration on Regina, but instead found her mind going back to her conversation in the tea house with

Stan Loewry—his voice in the small space, his manner relaxed and pleased, as if he liked nothing better in the world than sitting in the little house with Emily discussing an old photograph and mythology.

A shadow from the doorway, preceding the person it fell from by the barest instant, rattled Emily out of her reverie. She had been less prepared but more willing to find Mr. Loewry standing there.

"Albert!" she said, when the boy's startled face was in the doorway. "Don't sneak up like that! You scared me half to death."

Albert's face spasmed and flushed. "I . . . I'm not sneaking. I just wanted to . . . come over." His eyes fell on the portrait of Regina.

Emily set the photograph down on the table and exhaled. "We're going to have to put a bell on you, Albert. Are you here to see Michael?"

"Um." Albert couldn't make his feet remain still on the threshold. "Um. No."

Emily gave Albert a questioning smile.

"I just wanted to come and see . . . the tea house," he said. "That's all. Sometimes I just like to come look at it. If I happen to be going by."

"You're always welcome to come here, whenever you want, Albert," she said, starting to feel a bit unable to sit still herself and sound polite. He was going to say something, something he felt strange about saying. She could feel it trembling from him, suddenly, some extra electric sensation along with his usual discomfort.

"So," he said, "are you alone . . . now?" he asked, not looking at Emily.

She took a moment to understand him, and withheld a grin. "Yes. Just sitting in the tea house by myself. Well, not anymore."

She felt warmth rise through her discomfort and enter her voice. After all, he was only believing what he'd been told. He was only showing his enthusiasm for the game. Had she really been almost irritated by poor Albert Dunne? It seemed so unfair to her, then, but she also couldn't help entertaining a certain pride, occurring somewhere beneath the thoughts she acknowledged as her own. *He's only showing how much he believes in me.*

"Have you found any others?" Albert's eyes fleeted to Emily's.

"Others?"

"Other ghosts. Besides Regina. Any others besides the ones we've been, um, talking to."

The Indian warrior. The school headmaster. Mr. Walters, searching for his lost dog.

"Not just recently," she said. She began to feel strange discussing this with Albert alone, without Michael around or anyone else in the audience. The little groups gave her some release, allowed her to detach just enough to become the girl they all expected her to be now—the one with the gift, the one with access to another world. "They come to me, Albert. I don't find them. So far, anyway."

"Oh—right." Every time Albert's eyes flitted back to Emily's face, they lingered a little longer.

Emily stood up, and Albert nearly fell out of the doorway.

"Well, I should . . . go," she said. "I need to go, Albert. Back up to the house." She wondered where her control had gone at that moment. The girl sitting before a ring of spectators didn't stammer. She had reached a point where she hardly knew they were there, except for their expectation and apprehension.

"Okay," Albert said. "Sure."

Emily said, "Maybe sometime—" but Albert had already disappeared from the doorway. His hurried footsteps moved away down the drive.

Emily sat back down in her chair and looked at the portrait of Regina. She found herself longing to know the thoughts behind those dark eyes. She had so many questions of her own.

Ed Oakley, the boy who had wanted to know if his dog was in heaven at that first spirit-knocking session, stepped out of his front door and around the side of the house. His father, crouched over a bent mower blade, clucked his tongue. Ed's uncle John stood over him, looking at the bent blade with a faraway, amused frown. "The ideas they get," Uncle John said. "I can't even remember getting ideas like that. Can you?"

"That Naomi Stewart is an odd one. Never see her more than once or twice a month. Up in that big house. She wouldn't know if those kids were skinning cats in that damned garden house."

Uncle John squinted and hooked his calloused, weathered thumbs into his pockets. "That blade could be banged out."

"Yeah. Should."

Uncle John unhooked his thumbs. "The ideas they get."

"Crazy. You have enough money, you can be as crazy as you want. Hand me that hammer, John?"

Albert came home from Ravenwood after finding Emily in the tea house and stood in the middle of the shadowy living room, so much cooler than the outside. His heart had finally begun to slow down since he had hurried away from the estate. After a few long, slow breaths, Albert climbed the stairs and stood outside the closed door of his father's study. He shifted a bit on his feet; the floorboards shifted with him and creaked. His arms hung at his sides. He looked at the door and made himself stand still. No sound from within. He closed his eyes, turned, and went down the stairs.

Feet shuffled behind Albert in the room beyond the door.

Albert stood still on the staircase, not breathing.

The closed door opened behind him. "Albert?" his father said.

When Michael came to Emily with the idea of visiting Cat Pomeroy's grandmother, she refused. On the evening after Cat's visit, Michael found Emily in her accustomed place in the library, an enormous world atlas before her on the table. The atlas was open to a map of France; Emily trailed her finger along the northern border, on the frontier leading to Belgium. The area surrounding the town of Compiègne was circled in black ink. And beside the circle, their mother's handwriting: *October 10, 1918.*

"What was all that talk about never including adults, Michael?" Emily asked, closing the book. "About the risk?"

"I told that to *Albert*, Emily."

"You told everyone."

"That was before. Things have developed since then."

"No."

"Now, Em, listen, please—"

"No."

And so it went for a time. Finally, Michael said, "*Why* won't you do it?"

"Because it can only lead to trouble. And . . ."

"And what?"

"And it's not nice. Tricking people."

"Tricking people? Em, these people want to see you perform, that's all."

"Fine. Then let's tell them how the trick is done. Tell them it's a show."

"Now, Em, be reasonable. Does a magician tell the crowd how his tricks are done?"

"Are we magicians now, Michael?"

He blinked. "Of course we are. You know that." Michael paused. "Is it because you're afraid? That's it, isn't it? You're afraid to—"

"Don't try *that*, Michael. I *am* afraid of what Mama will say if she finds out we've been fooling somebody's grandmother. And don't tell me she won't find out."

"She won't, Em. That's part of the deal—I made that all very, very clear. Besides, Cat's grandmother knows about what's been going on here at the tea house; she could already have told Mama about that. And if anybody around here ever got a chance to talk to Mama, she may have. Cat's grandmother wants to think a ghost is visiting her—what's the harm? You could be the haunted grand-daughter she never had."

Emily smirked at her brother.

"I can't do it without you, Em."

"All right," she said, and closed the big atlas with a thud. "That's enough. One time."

Michael bowed before her. "Of course. You won't regret it, Astonishing One."

. . .

Emily walked out into the dull heat of another July morning. She went behind the house, to the stands of trees and shade clustered along the creek branching off from the river and winding around Ravenwood, forming its northern boundary. The estate's old water tower loomed up out of the trees, a forbidding granite spire that fed the estate until city water made it out here, a few years before the twins were born. Now locked up and full of a rotting stair-case Emily's mother said should have been replaced years before it went out of use, the tower looked like a place for a medieval pris-oner to Emily, someone unjustly held in chains in the dim light from the little window in the rock face of the tower—a dethroned prince, a betrayed lover. Emily passed under the trees and into the solid shadow of the tower, ran her hand on the rough stone, and continued down through the dense grasses and weeds grow-ing wild here down to the creek. The ground felt spongy from the rain a few days before. The layer of soft mossy life and decay gave way to mud and stones, a gently buzzing place of insects and frogs. Emily thought of the goddess Persephone and her underworld of shadows, of how this place seemed lulling in its tranquil hum, for-getful, not so much a denial of memory as a distraction from it. If she really were to meet Regina at Ravenwood, Emily thought this the best place. Regina in a light summer frock, holding the hem up over her bare knees and wading in the creek, watching Emily with those dark, questioning eyes, a real being out of time, young and slightly tanned from the sun, disturbing the water and clouds of tiny nymphs lighting there in the shallows. Real and showing a damp shimmer of perspiration on her forehead and along her neck when she moved into a patch of sun. Emily would be ready to meet Regina now, she felt certain. She would wade out into the water to her and welcome her home.

She bent to the water and put her hand in to feel the goose bumps of the sudden coolness and touch the slimy rocks at the bottom. She withdrew her hand and turned back toward the trees, passing back under the stone tower and around the house, the sleepy bustle of the creek dwindling behind her.

Mr. Holt, their tutor, stood in the middle of the drive, facing the tea house and studying the little brick building with some interest. He was a stocky man in his mid-fifties with white, unruly hair. He wore a white shirt and vest, and held a large pad of paper under one arm. His right elbow rested on his hip; his right hand held a long brown cigarette at an angle away from his body. As Emily approached, Mr. Holt brought the cigarette to his lips and took a deep drag on it, then exhaled a large cloud that hung about him as listlessly as the boughs of the trees all around.

"Good morning, Emily," Mr. Holt said. He did not turn toward her.

"Good morning, Mr. Holt. You're here early today."

Mr. Holt turned from the tea house as if suddenly reminded of his manners. Mr. Holt often joked and was not afraid to laugh loudly from time to time. "Yes, a bit early. I'm very interested in this little house of yours, Emily."

"Really? All of a sudden?"

"Yes, all of a sudden. I never really looked at it, you see. I have walked by this place a hundred times and not *seen* it. Funny how that happens, don't you think?"

"Yes, very," Emily said. There was something strange about

standing out near the tea house with Mr. Holt. Something much more provoking than his lessons on history and literature.

"I've seen it now. And now, in this ungodly heat, I want to paint it."

"Paint it?"

"On canvas, I mean. I paint, in my spare time. Actually, I tutor so that I can eat, and I spend the rest of my time destroying and rebuilding myself with this painting nonsense."

"Oh." Emily pointed at the pad under his arm. "Going to sketch it first?"

He looked at the pad as if he had forgotten it. "Yes, that's right." He drew a pencil from his shirt pocket. "I'm going to sketch it so that I can better understand it."

Emily turned to face the tea house. "Do you believe in ghosts, Mr. Holt?" she asked.

He frowned with pleasure. "Where did that come from?"

"I've been wondering if I believe in ghosts, that's all. Do you?"

"No," he said, looking at the tea house. "I suppose this place is haunted?" He crossed his arms and tapped one long finger on the edge of his sketch pad.

"Of course it is. Look at it." Emily moved closer to the tea house. "And what if I told you that not only is one ghost in there, but that it's filled with ghosts? More ghosts than you could imagine?"

Mr. Holt laughed. "I thought you hadn't made up your mind about ghosts."

Emily shrugged.

"What is this all about?"

"Nothing," she said. "Just wondering about what you believed."

"Taking up an interest in the subject?"

"You could say that, yes."

"Belief is a funny thing, Emily," he said. He walked to the tea house and looked through a window. "Can't see anything, but that's to be expected. They are ghosts, after all."

"Exactly."

Mr. Holt knocked on the door three times, and the sounds bounced dully within the tea house. "Hello? Hello there?" He shrugged at Emily, and stepped away from the door. "I guess the dead aren't taking any visitors today."

"You have to knock just right. You have to know how to do it."

"People spend a great deal of time trying to figure out what they believe, then trying to become familiar with all of it, only to have to figure what they believe all over again. Arthur Conan Doyle—the man who wrote all those Sherlock Holmes stories?— he believed in faeries, among other things. Imagine that."

"May I see your sketches, Mr. Holt?"

Without pausing, he took the pad from under his arm, opened the cover to the first page, and handed the pad to Emily. A sketch of City Hall, a remarkable likeness, with a tiny image of William Penn's statue on the steeple. A date appeared in the corner of the sketch, four days before. The second page revealed a horse-drawn carriage—the driver stood on the sidewalk, buying a newspaper from a vendor.

"Where is this from?" Emily asked.

"Market Street. I was looking for something to draw quickly, and this is what I found. Looks like an old piece, with no autos in it, doesn't it?" The date in the corner of this second sketch was of two weeks before.

When Emily turned to the third sketch, done earlier that morning, she laughed out loud. There was the groundhog, rendered in dark ink and peering from between the soft blades of long summer grass.

"Wonderful!" Emily said. "Look at him! How did you get him to pose for this?"

"I didn't have long. I got the gist of him while he was there. I believe I understand just how that fellow thinks."

"It's perfect—this is the best one."

"Better than City Hall?" Mr. Holt said. "I worked much harder on City Hall."

"They're all beautiful—but look at him!"

"If you like it so much," Mr. Holt said with pleasure, "why don't you keep it?"

"I couldn't—"

"You will." Mr. Holt took the pad from her hands; with one motion, he tore out the sketch. He placed the pad under his arm and offered Emily the drawing. "There. You've got to take it now, or I can't imagine what will become of it."

Emily beamed at the sketch.

"Happy belated birthday." Mr. Holt looked at his watch. "Now, if you please, go and see what your brother is up to. Class begins in just under ten minutes; I expect you both to be there."

Emily found the door to Michael's room open. He sat up in bed, his hair messy, bent over his notebook, scribbling with a pencil. When he finally noticed her there, he looked up and his eyes moved past her, still following where his scribbling had been leading him. His eyes focused. "Mr. Holt is here, I guess."

"He's waiting downstairs. Time to take a break from stories, for now," she said.

"Right. Time for different stories about dead people." Michael made another short line in his notebook and snapped it shut with a soft and contented clap.

obert Ward sat on the second-floor gallery looking out over the river and smoking a long, thin cigar. His hair was completely white by then, his face heavily lined. His eyes shone with a dull luster as he picked up the bottle of whiskey his wife had called cheap rotgut and filled his glass. He held the glass up to the sun, turning it like a curious idea. Robert spent more and more hours up here on the gallery in the three years since Elaine died, racked and pale from tuberculosis. He sometimes tried to think of her as the nineteen-year-old girl he'd married, twenty years before, but from that time he mostly remembered fancy layers of petticoats and delicate hands that had never lifted more than a brush in her father's house. She remained to him as the mother of his children, the person who had gotten to know him too well. He drained his glass and set it down beside his chair, then propped up his crossed feet on the balustrade as if sitting on the porch at a general store, the embers of his cigar glowing and puffing.

Regina found him there, as she often did. She wore a light,

embroidered summer dress and had brushed her long dark hair thoroughly that morning. Robert liked to run his fingers through her hair sometimes when they sat on the gallery and call her his doll. Ever since she had turned sixteen a few months before, he would sometimes reflect out loud about the gentleman callers who would be sniffing around the house soon, how he would bring them up here to the gallery and see what they had to say. "In whiskey *veritas*, dear."

Regina settled into the chair beside Robert. "I've had one of my dreams again, Daddy," she said.

Robert turned from the river and reached out to stroke her hair. Regina sat forward, cocking her head and meeting his fingers. "Mother, again?" he said.

"Yes. She came to me along the river."

"And what does Mother have to say these days?"

"She's worried about you. She thinks you're lonely."

Robert gave a gentle laugh. He took his hand from Regina's hair and turned to pour himself another glass. "Who the hell isn't, my love?"

"Daddy—"

"Your mother loves you," Robert said, sitting back with his glass. His voice softened. "She still loves you. She will be waiting for you, when the time comes. But you tell her for me that I'd prefer she worry about somebody else." He raised the glass to his lips. "Would you sing your old dad a song?"

"What would you like to hear?"

"Sad and lonely sounds about right. Break my heart, darling."

Regina sat up straight in her chair. She sang in a high, sweet lilt, not quite on key, but she held the notes an instant on her tongue before breathing them out into the light breeze from the river. Robert turned his glass and his eyes gleamed.

A Rose tree in full bearing,
Had sweet flowers fair to see,
One Rose beyond comparing,
For beauty attracted me.
Tho' eager once to win it,
Lovely blooming trees and gay,
I find a canker in it,
And now throw it far away.

Robert's son Jonathan stepped out onto the gallery. He had been visiting one of the other families along the river. His dress shirt was opened at the throat, his necktie hung in his fist. Jonathan was home between his freshman and sophomore years at the University of Pennsylvania, where he studied the mysteries of what he called the family money business. Regina broke off her song and smiled at him. *Don't.*

"Ah, Jonny," Robert said. "How was the pig roast?"

"It was a very nice dinner party. Small. You should have come, Gina." Jonathan never looked away from his father.

"Well, I hope you gave my regards. Did you see that girl . . . ?"

"Gwendolyn McEntyre," Jonathan said. "Yes, I did."

"I'll bet you did," Robert said. "Sit down, have a drink."

"Thank you, Dad. No."

"You going to marry that girl, Jonny?"

"We'll see," Jonathan said. "Not before I'm done school, anyway. Gina—"

"And when are you going to kiss her? Before or after the first child comes along?" Robert grinned at his son.

Jonathan turned to his sister and spoke in a soft voice. "Gina, I wonder if I could have a moment with Dad."

"I've only just sat down," Regina said. *Don't,* her eyes said. *Let it alone.*

"Gina. Please."

"It's all right, sweetness," Robert said. "We're going to discuss manly things a young lady like yourself shouldn't hear." He winked at her.

"I'll be back soon," she said, and touched his hand. She stood up and tried to hold her brother's eyes, but he looked away until she left the gallery and went down the hall to the main stairs. Jonathan watched her go. He listened to her footsteps fade away. The wind off the river stirred Jonathan's collar and tossed the smoke from Robert's cigar into a brief dervish. The afternoon light lay flat on the house and the gallery, bracketed in deepening shadows.

Jonathan turned to his father, who looked out over the river. "Do you really think it's a good idea to have her sit with you while you empty that bottle?"

"I ran out of good ideas a long time ago, Jonny. For God's sake, sit down." Robert raised his glass to his mouth.

Jonathan remained standing. "And do you think it's a good idea to encourage this talk about Mother and dreams? Gina is an impressionable girl, Dad."

"Sensitive, I'd call it."

"She is no more talking to Mother in her dreams than you or I," Jonathan said.

"Do you think I don't know that?" Robert said. "Is that what you think?" He seemed tickled at the notion.

"Where are the help?" Jonathan asked.

"'The help' got the morning off. I wanted some peace around here. Ellen and Ruth are bigger busybodies than you, son. They will be here in an hour or so for supper—don't you worry."

"I won't be here."

"Well, there you are." Robert picked up the bottle.

"Has Gina been wandering again, Dad? That's why we need Ellen and Ruth around. The place can fall apart otherwise, as far as I'm concerned. And all this talk about Mother coming to visit her isn't helping, Dad. In her condition."

"Her condition is fine. There's nothing wrong with that girl but that she's too soft-hearted. Not like you and I, eh, Jon?" He poured some whiskey into his glass.

"How many lucky falls down the stairs do you think she has? We should change the lock on her bedroom door, get a new key."

"I've lost track of all the keys and locks around here, too," Robert said, taking a sip. "Say, Jon, did you tell that girl, Gwendolyn, about your plans? Does she know your right and proper intentions?"

"I told you I don't have plans or intentions."

"Not you, Jonny, no. Maybe you should. You are the most bloodless young man I've ever seen. Now sit down and have a drink with your father."

Jonathan tossed his tie on the chair and folded his arms.

"So is it love or money, Jon? Just what kind of living has this sweet thing grown accustomed to?"

"Gwen doesn't have much money, Dad. We're the rich ones around here, remember?"

"Good for you. Hope for you yet. People worry about money so damn much."

"You have me to worry about money around here, Dad."

Robert's eyes lit up behind the dull whiskey glow. "Let's not forget whose money we're discussing, my boy."

"Never, Dad. Never." Jonathan looked down at his father, the anger in his eyes spent, exhausted only for the moment. A stranger walking out onto the gallery at that moment might have mistaken the look for tenderness.

Robert's face warmed up again with pleasant amusement. "Will you do me one favor, son, should I go to my reward before you marry that nice girl? Would you give her a shovel for me? You should both hold it in your wedding picture, because you're going to dig that hole together."

"You're drunk and the sun hasn't even gone down." Jonathan picked up his tie.

"This will all be yours, once you have your education and are a man and take your sweet young bride." Robert refilled his glass. "I wish you a long life, son. *Domine, miserere nobis.*" Lord, have mercy on us. He took a long drink.

"Amen," Jonathan said, and went back into the house.

Jonathan found Regina in her room, sitting on the bed with her hands folded. Her four-poster bed loomed up around her, the transparent white curtains catching some sun from the window, the light making the bed and the room and Regina like visions out of memory. Regina looked up, expecting him.

"He's lonely, Jonathan. Why must you provoke him?"

"I don't want you sitting out there with him when he's like that, Gina. It's not good for either of you."

"He'll be sad, alone out there."

"He'll be passed out in ten minutes."

"I had another dream—"

"Gina, please. Have you had any rest since this morning?"

"I haven't needed it, Jonathan."

"If you don't rest you'll be more restless tonight, Gina, you know that. Have you been walking at night lately?"

"Not as much," Regina said, lying back on her bed and curling up.

Jonathan stroked her forehead, her hair. "Have you been forgetting again?"

"Not so much. It's better now."

"Rest. Ruth and Ellen will be here soon to see to supper. I have an appointment in the city. I have to catch a train."

Regina already seemed to be falling asleep. "'Night, Jonathan."

He bent to kiss her on the head and went out into the hall, closing the door quietly behind him. He looked a moment at the keyhole in her door, the key lost years before. After checking his watch, Jonathan went downstairs and made sure to lock all of the doors to the outside. As he left the sunporch, a view of the back lawn and the place where the grass gave way to the steep fall to the river below caught his attention, the water darkening in the late afternoon light. Jonathan turned toward the front door and hurried for his train.

. . .

Regina sits up in her bed, the smell of earth and cold brick in her nose. Mother. She must descend to meet her, follow her voice—descend down into the house, down into the earthy smell, descend and emerge to meet her by the river.

Jonathan. He loves but does not understand. He cannot meet her. He's home but cannot come home.

Regina must go where she knew she shouldn't as a little girl, the place Mother told her to forget. The dark place, below. She would go there now. She must. Mother calling, from outside. On the river.

She finds herself in her father's room, standing at the bookshelf, already holding the long iron key her father has forgotten, the hands and heart under the crown on the key cold but not dead. She had seen him put the key there years before, when he did not know she saw, when she was as quiet as a shadow in the hallway, and then she had forgotten it and he had forgotten it. And then Mother in the dark said, The shelf, the key. Regina.

She finds herself at the top of the stairs. The light from outside becomes more golden, slow and soft. She finds herself on the sunporch. Hand on the doorknob—holding fast. In the kitchen. Motes of dust from the pantry, dancing.

The basement stairs. The corner. The dark corner.

She nearly drops the long iron key.

Cold metal. Earth and bricks. Descending to meet her. In the dark. The basement. The earth. Her fingers on the bricks. Damp. Cold.

Mother calling.

The bricks. The long dark.

The little house. Light. Another door.

Outside. Grass, river breeze. Father's feet propped on the balustrade above, Father's head laid to the side. Peace.

Mother's voice, harder to hear in daylight, coming from somewhere, from all around.

Regina closes her eyes.

Mother.

One step . . . two. Three?

Hear the voice. Know it.

One step. Two.

Breeze from below. Water. Earth.

Mother. By the river.

One step.

Two.

The ground flips sideways.

The rocks, the water.

For one instant, Regina's feet leave the earth, and all she knows is water and sky and Mother. Calling.

PART THREE

11.

THE CIRCLE OPENS

EMILY AND MICHAEL SAT IN MRS. POMEROY'S PARLOR, A grandmother's place of lace and china. A cold porcelain crucifix hung over the doorway. Mrs. Pomeroy and her friends were arrayed in chairs around the room and observed the twins, who wore fine clothes usually reserved for church and family visits. When Michael first descended into the front hall at Ravenwood in his blue suit and Emily followed in a flowered dress and polished shoes, their mother looked up from her newspaper and greeted them with raised eyebrows. "Having tea with the governor, children?"

"Catherine Pomeroy invited us to lunch at her grandmother's house," Michael said.

Emily said, "We thought it would be fun to dress up a little."

"You two certainly have strange ideas about fun. A little old for dress-up, aren't we?"

"Adults play dress-up all the time," Michael said.

Mrs. Stewart disappeared behind her paper. "Fair enough."

As Emily and Michael walked out of the east entrance and onto the street, they saw Mr. Loewry pulling up in his two-tone brown automobile. They waved, and he waved, and the twins went on their way.

"I wonder if he feels guilty?" Emily had said.

"Who?"

"Mr. Loewry."

"Guilty about what?"

"About Daddy. About not seeing him again before . . ."

"How should I know what he feels? What's the difference? He's here now—he and Mama can sit around and remember what it was like to be young."

"No need to be so touchy—"

"I'm not *touchy*, Em." Michael moved ahead in long, tense strides. "We've got more pressing things to think about, that's all."

In Mrs. Pomeroy's parlor, Emily and Michael sat side by side with cups and saucers on their laps. The ladies took turns asking the twins questions and making satisfied sounds at the answers, while breaking off into details about their own lives. The ladies took a surprising interest in the twins' birth date.

"June twenty-third?" Mrs. Pomeroy said. "Ah." She had a soothing voice, like water tumbling over small pebbles. "You are Cancers: very sensitive, very impressionable." Mrs. Pomeroy was tremendously heavy, the biggest woman Emily or Michael had ever seen. Mrs. Pomeroy, the twins discovered, had taught Latin and ancient Greek at a women's college in Massachusetts in the years before her marriage, many years before she was widowed. Mrs. Pomeroy was an apostle of beautiful things. In her days as a teacher, she had often battled with the administration to place art and culture over budget and politics. "We are here in this world for the beauty," she told the twins. "We must endure the ugliness." Around her neck, Mrs. Pomeroy wore another large crucifix, this one silver, with an intricately detailed and suffering Christ. Emily half expected His blood to drip into her hostess's tea. She tried not to stare.

"Twin Cancers," Mrs. Pomeroy said.

"Connected in birth, connected in spirit," one of the Misses Irving said—a small, thin woman, who blinked infrequently and shared the couch with her sister. Miss Sophia, the one who had spoken up, had encouraged the twins to call her and her sister, Miss Rose, by their Christian names to avoid confusion.

"Which one of you was born first?" Miss Rose asked.

"I was," Emily said, "by a few minutes."

Miss Sophia and Miss Rose nodded at one another. The resemblance between them was so close, an unknowing person would have picked them out as the twins in the room. Even the deep pattern of lines around their eyes seemed to match. They had lived together for many years and gave the effect of two different moods in the same well-mannered person. Miss Sophia was a retired librarian and an amateur historian with an astonishing capacity to recall minute details of books she had read long ago and people many years in their graves. "It seems to me," Miss Sophia said, "that memory is the most useful thing about people."

Miss Rose was a classically trained cellist who had studied in Germany and France as a young woman. "I play violin, myself," Miss Sophia offered, "but nothing like Rose."

Miss Rose shrugged.

"Her instructor told Papa that she could have played in any orchestra in the world, if she were a man," Miss Sophia said.

All of this before returning to their father's house to care for him in a slow decline that lasted decades—reading to him from the newspapers in the morning and playing for him in the afternoon.

In a high-backed wooden chair sat Mrs. Lattimore, a light-skinned black woman with brilliantly white hair, an imperious presence, and a terse, self-conscious British accent. "You are very bold," she said to Michael, watching him over her teacup through a curling veil of steam. Mrs. Lattimore was the daughter of a merchant from Barbados. She had gone to England to work as a governess and teacher in the family of one of her father's business associates for a few years, learned everything she could about British civility and culture, and returned to Barbados to marry another of her father's merchant acquaintances, who had brought her to the United States twenty years ago. "And you," she said to Emily, leaning forward, "have an old heart. Very old. Anyone can see that."

Emily and Michael were amazed that the ladies did not ask any questions about spirit knocking, other than when Emily had realized her talent and how often she practiced it. This acceptance before the fact surprised the twins almost as much as the ladies' willingness to tell their life stories in brief, as if out of custom. Emily and Michael had watched their own mother hesitate to even introduce herself on the odd occasion a stranger confronted her.

"My mother was often visited by my father in her dreams after he passed away," Mrs. Pomeroy said. "And sometimes he would lie in bed with her when she couldn't sleep. She said she could sense him there, like she had for years and years before he passed on."

"When we were still girls," Miss Rose said, "there was a man in the neighborhood who had seizures and spoke in tongues."

"He would convulse and twitch," Miss Sophia added. "He said that he felt God pressing down on him—that God was shouting at him. Some of the people said that when it was on him, he saw things in the future—and that if he saw a person in a golden light, that person's time was coming."

Miss Rose sat up. "Grace," she said to Mrs. Lattimore, "tell Michael and Emily about your grandmother."

Mrs. Lattimore lowered her eyelids on Miss Rose and raised them on the twins. "To her the living and the dead were all the same," she said. "She taught my mother that the dead are part of the air all around us; their blood runs in the rivers and in the ground and through our bodies. My grandmother taught my mother some very old things." Mrs. Lattimore sipped her tea.

"Yes," Mrs. Pomeroy said. "My mother had many charms, also, and she left me this"—indicating the crucifix around her neck— "which was used in the daily devotions of Benedictine monks." Mrs. Pomeroy took the crucifix in her hand and closed her eyes a moment. "My Tom died in 1909, in a hunting accident," she said. "A card reader in Boston had told me that a terrible misfortune would befall me, and I waited and prayed and waited. I looked for signs." Mrs. Pomeroy dabbled in the reading of tea leaves, as well as palms and tarot cards, but said she considered herself purely an amateur. "I waited, and sure enough, less than a year later, Tom was hunting with his brother, and . . . there was an accident."

Mrs. Lattimore sipped her tea and watched Emily. "My husband's been dead for six years," she said in her studied voice. "A woman who accused him of fathering her child poisoned him."

Mrs. Lattimore made a disgusted sound; her eyes sparkled. "She poisoned a glass of whiskey Carl was drinking, and that killed him quick." She finished the last of her tea and placed her saucer on the tiny table in the center of their circle.

Emily and Michael sat speechless. They had never known adults to speak this openly before, and were uncertain of the proper response. For want of any handy revelations, they commented on the ladies' remarks only in the form of nods and interested looks.

"We never married," Miss Rose said. She waited a respectable moment before continuing, watching the children. "Our father wanted us to be ladies . . . he wanted us to know about a better world. Music, books. And then he was so sick for so long."

Miss Sophia cleared her throat and leaned forward, her voice hushed. "Now, Mrs. Nerova's husband—" she said. Just then there were heavy footsteps on the front porch and three quick knocks on the door.

"Careful," Mrs. Lattimore said. "She can hear you thinking."

"Come in, Basya," Mrs. Pomeroy called. She gave Emily a pat on the knee that said everything would be just fine. "Mrs. Nerova is an artist. A sculptor. Very passionate."

"Keeps her work locked up in the basement, hidden from the world," Mrs. Lattimore said.

"Her great-grandmother was a countess, you know," Miss Rose said. "Long story. Very sad."

The front door swung open and a sturdy little woman came quickly through the living room, the deep folds of her skirt swirling about her. She was round and compact, and somehow gave the impression of great size. Her graying blond hair was pulled up behind her head in a hasty ponytail. The woman squinted at

Emily and Michael, who fought the urge to shrink into their seats. She carried a box bound up in string under one arm, which she set aside.

"This," said Mrs. Pomeroy, "is Mrs. Nerova."

"Hello," Mrs. Nerova said in a thick Slavic accent. She chose a chair and sat down. Miss Sophia had gotten up and filled a cup for the fierce little woman. As Mrs. Nerova began to sip her tea, Mrs. Lattimore said, "We were just talking about our husbands, and we've told about all but yours—"

"That *bastard*," Mrs. Nerova hissed, setting her cup on the saucer before her with a clatter. "That old *bastard*." Mrs. Nerova leaned toward Emily. "Are they talking about him, these hens?"

Mrs. Pomeroy said, "Of course not, Basya—"

"Have they told you *I* killed him?" Mrs. Nerova asked the children, pointing her chin at them. "I did—don't let them tell you different. I killed him, and I wish I could dig him up and kill him again. I would cut his heart out." Mrs. Nerova picked up her cup, sipped from it, and set it daintily back on the saucer.

Mrs. Pomeroy said, "Basya, please."

Mrs. Lattimore laughed, making the cup and saucer in her hand ring. "Basya," she said, "you did not kill that man."

"I *did*, I *did*. God *damn* it." Mrs. Nerova stood up and addressed the two young guests. "I prayed ten years—*ten*—I prayed and prayed." She knelt down. "I prayed, 'God, God Almighty, please, *please* kill that rotten old bastard! Please, set me free, deliver me!'" She stood up and shook the creases out of her skirt. "And finally— *boom*—God heard me, and I am so, so grateful."

"Basya," Mrs. Pomeroy said, absently touching her crucifix with her fingertips.

"He had a massive stroke," Miss Sophia told the children.

"His third," Mrs. Lattimore said.

Mrs. Nerova resumed her seat and sipped her tea. "He's dead, that's what counts."

"He's been dead eight years now," Mrs. Lattimore said.

"If he were standing here now," Mrs. Nerova said with dignity, "I would cut his dirty heart out." She took another sip of tea. "Now." Mrs. Nerova produced a silver pie cutter from her box and pointed it at Emily. "Who wants cake?"

The ladies passed pieces of soft, crumbling apple cake all around on small plates with blue images of wispy trees. The ladies ate their cake and discussed it for a polite while. Finally, Mrs. Nerova fixed an appraising, challenging look on Emily. "So," she said, "you are the ghost twins?"

Emily blushed. "Yes, ma'am. You could say that."

"I could say that," Mrs. Nerova said. "I could say lots of things. When were you born?"

"They are Cancers," Miss Rose volunteered.

"You are doing this how long?" Mrs. Nerova said.

"Over a month," Michael said.

Mrs. Nerova looked at Michael and then at Mrs. Pomeroy. "What about him?"

"He assists Emily," Mrs. Pomeroy said. "Isn't that right, Michael?"

"Yes, ma'am, that's right."

"*Assist,*" Mrs. Nerova said. She placed her plate and saucer on the tiny round table. "Assist. You have no ghost?"

"No, ma'am."

"You are like gypsies, you two?" Mrs. Nerova said. "You *assist* people finding ghosts?"

THE GIRL WHO WOULD SPEAK FOR THE DEAD

Emily steeled herself by thinking, *If it gets too bad, I can just say I can't do it anymore. I can say that I can't do it anymore, and that will be that.*

Mrs. Nerova stood up. "Okay. Enough talk." She took the plates and saucers from the others and gathered them together on the table. "Now," she said, turning toward Emily, "you bring ghost for us."

"We've never tried this outside the tea house," Michael hurried to say.

"Tea house?" Mrs. Nerova said.

"We have a little playhouse at home," Emily said. "I contact Regina there."

Mrs. Nerova looked at Emily and raised one eyebrow, gathering her forehead in deep creases. "You are rich, yes?"

"Yes, ma'am," Emily said.

"How nice," Mrs. Nerova said, looking at Emily with hardly a blink.

Emily fought the urge to look away. "Yes," she said. Then, raising her chin a bit: "We have everything we need."

"And more, I'm sure," Mrs. Nerova said, as if she'd heard all she needed to know. "Go on. The playhouse."

Emily drew a breath. "Regina died near the tea house. She reached me first there."

"Do you think you can do it here?" Miss Sophia said.

"I will try," Emily said, grateful to turn to someone else.

Michael gave Emily a meaningful look of encouragement, then stood up. "We'll need a moment of silence, please. Also, you must all want Regina to come to us. Emily needs your help. If we could all concentrate."

· 113 ·

The ladies lowered their heads and closed their eyes. Mrs. Pomeroy did so first, folding her hands in her lap. The sisters followed suit, looking penitent in the soft light from the window behind them. Mrs. Lattimore touched her temple in deep concentration. Mrs. Nerova, last to close her eyes, dropped her lids and took a slow breath.

Michael resumed his seat. "Remember," he said, "one knock means no, two knocks, yes." Michael let the moment spin out into another and another, listening to the steady tick of Mrs. Pomeroy's clock in the next room. "Regina?" he said. The name hung in the air above them. "Regina, are you with us?"

Emily sensed the five ladies straining to hear anything at all.

A single knock sounded. Emily counted an instant off in her mind and let the tension play out into more quiet. A second knock followed and settled around them into silence.

"Welcome, Regina," Michael said. "We are so glad to have you with us again."

Emily felt everyone relax, down to herself and Michael. The ladies glowed with it; she felt them settle into their chairs. The magic had worked again—the magic would always work again.

12.

THE SPIRIT OF LONELY PLACES

ONE WEEK AFTER THE MEETING WITH THE LADIES, EMILY found herself unable to stay inside the house. She went downstairs and out into the afternoon sun. Another unforgiving August day, but she welcomed the sunlight on her face. She crossed the lawn to stand on the high riverbank. There were no boats on the water and few geese, making the Delaware seem desolate.

In Emily's book of make-believe, she had recently read of the Wendigo, haunting forgotten places where people lost their way. When a traveler walks through a forest or across hills or through an icy, northern waste, the book said, the Wendigo follows him—a watched feeling, a sense of pursuit—forcing the traveler to look over his or her shoulder, or to stop and listen. But the cleverness and speed of the Wendigo is too great, and it never allows the traveler to see more than a shadow of itself; the Wendigo's voice is only a soft sigh on the breeze or the long, low moaning of the wind at night. Some stories told of a towering phantom, a harbinger of death—others painted a flesh-eating monster, stalking hunters in the northern woodlands. According to the book of make-believe, the spirit of lonely places took on many forms.

Looking across the river, Emily imagined that the shadowy Wendigo could be anywhere around her: in the tall grass along the water's edge, in the shrubbery around the mansion, across the river on the New Jersey side, slipping through the trees, able to make out every detail of her face despite the wide expanse of water between. The Wendigo might even have been in the tea house while she stood squinting in the sunlight, perhaps with its face close to the window, disguised by the reflection of the trees along the river and the blue sky overhead, its breathless form perfectly still. She had walked out here to look at the river but now felt compelled to turn away. The lonely quiet sent her mind back to livelier times, full of change.

After meeting with the ladies a week before, Michael had been exuberant as they made their way home. "I thought that Mrs. Nerova was going to ruin everything," Michael had said. "But once you got started, I think we had her more than the rest of them."

"Yes. Maybe."

"*Maybe?* I don't think there's any maybe about it. You were there, Em—they couldn't take their eyes off you."

The ladies had greeted her and embraced her so warmly, so lovingly. There had been no fear in them, unlike the children, who treated a spirit-knocking session as a test of courage. Somehow even this was not quite right—that the ladies had been fearless. Emily sensed that whatever fear they brought with them, it was certainly not of her, or even of the ghost she claimed to bring with her. She knew, even then, though she could hardly tell herself so, that the fear the ladies sat down with on that afternoon had been tended so long it had become hope.

On the riverbank, Emily began imagining what it would be like to be the Wendigo itself instead of the traveler. To see the traveler stop and listen, becoming so still; to move unseen in the shadows and be felt in the oldest parts of the traveler's mind. She turned toward the house and looked at the gleaming windows and the deep black of the shutters, seeing the place as an unearthly visitor from a distant tundra might. She considered the third-floor gallery with its guarded shadows and the leaf-dappled sunlight dancing on the balustrade. If she were the Wendigo, she would watch from behind the thick, molded posts, her face barely perceptible in the shade and invisible in the dappled light. She would wait for a lonely traveler to appear on the riverbank. And if the traveler went to the house, moving out of the sun and into the shadow of the mansion, and crossed the porch boards, accompanied by the intimate echoes of his own heels, and ascended through the house—first floor, second floor, third floor—and walked out onto the third-floor gallery in hopes of catching the Wendigo at her game, he would find himself confronted by the deserted gallery, a remote horizon, and the faint sound of an occasional stray breeze in the heat, sighing just loud enough to be heard.

Dusk gathered to its fullest before vanishing beneath the twilight. Emily came through the house to a back staircase, running her hand along the cool plaster wall beside her, still wandering like a stranger in her own home. At the top of the staircase, she heard the voices of her mother and Stan Loewry. The staircase stood at the end of a short hall that passed the sunporch; nothing could be seen going on in there from the foot of the stairs, but a turn of acoustics brought voices through the doorway and around the interceding wall. Emily crept down the stairs, placing her feet at the edge of each riser to avoid the squeaks waiting down the center of the staircase.

"I remember how he would tell me, 'Now, be reasonable, Stan,'" Stan said. "In that rational voice of his."

"Yes," her mother said. "He was always telling me that, too."

"He couldn't understand that he was the only reasonable one around, and that he would just have to be patient with the rest of us."

Emily knew they were speaking of her father; he had told her more than a few times to be reasonable herself.

"And when the War came?" Stan said. "What did he say about that?"

"Nobody liked the War, Stan."

"But we would all have to rise to the occasion? Do what we could?"

"Stan . . ."

"But he did say that?"

"Yes, Stan, he did. And that is why he volunteered."

Emily sat down on the bottom stair and rested her chin in her hands. She had been six years old when her father left for Europe; she vaguely remembered him in his dress uniform. Emily's boyish-looking father, at the age of thirty-seven, had been transformed from a gentleman doctor into an army surgeon, rank of major. As Emily recalled, the uniform made him look younger, not older.

"How close did you get to the fighting?" her mother said.

"Not very. But if you were anywhere near it, you heard the

artillery all the time. Day and night, shelling. Sounded like the world was ending. Suddenly it seemed like all of Europe was running in every direction, like they had all gone crazy. This was more so near the front, of course. I had been there three years when the War started, and I had become used to a certain Continental ease." Stan tossed the words away as if they meant nothing to him. "Of course, the best way to experience a war is on an account provided by Dad way back when. Made things much more comfortable."

They were quiet a moment. Emily gazed at the wall.

"I followed the battles awhile," Stan said. "I was drawn to the fighting. I never thought it was glamorous. I knew some who did. But I found myself following it. It was then that I got accustomed to the constant shelling. I remember thinking, 'My God, will they never run out of ammunition?' By then Dad was very deeply involved in iron, and had gotten into munitions. Lots of contracts with the Brits. So I would listen to the shelling, and think about the men dying nearby, and I would think about Dad busily making shells and God knows what all else, and I would receive another check with his accountant's return address."

Emily heard Stan set his cup down. A long, still moment followed the sound of cup and saucer. She sat rigid, fearing that even her breathing might betray her.

Stan said, "How were the children, when the news came about Donald?"

A chair creaked; her mother cleared her throat. "That was the hardest thing. I always thought the hardest thing would be going to sleep alone and waking up alone, but telling Emily and Michael was hardest. I received the telegram on a Monday. It said that Donald had been killed on October tenth, less than a week before.

That was another thing I remember—feeling so strange. Doctors aren't supposed to die, for one thing. And Donald had been dead almost a week, and I hadn't known it. The idea that Donald could be gone, and that I could walk around for a week not knowing. I took the letter upstairs before I opened it—it was clearly post-marked and official-looking. And I had that sinking feeling. That feeling when you know something terrible has happened but there's still time to believe, for a moment, that it hasn't? And you think, 'Don't be silly, everything is fine, this is nothing,' and usually, that's right. After all, he wasn't a soldier, he wasn't fighting in the trenches. But then, sometimes, it is something."

Emily stifled a sudden choking sound in her throat. She placed a hand over her mouth and looked at the floor in surprise.

"Yes," Stan said.

"So I took the letter upstairs and I opened it. And there it was: *'We regret to inform you.'*"

"Naomi, you don't have to—"

"No, please, Stan. I read the letter, and I wouldn't let Mary into the room. I heard her crying out in the hall already, so I knew she'd seen the envelope. I remember how angry that made me. That woman does not cry often. I thought about going out into the hall and firing her, Stan, God help me." She laughed. "Imagine that, after she'd been a mother to me. I opened the door, and Mary looked at my face and she knew, and we sat on the bed together and cried and cried." She laughed a little again.

Emily covered her face with her hands. Her body shook.

"I was so mad at him for leaving the twins and me to volunteer, all for his damn ideas about duty. It took a long time to make my peace with that."

"Duty was the only reason he left?"

Emily thought she heard regret in his voice even before he'd finished the question.

"Yes, Stan," her mother said.

Someone picked up a cup. Soft clatter of china and silverware.

Her mother cleared her throat again. "After a few hours, I told Emily. I thought, no point in keeping it from her; she was going to see Mary and me moping around the place, and anyway, she had a right to know. Michael was a very bright little boy in his own way, but Em . . . she was always an old soul."

Emily rubbed the palms of her hands against her eyes.

"I asked her to help me tell Michael. We told him together. He didn't say a thing. It was terrible: he sort of closed up right in front of us—his eyes, his mouth, his whole face. When we tried to hug him, he was so rigid, squeezing his whole body together. He didn't talk for a few days. I almost called in a doctor. But he ate, so I waited. And eventually, he talked. For a long time, he didn't want to talk about his father at all, and I never forced him."

Quiet. Uncovering her face, Emily clasped her hands together and waited.

"Before you left for Europe," her mother said, "you and Donald fought." She waited a moment. "Isn't that right?"

"Yes. He told you?"

"He seemed very upset, and when I made some remark about it, he was very short with me. Donald wasn't often like that."

Stan sighed. "Donald and I disagreed about a lot of things," he said, "you know that. Of course, there was politics. Donald never liked some of my friends, and when they came to school, he kept his distance. He always said, 'All you rich kids, running off with the socialists in tuxedos and sport coupés.' Of course by then, *he* was something of a rich kid, too, but his father had never let him feel like a rich kid, and he never really felt part of our little Princeton clique. 'All your talk about "social injustice" and the "working man"—not one of you has ever had to work a day in your lives,' he used to say. 'And you, Stan,' he'd say, because of course I was the worst example, 'how do you think the slaving masses feel about a wealthy brat who is always trying to find either a drink or a girl, and has all the money and time in the world to do it?'"

"He was unfair at times," Mrs. Stewart offered.

"No, that was pretty fair, I thought. Even then. It's not that Donald was uncaring, Naomi—I never thought that. He believed in the flag and the old republic. I didn't. But at least I believed in something in those days."

"And now?"

"Ask me again tomorrow."

Quiet. A chair shifted. A cup clattered, picked up or put down.

"And that night in the library?" her mother said.

"When I went in to see him, he was drunk—I guess you knew that at the time—and that caught me off-guard. The man wasn't much of a drinker. Donald was sitting at the table with his feet up and looking out the window. He had a tumbler of gin in his hand, and I looked at him, and I knew right away he was as drunk as a lord. So he just kept looking out the window, which was frosted over—it was a brutally cold night, remember?—and he said, 'Sit down, Stan. Drink?' I told him he was way ahead of me, and he laughed. I remember that laugh sounded so unhappy. I knew I should leave before something unpleasant happened. But I couldn't, because something very unpleasant had been building up for some time by then, and I guess I wanted to finally see how it would be."

"I did hear the shouting," Mrs. Stewart said.

"Yeah. We talked for a while, and I had a drink or two. He only seemed to half listen to what I said. There was another conversation he wanted to have, about all of the things that had changed between us, and I was feeling ready for that conversation myself, because I was tired and sad, too. Finally, he started in: 'So, you been out with your crusader friends?' And I said, still trying to make a joke of everything, 'Yes. We're planning to overthrow the government—I can get you in on the ground floor.' Donald laughed. 'That would be perfect, Stan, that would be just right for you. Overthrow. Isn't it funny how those who have everything, who could have *anything*, still want what other people have? Isn't it funny how that is, Stan? People will do anything—especially these funny people with everything they want—they'll do *anything*.

"'They'll betray, steal, whatever it takes.' And then he said that I had a fine nerve criticizing Rockefeller, Morgan, my father— that I was put together just like those men, men who never finish acquiring. He said that I simply tried to take whatever I wanted. He was mostly right about that, too. And then he got out of his chair and he paced around, still shouting at me. I was getting awful mad myself, by then. Mostly out of guilt. And then he picked up that little goddamn statue of Jefferson he always had around, and I thought he was going to throw it at me. I used to call Jefferson 'the Great American' to get under Donald's skin back at Princeton. So at that moment, when Donald was standing there with Jefferson in his hand—and to this day I don't know what he had in mind to do with it—I said to him, 'Are you going to work me over with

Saint Thomas there?' I think I wanted him to throw it at me, to just heave it at my head and be done with it. But he said, 'Get out of my house.' I went right for the door, and he said—I remember this very clearly—'Don't say good-bye to Naomi, Stan. Don't say a word to her. Just leave this house.' And then—I shouldn't tell you this, Naomi, but I felt like killing him then, when he said that. So I left."

A long quiet followed. When Mrs. Stewart did finally speak, she said, "Would you like some fresh air, Stan?"

"That would be very nice."

Emily hurried softly up to the small landing where the staircase turned left. She stood just beyond the corner of the landing and listened. Below, Stan and her mother walked out of the sunporch and within several feet of the foot of the stairs, still warm from Emily's presence, and through the house toward the front entrance. The front door opened and closed, and a great stillness filled the house. Emily came back down the stairs and looked at the two chairs where Stan and her mother had been sitting. Two empty glasses stood on the table.

13.

BRUSHSTROKES ON CANVAS

ON A BRIGHT WEDNESDAY MORNING, MR. HOLT SET UP A stool and an easel on the grass just beside the cobblestone drive. After arranging his palette with gobs of color and placing a clean, white canvas on his easel, he stood on the cobblestone drive and looked at the tea house, his eyes squinting, his fingertips at his lips. He circled the tea house, his eyes moving over the door and windows and bricks and roof. His fingers tapped at his lips. He came around to his easel, regarded the empty canvas, looked again at the tea house—now at a two-thirds angle in his view—and returned his attention to the canvas. He picked up his palette, dipped his brush into the colors congealing there in heaps, and raised it to the canvas, beginning to break up the expansive white with strokes of color.

Emily opened the door for Mr. Holt when he knocked.
"I saw you painting out there a little while ago," she said.

"Why didn't you step out to say hello?"

"I didn't want to disturb you. Also, I'd rather not see the painting until it's finished."

"I left the canvas out on the porch to dry, so you might want to be careful about going out there. Now, where is that brother of yours?"

"Upstairs; I'll get him." Emily shut the door behind Mr. Holt, and the tutor stood in the middle of the main hall, hands in his pockets. The man seemed forever prepared to ponder the things around him, however familiar.

Emily stopped and turned back. "Mr. Holt," she said, "can I ask you a question?"

"Of course. Your mother pays me to answer questions."

"It may seem a little odd."

Mr. Holt raised one eyebrow. "All right."

"What, exactly, is a socialist?"

"You are the strangest girl," he said, as if to himself. "What would make you ask me that?"

"I hear about things," she said. "I know that it's politics and all that, but I want to know more about it."

"Thinking of becoming a socialist, Miss Stewart?"

Emily frowned so he would know she expected a real answer.

"Well," he said, "that is a bit like asking what a Buddhist is, isn't it? I mean, I could tell you what I think a Buddhist is, and what the books I've read say a Buddhist is, but in the end I can only give you my best impression of a Buddhist." He paused and watched her eyes. "And you accept this?" he asked her.

Emily nodded.

"Well then, a socialist—" Mr. Holt turned on his heel and

walked around in a small half-circle, his hand on his chin. "A socialist believes that things like factories or land shouldn't belong to companies or the wealthy, but that such things should belong to the people—that is, everyone. They want a government that does not reward profit or property, to create a society where people work for the good of the whole." Mr. Holt did not seem quite as glad as usual to pass on information. His voice—which he could easily project across a large room—was restrained, as if his ears were sensitive to the echo of his words in Ravenwood's grand front hall. "Does that answer your question?"

"Yes. May I ask another?"

"Of course."

"Are you a socialist, Mr. Holt?"

He laughed and shook his head. "No, Em, I am not. I am not because—well, that is very complicated. Let's just say that I don't have the optimism that sort of thinking requires." He paused, then added, "I am far too cynical about human nature to believe a society like that can exist. I wish I weren't. I may have been able to muster some optimism when I was younger."

"Are there many socialists?"

"More than you think. A bunch of them in Russia got together and overthrew the tsar a few years back. There are some who would like to do the same thing here." Mr. Holt's eyes twinkled. "I wonder if I could ask you a question, then?"

"Go on," Emily said. She folded her arms.

"Does any of this have to do with Mr. Loewry?"

Emily's mouth snapped shut.

"Because it just so happens that Mr. Loewry used to write for a socialist newspaper in Philadelphia, several years before the War started in Europe. You see, I've known one or two socialists in my time and seen one or two socialist newspapers. Anyway, that paper's gone now—they're all gone: the government shut down all those newspapers and magazines when we entered the War. As I say, I was never a socialist myself, but I've read a few of Mr. Loewry's articles. He was quite a firebrand. Passionate. He never wrote under his own name, naturally—but, as I say, I knew one or two people who knew quite a bit about local socialists. I imagine his father must have found out, too. I can't believe the old man didn't disown him. Blood *is* thick, I suppose." As he spoke, Mr. Holt turned on his heel, still taking in the details around him. He turned fully and faced Emily. "Now," he said, "ask yourself this, if you can spare a moment from tracking ghosts around here: What would make a man like that, a man with so much wealth, thanks to the toil of I don't know how many faceless people in his father's factories—what would make this man write anonymous articles calling for the end of the workers' slavery and for a world where the only exchange rate lies between brotherhood and kindness?"

Emily, out of responses, met his question with a look of no answers.

Mr. Holt looked at his watch. "Better call your brother, Emily. We'll talk old politics another time. The day rapidly escapes us."

14.

PERSONAL EFFECTS

ANOTHER ROUND OF INTENSE AUGUST HEAT SETTLED OVER Ravenwood, hot and muggy with long afternoons. By the end of the first week, Emily and Michael had met with the ladies three times. In the first session, the ladies had asked familiar questions of Regina: Are you with your family? Do you miss the world? Are you at peace? Emily took in the ladies' sighs and whispers after each answer, almost as if they willed the knocks, not her. As if she really were only an instrument. This sensation did not unsettle her; it was a source of great comfort. For Michael, each session was like a stunt, even when the twins had gotten comfortable and there seemed little chance that the ladies would suddenly dispute the whole business. It was all a grand experiment, careful, calculated, and revealing. Emily could forgive him this, somehow, but couldn't indulge in these feelings herself. She focused instead on the ladies' appetite for spirit knocking, on their smiles, and on the idea that when they lay down in their beds at night, everything they'd left behind in their lives wouldn't seem so far away. And the ladies' eyes when they looked at her, their hushed voices, almost like joyous bows before her—though Emily found herself unable to dwell on such things for long without reminding herself of the ladies lying down in their lonely beds at night.

The ladies—who often fulfilled all the expected roles of civility—never once asked after their mother, or how things were at the house. The closest the ladies had come to discussing the twins' family came on Emily and Michael's second visit to Mrs. Pomeroy's parlor, where their hostess told the twins, in reference to their dealings with the world beyond, "We know how much loss your family has suffered." Cat had communicated the twins' wish of discretion and secrecy, and sometimes it seemed to Emily that the most astonishing thing of all was how dutifully the ladies honored it.

And the twins learned more about the ladies. Mrs. Pomeroy's lovely speaking voice came with a matching singing voice, which they discovered when she sang an old French hymn. Mrs. Lattimore had sailed along the coast of South America in her father's ship as a young girl, and she had watched whales breach and dive at sunset, and seen sharks pull thrashing seabirds underwater. Mrs. Nerova's great-great-grandmother, not her great-grandmother, was supposed in family lore to have been a countess disowned by her father over an affair with a sailor. Miss Sophia gave this last detail to Emily and Michael, with some tone of apology and an eye on Mrs. Nerova, who sat impervious, looking bored. "All done," Mrs. Nerova said. "All gone, anyway."

Miss Rose leaned toward the twins. "The Revolution, you know. No more aristocracy."

"The Bolsheviks," Miss Sophia added, "swept away the old Russia. So even if she hadn't met that sailor—"

"Is better this way," Mrs. Nerova said. "What else they take from me?"

For the second session with the ladies, Michael hinted that they should bring out some of their menagerie of ghosts. Emily suggested that Michael's ghosts were riskier than Regina, who was at least a real dead person.

"Em," Michael said, "those ladies are not trying to prove that you can't do this. If they were, we'd already be finished. All of this means more to them than it ever could to you or me."

Emily's eyes were on the water, her arms wrapped around her shins. "I know that, Michael. Don't you think I know that?"

"So, which ones should we use next time?" Michael said. "The poet? The nun?"

At the ladies' second spirit-knocking session, Michael introduced some ghosts from the notebook, suggesting to the ladies that while Emily had discovered she could reach beyond Regina, she was still learning to feel the presence of the dead inside her, and that at times the responses of these less-familiar spirits were murky and confusing. "This way," Michael had told Emily, "if you're not sure how to answer, for whatever reason, you can put on a troubled look and I'll rush in and calm the old girls down with a lot of talk about 'murkiness' and 'confusion.'"

The ladies, delighted with these additions, sat in a hush around Emily as the knocks echoed in their empty teacups. At the end of the third session, after the ladies had avidly questioned the poet—whose answers Emily made increasingly delayed—Mrs. Nerova got out of her chair and knelt before Emily, taking the girl's hand. "Emily," Mrs. Nerova said, "you maybe could reach others? Besides poet and soldiers and this nun?"

"It might be . . . possible," Emily said.

"They have always come to her first," Michael said.

"But you maybe *could* reach anyone?" Mrs. Nerova asked her.

"Maybe."

Mrs. Pomeroy closed her eyes. Mrs. Lattimore sat back in her chair. The sisters looked on, sitting very still.

"I might be able to reach anyone," Emily offered. "It might take some time, but—"

"You maybe could reach a father? A mother? A son?" Mrs. Nerova asked. She leaned closer to Emily, holding the girl's hand in both of her own, her grip gentle but strong and braced by the sturdy bones in her pudgy fingers. "A husband?"

"Possibly," Emily said.

Mrs. Nerova, her back to everyone else in the room, showed Emily a face that was there and gone in an instant. It almost broke Emily's sense of control. In this face—which Emily imagined Mrs. Nerova had shown to no one else in the room, if to anyone, ever—Emily saw a much younger and much older Mrs. Nerova. Emily fought the urge to look away from such intimate exposure out of an impulse of propriety.

"I will try," Emily said. "We will try."

"Wonderful," Mrs. Nerova said. "Wonderful, wonderful—you take time, come back when you ready!"

At the fourth spirit-knocking session with the ladies, Emily and Michael came prepared to put on their greatest performance.

The children had sat by the river and talked, going over the possibilities. As Emily and Michael walked to Mrs. Pomeroy's house, Michael tried to sort through all they had discussed. "So they have to keep the questions simple—that's the beauty of yes and no—but if they want to get into twenty questions and try to drag specifics out of you, go into your act about the 'foggy connection' with anyone besides Regina."

"I know the act, Michael."

"All right, all right. You've got to figure that these ladies are going to want to talk to their husbands, and they're not going to want to prove you in the wrong—it's like selling black cats to witches, Em!"

In Mrs. Pomeroy's parlor, the ladies sat in their accustomed ring, dressed as if for a funeral. Michael said to all gathered, "Emily has spent a great deal of time in the tea house preparing for this meeting." The truth was that Emily had not been any closer to the tea house than the edge of the cobblestone drive since the last spirit-knocking session held for the children of the neighborhood. "She has made many attempts, and has been successful in contacting a spirit who did not contact her first."

The twins both felt the change in the room. The ladies, unmoving, seemed to become more still; the pauses between the ticking of the clock in the other room and Michael's words became short breaks of bottomless silence.

"It was the spirit of our grandmother on my mother's side, Gwendolyn Ward. She died in 1919 of influenza, in a small cottage behind our home."

The ladies nodded at this—they had lost family and friends to the same disease. The twins knew for certain that their grandmother

PAUL ELWORK

had died in the cottage behind the mansion, and they knew it had probably been in 1919. Emily seemed to remember her mother saying on more than one occasion that she and Michael had been only eight years old when Grandmama died. Emily and Michael were not quite sure whether she had died of influenza or pneumonia.

Michael took his chair and Emily spoke up. "I was only able to keep brief contact with her, and could only ask her a few questions each time," she said.

"The task was very exhausting," Michael added.

"And I need more rest than usual afterwards," Emily said.

"We won't tax you too much, dear," Mrs. Pomeroy said.

"We will try only little bit," Mrs. Nerova said.

"None of this can be hurried," Mrs. Lattimore said. "The dead can be as difficult or easy as they please."

Nods and a general rustling of agreement followed.

"We can only search for one spirit for each of you," Michael said. "It will still be a strain for Emily, but she feels prepared to make the attempt. So think carefully about who is to be contacted, and we may need to work on any of them for several sessions, and we may not be able to get all of them in this afternoon. As always, Emily will need all of our help, and we will all need to put as much of our energy as we can into reaching out. We must all *want* Emily to contact these spirits, and we must all try our best from the start."

The ladies had drawn straws before Emily and Michael had arrived. Mrs. Nerova drew the longest straw and went first. She sat down in a chair before Emily, a pained excitement transforming her—the resolute and flinty Mrs. Nerova sat before Emily a fussy and nervous girl, smiling in the hopes that everyone liked her. Unlike the secret face Emily had glimpsed, Mrs. Nerova radiated this youthfulness, and all of the other ladies beamed in the presence of it.

"What spirit have you chosen, Mrs. Nerova?" Michael asked.

"My husband," she said.

The ladies showed no response; the choice was no surprise to them. Their approval and deference reminded Emily of a group of bridesmaids clustered around a young bride, full of hope, at one of the few weddings she and Michael had ever attended, a few years before.

Emily half expected to see a silver pie cutter in Mrs. Nerova's sleeve. "And you brought something of his with you?" she asked.

Each of the ladies had a small bag beside her containing some item once belonging to the departed. Michael had suggested the ladies bring these things as an experiment, to see if contact could be made more easily using these objects.

"Yes," Mrs. Nerova said. She produced a tarnished flute. The keys of the flute creaked in Mrs. Nerova's hands.

"You never said your husband played the flute," Mrs. Pomeroy said.

"He had since he was little boy. But he hardly ever played it."

Emily reached for the flute. A faint tremble moved through Emily's hands as she touched the cool metal of the keys, of the flute's throat. For a moment it seemed to Emily that it carried some sort of a lingering charge that swept over the surface of her hands and into her body.

"Now," Emily said, "what was his name?"

"George Gregorivich Nerov," Mrs. Nerova said.

Emily wrapped her fingers around the flute and closed her eyes. She began counting in her mind. When she reached twenty, Emily opened her eyes and found Mrs. Nerova watching her, her look of excitement appearing strained to Emily. Mrs. Nerova's features took on a sallow glow and her eyes trembled in her face. It still wasn't quite the secret face, but something much closer to it.

Emily suppressed the impulse to reach out and take the woman's sturdy hand and released a long breath. Mrs. Nerova ran her tongue over her dry lips and glanced around at the other ladies. No one moved. Mrs. Nerova looked back at Emily. She said, "George . . . are you here?"

Emily appeared to listen for something very far off in the distance. After another drawn-out moment, one knock struck the air. A second knock, following slowly after, filled the small parlor, and the ladies cocked their heads as if they had never heard the strange sounds before.

"Mrs. Nerova," Emily said, amazed at how calm her voice sounded, "we can begin. What would you like to ask first?"

"Can," Mrs. Nerova said, in a cracked voice. Her eyes moved down to her hands, then to the flute Emily held, then out into the other room. Looking past everyone gathered around, she said, "Can you forgive me, George?"

Emily felt a catch in her throat and choked it down. She let the silence play out, willing her suddenly hectic heartbeat to settle down. *Breathe. Wait.* Her throat opened and her eyes cleared; she felt that even Michael could no longer bear the anticipation— though he must have known what her answer would be, the way one always knew that the hero in an adventure serial would survive, however treacherous the odds. Emily sent a single knock out into the electric air of Mrs. Pomeroy's parlor. Another followed, a brief and open sound.

A small tear rolled down Mrs. Nerova's cheek.

She has been waiting years for this. All of that time. Emily hauled her voice out of her chest and asked, "Would you like to ask another question or two, Mrs. Nerova?"

"Yes," Mrs. Nerova said, "yes, all right." She asked two more questions and the color returned to her face with the responses. Her husband was no longer angry, and he had left his pain on earth with all of his bitterness. Mrs. Nerova reached out and drew the flute from Emily's fingers. Gratitude shone from her like the corona of youth.

Emily blinked, and a tear rushed from her own eye. She shook her head slightly in an anguish of happy confusion.

The ladies sat in holy quiet.

Michael watched his sister in undisguised awe. He came to her side and wiped the tear from her face. "Can you go on?"

Emily nodded.

Michael looked her in the face, his back to the ladies. He raised his eyebrows. *Bravo!*

She gently waved him away. "I'm fine," she said. "We have much more to do today."

Mrs. Lattimore's turn followed. She brought a crooked piece of china that had passed from her mother-in-law to her husband. "I broke the plate a few years ago, but I kept the pieces in a drawer in the kitchen." She handed Emily the broken china while looking her in the eye, and Emily was afraid her hand might again tremble, but her breath was even and her hand steady. Mrs. Lattimore did not shed tears and looked at Emily throughout. She spoke firmly, carefully, to the air around them.

"Are you restless still?" she asked her dead husband.

A single knock. *No.*

"Are you one with God at last?"

Yes.

"Do the angels sing, like they told us at school?"

Yes.

Emily touched her forehead and leaned forward as a signal to Michael. Her brother came to Emily's side and took her hand, whispering in her ear. Mrs. Lattimore watched on in her steady gaze.

"Are you all right?" Mrs. Pomeroy said from her chair.

"I'm fine," Emily said, passing a hand over her eyes. "He's slipping away . . . I can't hold him."

"That man," Mrs. Lattimore said, "was always a difficult one. Carl had a heart of iron and fire." Mrs. Lattimore stood up from her chair. "It's all right, child," she said to Emily, touching a stray lock of Emily's hair.

"Please bring me some water, Michael."

Michael went to the kitchen and brought a glass back to Emily, handing it to her and placing his hand on her shoulder. When Emily finished her water, Michael brought another chair so that Miss Sophia and Miss Rose could be seated before Emily. From her bag, Miss Sophia took out a maroon sweater, worn at the elbows. Miss Rose brought out a pair of cracked leather shoes.

"We want to reach our father," Miss Sophia said. "Samuel Clayton Irving."

Emily held the sweater draped over her legs and balanced the shoes on her knees. The quiet moment, then the look from Emily that Samuel Clayton Irving had joined them in Mrs. Pomeroy's parlor.

Miss Sophia asked the first few questions, and Miss Rose nodded along.

"Are you at peace, Papa?"

Yes.

"Can you wait for us, where you are?"

Yes.

"Have you forgotten your promise?"

No.

After the single knock had settled into quiet and clock ticks, Miss Rose sat up and spoke. Her voice was hushed, barely audible. "Do you understand why I couldn't tell you?"

The double knocks bounced with firm assurance off the walls around them, and Miss Sophia took her sister's hand.

When Mrs. Pomeroy sat before Emily, the chair squeaked loudly beneath her girth. She had given Emily a crumpled brown hat to hold. Mrs. Pomeroy touched her silver crucifix. "Don't strain yourself now," she said in her beautiful watery voice.

Emily shut her eyes so she would not have to see Mrs. Pomeroy looking at her so pleasantly. She touched the hat with tentative fingertips. Mr. Pomeroy had put this hat on as he walked out of his front door, had hung it up at the end of long days, had removed it on Sundays, baring his head to the vaulted church ceiling above. The hat had sheltered a head that had sheltered a mind that had sheltered a whole person. She prepared herself to open her eyes and look at Mrs. Pomeroy, a much more daunting task than keeping her hands steady or holding out for just the right inflection in the timing and delivery of her knocks. It was a question of happiness, she reminded herself; it was another chance to replace death with joy and hope. She nodded once.

Mrs. Pomeroy cleared her throat. "Tom? Can you . . . Can you see now why it all had to be, from where you are?"

One knock, a second, and Mrs. Pomeroy lowered her head, taking firm hold of her crucifix, preparing to ask another question as the knocks rang out of the room and quiet settled back in.

15.

ARCANA

A FEW DAYS LATER, EMILY FOUND HERSELF IN A LISTLESS mood. Their last session with the ladies stayed with her even when she was not replaying bits of it in her mind, creating a nervous energy in her that made sitting still out of the question.

Very soon the school year would begin. As she wandered through the quiet house (her mother and Mary had gone downtown to attend to some banking affairs; Michael had gone to visit Albert Dunne), Emily had begun to play with the idea that the whole business of spirit knocking was purely summer magic, something that could not withstand the clear realities of mathematics and grammar. It seemed to her that it must die a reasonable death from exposure.

Following the angles of the third-floor halls, Emily came to her mother's bedroom, beyond the closed doors of unused rooms. She rarely ventured into this room when her mother was at home. When her mother was home—particularly when her mother was inside the room—it had a suffocating sense of a place made only for one person, a room that shrank when Emily entered. When her mother was away, the room became just a room, rather simple and unpretentious, boring. Emily walked to her mother's bedroom door and placed her hand on the knob. She closed her eyes and pictured her mother's room: the four-poster bed, the view of the river, and the shadowy painted portrait of Robert and Elaine Ward. Robert stood in a white suit jacket and held his wife, who wore a yellow dress and bonnet, in his encircling arms. Emily turned the knob and stepped into the room. The faces in the portrait seemed to watch her from the distance of all they had known and all she could never know.

Emily went to her mother's dresser and looked at herself in the mirror looming up from behind it. The top of the dresser was clear, with only a bottle of perfume and a comb sitting off to the side. Emily consciously noticed this arrangement for the first time. There were no photographs in frames of different sizes, no small pictures tucked in the narrow space between the tall mirror and the dark frame surrounding it, no jewelry or music boxes, and no trace of dust. It occurred to Emily that someone who kept the top of their dresser so clean must keep many things in the drawers below. Emily went down on one knee and opened the bottom drawer of her mother's dresser. Finding folded layers of underwear and hosiery, she shut the drawer after running her hand beneath the clothes to detect anything hidden under these private things. She understood that she should leave her mother's room immediately, by every code of conduct that had been drummed into her. But such things were thin abstractions in the face of her now-whetted curiosity. She thought of Mr. Pomeroy's crumpled brown hat, of Mr. Irving's worn sweater and cracked shoes, and waved it all away as irritating and irrelevant distractions.

The second drawer from the bottom had some blouses folded to one side. Two large photograph albums, stacked together, occupied the other half of the drawer. When Emily pulled the drawer out, the weight of these albums almost caused it to drop into her lap. The albums were familiar; she had seen them shown on the rare occasion of a visiting friend or relative. She had looked through them on several occasions herself. She knew what they contained: lots of pictures from her father's camera—of her mother, her father, herself and Michael; scenes of the river, the seashore, Christmas mornings. Without disturbing anything inside, she closed the drawer with a snug bump.

Emily noticed the brass keyhole above the top drawer handle and seized it out of the familiar subconscious landscape in her mind. Before she even pulled on the knob, Emily knew what would follow: the brass keyhole whispered a premonition to her. The drawer gave only a short distance and stopped with a soft thud, the inversion of the sound the other two drawers had made when closed. On impulse, Emily took the knob again and tugged on it, as if some sorcery of persistence might cause the locked drawer to open. Emily understood that locks existed for privacy and protection, of course, and that locks on houses kept out the world at large. It was not lost on Emily that locks on interior doors, cabinets, chests, and dressers protected those within the locked doors of a house from one another.

Emily and Michael sat in Mrs. Pomeroy's parlor, surrounded by the ladies. Emily had put up some resistance when Michael approached her, letting him know about her notions of spirit knocking falling away after the start of the school year.

"But I thought we were ending all of this," she had said to Michael.

"Em, we did not say that. When did we agree to that?"

"How many times can we go through this routine with them?"

"Evidently as many as we like. Those old ladies love you. How can you begrudge them that? We don't even have to perform this time, unless you want to. Let's go and see what happens. At the very least there will probably be some pie. Don't worry. I don't intend to spend the rest of my life in that parlor with those five old women. There is a whole world out there, Em."

"All right, Michael. But here's the agreement: we go and see the ladies, and if the mood strikes me to entertain them, we will. And if the mood strikes me to tell them once and for all that I won't be doing this anymore . . . that I can't do it anymore . . . then that's what I will do. Agreed?"

"All right, Em. You're the spirit knocker. Just give me some kind of sign if you're about to do something rash."

"You'll know just before it happens."

"That's all I ask."

The ladies were especially pleased to see Emily and Michael. Mrs. Nerova watched Emily with bright eyes, as if ready to present her with a gift she had worked long to craft. Mrs. Lattimore explained the ladies' mood to the twins. "We thought," she said in her imperious manner, "that we might do something special this afternoon. We thought it might be useful to allow you the opportunity to experience something different. But first we should establish just how different it is. Have either of you ever had your cards read?"

They had both heard of gypsies reading the future in all sorts of things—cards, tea leaves, crystal balls—but they had never watched anyone actually do it.

"This should be interesting, then," Mrs. Lattimore said.

Mrs. Nerova said, "I will read, all right? She reads cards," she said, indicating Mrs. Pomeroy, "and she reads cards," indicating Mrs. Lattimore, "but I will read today." She turned to Michael. "Maybe I will read for you, too—we'll see what happens."

"I would be much more interested to see Emily's cards read, Mrs. Nerova."

"Me too, me too," Mrs. Nerova said, producing a deck of cards from her pocket.

"The tarot is very old, going back to ancient times," Mrs. Pomeroy said.

"Yes," Mrs. Lattimore said, "they are older than Christ, older than Moses."

"Enough history," Mrs. Nerova said. "This is no game, children. Understand? This is serious, very serious. Everything is in these cards: the stars, the world, life, death. Understand? Otherwise, forget it." And she collected her cards up, which she had begun to shuffle, as if she were ready to tuck them back into her purse.

The twins assured Mrs. Nerova that they understood the gravity of the situation.

"I think we can begin, Basya," Mrs. Lattimore said.

Mrs. Nerova gave the cards one last brisk shuffling; the cards came together in a blur and a series of short, fast reports. "Simple. Nice and simple. Some like it fancy," she said with light scorn, her eyes flitting up toward Mrs. Pomeroy and Mrs. Lattimore.

Mrs. Nerova deftly laid seven cards out in a colorful V arrangement, pointed toward Emily. "No dancing around," Mrs. Nerova
said. "Let's see."

The ladies leaned in on all sides.

Mrs. Nerova placed her finger on the leftmost card. It had a
Roman numeral XII at the top and featured a man hanging upside
down from a gnarled tree branch by one ankle, a heavily knotted
rope keeping him in midair. The expression on the man's face,
despite his precarious position, was one of mild amusement. His
hands were folded behind his back. Across the bottom of the card,
in an old-fashioned-looking script, read the words *The Hanged Man*.

Michael shot a look of merriment at his sister. The ladies all
responded with pleased chuckles and nods.

"Shhhh," Mrs. Nerova hissed. The ladies quieted down.

"Is that good?" Emily asked Mrs. Nerova.

"It's not bad—it's good, yes, it's all right. This card says you are
in between things, uncertain. These cards don't lie. You have big
choices ahead. Soon."

Mrs. Nerova moved her finger to the next card. There was something of a subdued flourish in the motion of her hand—her fingers moved over ancient arts, steeped in mystery. The second card,
number IV, revealed a handsome man on a jewel-studded throne, a
scepter in his right hand. He wore a heavy golden crown and copi-
ous purple garments. Only half of the man's face could be seen; in
this half, the leading edge of a deep frown revealed itself. The script
at the bottom named the card *The Emperor*.

"A man of influence, eh, of *reputation*. A recent acquaintance of
yours, maybe? This man comes as an advisor, yes?"

Emily remained quiet.

The next card featured a smirking young man gathering up three swords; two more lay at his feet: *Five of Swords*. In the background, two swordless men skulked off.

The ladies made concerned noises; Mrs. Nerova silenced them. "Not good. A bad time is coming."

"Basya," Mrs. Pomeroy said.

"What? I read the cards; I tell what they say. You want *lies*? You want lies, you read. I will not be the false friend. But someone may be," Mrs. Nerova said to Emily, touching her finger to the smirking young sword collector. "Someone may work against you. Without your knowledge?"

Emily hid her thoughts behind a closed face, watching Mrs. Nerova.

"You are young," Mrs. Nerova said. "You feel trust. Hope? Yes. But be ready for the bad. You must be careful *here*." Her finger departed from the cards and tapped her careworn temple—twice. "And *here*." The sturdy finger swept down and jabbed—once—at her heart. "The real ordeal is waiting."

The fourth card showed a woman dressed in blue robes, holding a scroll in one hand and wearing a silver crown. The card was marked number II and named *The High Priestess*. "Ah," Mrs. Nerova said. "This card is about your, eh, *abilities*. You are gifted child, you have special talents, you understand about spirits and stars. You have long memory. Your talents serve you well. But we already know this, yes? There is good here. You have, eh, *intuition*. This you should trust."

The fifth card: *Knight of Swords*, inverted. On its face, a knight—bearing a raised sword and a determined expression—rode his black charger upside down toward Emily.

Mrs. Pomeroy released a breath of surprise. Mrs. Lattimore made a small, concerned noise.

"Shhh," Mrs. Nerova said. She glanced at Emily. "Not so good. This says more about deception. Beware of liars. Especially after this card"—she tapped the Five of Swords—"be careful."

Emily's thoughts whirled. *Just a game, like our game. Just an old game.*

Mrs. Nerova touched the sixth card. On it, a naked Adam and Eve stood before an apple tree holding hands, while an angel prepared to fire an arrow from a cloud at the woman and a serpent coiled around the trunk of the apple tree: *The Lovers.* "Ah, yes. An important decision, very soon," Mrs. Nerova said. "An important choice. You have the sight. You can choose. Trust your sight."

A card numbered XVI, showing a burning tower being struck by lightning, completed the array. Mrs. Nerova looked at this last card in silence for a moment, fingering the edge of the card. "*The Tower.* Big things are coming—dangerous things—prepare yourself."

Emily felt her tongue become cottony. She looked about at the other ladies, who each watched her with sympathy and concern.

"You will be accused," Mrs. Nerova said, "but you are not guilty. Things will change. You must be ready. But we must always be ready, yes? It's not all bad. You may find release in the trial." She sat back. "What does it mean?" Mrs. Nerova said, waving her hand over the cards. "You have things that you can do. You have good friends and not so good friends. A bad time ahead, but a good time will come, and before you think. It means: 'Be careful!' The cards say, 'Be careful, trust yourself.'"

Emily looked at the seven cards before her. The Hanged Man's smile held more wry amusement than good wishes; the Emperor's frown was too dark to advise mere caution; and the sword-collecting young man's sidelong smirk suggested that, given everything that had ever been and ever would be, even trusting herself was a dangerous choice. The High Priestess, seeming least prepared to give counsel, looked out at Emily with a tight mouth and large, dark eyes.

As the twins made their way home, Emily thought that of all the cards laid before her, the Lovers seemed to speak of the greatest potential harm. No other card seemed to warn of such precarious vulnerability—not the Five of Swords, not the Hanged Man, not even the Tower. The Lovers had thrown their lots in with each other—they looked one to the other, their backs to the arrow and the serpent, not in ignorance but in faith in one another and in themselves. This choice was their belief and everything would follow from it—and they smiled as if to say, *We know, we've known, we know.*

"Funny old cards," Michael said, as the twins walked home. "Did you let the old girls rattle you? Let's not forget who's in charge here."

"Who is in charge, Michael?"

"You are, Em," he said. "But I don't have to tell you that."

16.

THE GOOSE AND THE GRAVE

A WARM AND MILD AFTERNOON, THE FIRST SATURDAY IN September, only days before the opening of the school year. Emily and Mary took a walk around the estate, winding their route along the shady paths and byways. When they were away from the house and off on their own, a tone of conspiracy and play crept into their conversations.

"Mary, do you think there are ghosts at Ravenwood?"

"I am not a superstitious woman." This remark sounded in Emily's ear as an echo of her mother's manner of speaking—an echo that had come full circle back around to its source.

"It's too bad, really," Emily said. "It's such a perfect place for ghosts."

Mary pulled a thoughtful face. She folded her hands behind her and picked up her pace.

"What?" Emily said, following after.

"I was just thinking that everywhere is a perfect place for ghosts, everywhere that people have been."

Emily hurried to catch up with Mary. "You're thinking of a story, aren't you? You've got a ghost story and you won't tell me."

"It's really not a ghost story."

"It's something."

Mary raised her eyebrows.

Emily stopped. "Please, you have to tell it. To let on so and not tell is a cruel thing."

Mary moved on and pressed Emily's arm for her to do the same. "All right, then. Now I don't think this is particularly something your mother wanted to keep from you, otherwise I wouldn't tell it, and you could beg all day and night. And your mother is always saying that you're a young woman now, and that you should know about your family."

"*Mary*, please."

"All right." Mary gave Emily's arm a soft squeeze, a tactile echo: *All right.*

The two of them were close to a white bench standing in the shade of a rose arbor, along the western side of the house. Mary sat down, and Emily settled down beside her.

"Let's see," Mary said. "This is a story about your great-grandfather Robert Ward. It's about the time before he brought his family here, and some of the time after. The Wards were old Virginia plantation people and owned two dozen slaves, at least. One of these slaves was Adeline Ward. Slaves took their owners' names in those days. She was born just a few years after Robert—Robert was born in 1823, I believe. Robert's father, who your grandfather was named after, wanted Robert to be well-educated.

He saw to it that Robert received an education befitting a gentle-man. Robert eventually attended Harvard and went into finance. He had a great head for figures. Anyway," Mary said, taking a breath and softly expelling it, "Robert's father had all sorts of ideas about what his son should be. I suppose all fathers do. And one of the things Robert's father wanted his son to have was the dis-tinction of being a slave owner, and so, when he became a man, Robert was given two slaves and a fine horse as a present from his father. One of these slaves was Addie Ward. Robert had grown up with Addie; they were children together, and played together. So when Mr. Ward gave his son this gift, he was making Robert's playmate a legal possession, just like his horse and his house, with titles and forms to be transferred. Of course, in everyone's eyes all of Mr. Ward's slaves also belonged to his son, anyway—but this was official, you see, and made Robert uncomfortable. I should tell you, having drawn all of this out, that Robert loved Addie Ward and longed to take her away with him, somewhere. Somewhere his marrying Addie wouldn't stand as a betrayal of his land and his people. Of his father. Some castle somewhere far away, I suppose."

Emily could see the castle, and waves breaking on an old, rug-ged shoreline below. A place apart, where things could be pro-tected. Far away.

"Robert knew that in his father's world he could not love her, and for Robert, his father's world was all the world. Robert was still a very young man, and lived for his father's approval. His father knew his son was fond of Addie, of course, and that was why he made a gift of her to him. I don't think Mr. Ward would have done that if he'd known how strongly his son felt, though. Robert secretly wooed Addie the way he would have courted one of the daughters of Mr. Ward's friends. He came to her at night, far from the main house, whenever Addie would give him a moment to pour his heart out to her. Of course he did not have to woo her at all. In the custom of the time, she was his for the taking."

"Did she love him?" Emily asked.

"That's a tricky one. I don't know the answer to that, but I would like to think that she loved him. At least in that he loved her, whatever his faults. Now," Mary said, resuming, "Robert wooed her, and she was responsive to him, so the story goes. And they became lovers. You know what happens next. Addie became pregnant with Robert's child. This did not surprise Mr. Ward— he had known that his son was fond of Addie, remember, and such things weren't uncommon, anyway. The girl was kept away from prying eyes until the November night that she was to have the baby. It was a terribly hard delivery, and Addie was lucky to survive it. The baby wasn't so lucky. The baby was stillborn."

"Oh," Emily said.

"The baby was a boy, and Robert demanded to see his son. He raged at his father as he never had in his life, and put on quite a scene in the house. Mr. Ward was not pleased. Whatever he said to that young man that night, Robert stopped carrying on, and came down to the slave cabins all pale and quiet to see Addie and the baby. He ordered one of the other slaves who could work wood to make a coffin. When the coffin was ready, the little box was taken into the cabin. He loaded the coffin and a shovel into a wheelbarrow, and disappeared into the woods in the back of Mr. Ward's land. There was to be no more discussion of the baby in his father's house.

"Everything settled down. Robert went off to study, and time went by. Robert often visited home, and spent time with Addie, and Robert didn't court any of the daughters of his father's friends, or the ladies at school, or anywhere, as far as I know. Some men are like that—they get a woman in their mind, and that's that. They will destroy themselves and everyone else over her; they will let everything else fall apart. Some people find such things romantic."

Emily thought she had never heard anything so sad or beautiful.

Mary continued, "Time moved on. Robert and Addie got older. Robert visited his father's plantation and went away again, only to come back. One day, He married a pretty little woman he hardly knew—somehow his father got him to propose to her, and they were married. Robert was a passionate, emotional man, but terribly weak. Many people are. He married Elaine Milford in the 1860s, during the war. Robert had fallen off a horse as a young man and his leg was never the same—I guess you've heard about that. That's how he got the cane you see in some pictures of him. Anyway, he couldn't go to war, so he got married instead. Robert and Elaine had a family, as you know. He eventually left Virginia to move here, and built this house. And he brought Addie along, of course—she had been there before Elaine and would always be there, if it were up to Robert. When he left Virginia, Robert was in his forties, and so was Addie. Robert brought Addie to Pennsylvania, after all those years, even though his wife did not like her. Mrs. Ward wasn't deaf, dumb, and blind, after all. She recognized Addie as a rival—a winning rival—for her husband's affections. In spite of all that, Robert brought Addie to his new home. I guess you could say he was weak and then he wasn't. One day, though, your great-grandmother decided Addie should leave

Ravenwood. Somehow she convinced Robert to send Addie away, and he did—to a comfortable job in New York City with a friend that Robert admired and trusted. The one thing Robert would not do was send Addie back south, where she would be legally free— the war was over by then, but she would always be considered a slave down there. So Robert sent her farther north, to work for a very well-respected surgeon and teacher. She lived there for several years. Robert visited her whenever he could, on business trips that his wife knew were not business trips, and the story goes that once Robert asked Addie—begged her—to go to Europe with him, and she refused him. One day, Addie resigned from her post with Robert's surgeon-friend and left New York. She wrote Robert a letter saying she would be staying with her sister Rosaline, who was several years older than herself. Addie's sister was really a half sister, the daughter of Addie's mother, Joanna, and a freedman—a free colored man—who had purchased the infant from Robert's father and given the child her freedom. So, Addie went to Rosaline's place, and asked Robert not to come looking for her. She told him his place was with his wife. Rosaline had married a man named Norman some years before, and they had several children. One of these children was named Mitchell, the youngest in the family. Mitchell married a woman named Amanda Moreland and had some children of his own. Two of these children survived— children died often in those days, of infections, fevers, all sorts of terrible things. One of their surviving children was—is—named Norma. The other surviving child is me."

Emily had been gazing out over the grass—her eyes now snapped up to meet Mary's. Of course she had heard that Mary had a sister, though Mary herself never talked about her, and somewhere along the line had heard that the sister's name was Norma.

Mary laughed. "It's true."

"So . . ." Emily's eyes drifted away and snapped back to Mary.

"So Mitchell and Amanda Paterson were my parents, and Rosaline and Norman Paterson were my grandparents. And Addie Ward was my great-aunt."

"Does Mama know all of this?"

"Of course she does."

"Then why haven't you told me—"

"I'm telling you now," Mary said. "This is not entirely a story for a child, is it? But you are a young woman, Emily. Now," Mary said, as if she had finally come to the part of the story she had smiled over at the mention of ghosts, "the story goes that when Robert Ward was to come to his newly built home in Pennsylvania, he first went to his father's plantation with a shovel, a wheelbarrow, and a lantern well after dark. By then, as I've said, Robert was in his forties, and hadn't dug a hole in over twenty years, but he would do this without a soul's help. And Robert—supposedly on a business trip—traveled by train that night with Addie and the little box to Pennsylvania, hired a carriage from the station to Ravenwood, and buried the little box somewhere on the estate, just before dawn, in an unmarked grave. Or so the story goes."

Emily stood. "Where?"

"I don't know where. Addie didn't tell her sister that. In fact, my mother wasn't very sure about that part being true. But I think it is true."

Emily glanced over all her familiar surroundings, suddenly not quite so familiar. "Could be anywhere," she considered, looking down at the spot of earth beneath them. The thought of such a thing—the very idea of it—moved down through the oldest parts of her brain and along her spine, visibly sending a tremble through her shoulders.

"Goose walk over your grave?" Mary said.

Emily laughed, and the sensation was gone. She remembered when Mary had first shared this piece of folklore with her—that a sudden chill meant that a goose had walked over one's grave. Emily had protested that she didn't have a grave. Mary had gently pointed out that the goose is supposed to have walked over the place where her grave would one day be. Emily had been struck with an awful fascination, a thing less of the nerve endings than her irresistible chill, something that instead reversed the past and the present, leaving her standing in a lonely field of her own making, gazing down at an innocent patch of grass.

"And you're not having fun with me about any of this?" Emily asked in the rose arbor.

"I promise you, I am not. I didn't come to work here by accident, Emily. When I went into this line of work, I wanted to move away from Baltimore, for reasons of my own, and I came here to see the place and to apply for work, and what do you know? They hired me. The place got to me right away, and the story of the secret grave certainly gave it an appeal. The help of any old house are always full of stories about ghosts, hidden doors, you name it. There's a story about an underground tunnel here, for instance, that is supposed to lead from the house to a secret location on the estate. There have been some wild stories connected to that tunnel—pirate treasure, runaway slaves, all sorts of things. These stories are like a history of dreams, more than facts. They had me, right from the start." Mary stood up and brushed the wrinkles from her skirt. "And then there was your mother to care for."

Emily still watched the shades of a couple standing over a tiny grave in early morning darkness. The grave had been filled and stood as a heap of dirt in the lantern light.

"All right, Emily. Back to the present," Mary said, and started around to the front of the house.

Emily remained in the arbor. She sat down again and looked at the anonymous earth around her feet, beneath a carpet of lush grass and dandelions. Her blood and Mary's, somewhere in the ground. She felt the infant's coffin in the cool, moist soil, lying in perfect darkness.

Emily remained outside awhile, eventually getting up from the bench and walking along the path by the river. She considered places for the tiny grave: a copse of shaggy pines in the shadow of the mansion; behind the carriage house on the far end of the estate (a cavernous place, now that she thought of it); under the tea house. As she moved along the river away from the house, she caught the sounds of splashing and heard her brother laughing. He called out something and laughed harder, and though she could not tell what Michael said, she knew he was mocking someone, and that the someone was probably Albert Dunne. Emily chose her steps with care and came within earshot of Michael's words.

"At night, Al! They come upriver at night. Whoever heard of ghosts in the daylight?" Michael laughed and splashed.

"I don't see what daylight has to do with it," Albert said.

"Come on, Albert! Is this what you're made of?"

Emily stepped behind a tree several yards from where Albert Dunne stood, his back turned to her. Michael splashed in the river at the bottom of the steep bank, still out of Emily's sight. "Al! For God's sake, summer's practically over! Are you going to dive into this river, or what?"

Albert looked down toward the water. Emily could imagine Albert's face at that moment.

Michael's joyous voice rang up the bank. "Albert, you are the biggest coward I have ever known—how can you stand yourself? *You are disgusting!* Emily's *twice* the man you are!"

She burst into the clearing.

Albert snapped his head around, almost tumbling down the riverbank. He looked at Emily with hurt surprise, as if her presence made her partly responsible.

Emily stormed the bank and glared down at her brother. Michael paddled in a circle through the slow current. His clothes lay on the shore in a careless pile. He looked up at her with surprise for an instant, then grinned. "Hello, Em. Care for a swim?"

Albert stepped aside and slipped away, hurrying into the wooded shadows.

"*Shut up*, Michael," she said.

"Come on, Em, I'm just teasing. He is a coward, though—you know that—"

"Do you have to be so mean, Michael? Is it necessary to be so mean?"

"Settle down," Michael said. "Where's Albert?" he called to her, beginning to move away again in a lazy backstroke.

"He's gone. I guess the fun's over."

"He's afraid of ghosts in the river, Em. The ones who come up to the tea house."

"The ones you told him come up the river to the tea house?"

"The ones *we* told him about," Michael said good-naturedly. "I think he's afraid of the water, myself. Who's afraid of ghosts in the daytime?"

"It doesn't matter, Michael," Emily said in a hollow voice.

"He'll be all right. So, Em: Are you going to take a swim, or not?"

She looked at him a moment before turning toward the house.

"Don't leave me here!" Michael called after her. The sounds of him splashing in the river followed her back onto the cobblestone drive. "A drowned ghost—is that what you want? Turn your back and that's what you'll get, Em!"

Emily trudged toward the house, her shoulders stiff.

May 12, 1914

TUESDAY MORNING

Naomi Stewart found her brother Michael sleeping on the back porch at eight o'clock, his head tucked against his shoulder, his feet folded in his scuffed fine shoes, his hands folded in his lap. He looked as if he had fallen asleep only moments before, maybe after a pleasant morning walk, rather than a man who had probably slept a few hours at most after returning close to dawn, smelling of stale cigarettes and whiskey sweat. His suit jacket and pants hung in deep folds and the ghosts of stains rose up into Naomi's attention as she leaned in to brush the hair on his forehead. Close up, Michael's face looked fragile and worn for a man who had turned twenty-six only days before. Naomi sat down in the empty chair near Michael's and sipped her coffee. Donald had gone to his office over an hour before. The twins, almost two years old and usually up by seven, slept in. Naomi hadn't heard her mother stir at all that morning. Mary read the paper inside and listened to the radio. Ordinarily Mary would have joined Naomi for her own morning coffee, but she was the first to see Michael asleep outside and suggested Naomi might present a more forgiving face when he finally woke up.

Naomi felt his gaze and turned. Michael smiled at her, his eyes barely open. "Morning, sweet girl." Naomi, not yet twenty-one, never fully sure whether she should be his mother or his baby sister.

"Happy belated," she said.

"And many more." Michael winked at her. "Thanks."

"Did you enjoy yourself?" Naomi asked. Michael had been home from France only a couple of weeks before going to see a friend in New York for a day that turned into days. During his absence, Michael marked another year.

"I try as best I can."

"Emily and Michael enjoyed your cake the other night. They even blew out the candles."

"Well, there you see? You had a good time, too. Better to share the cake with those beautiful babies."

Naomi sipped her coffee and made no argument.

"I don't have to tell you what today is," Michael said.

Naomi nodded.

"He was nineteen. You're older now than he was, and here I thought you'd never be older than thirteen." Their elder brother, McEntyre, died eight years before on that day, fighting against the rebellion during the United States' occupation of the Philippines after the Spanish-American War. "Mac was the hope. The gentleman soldier. Now it's all up to you." Michael pulled out a cigarette and tapped it against the back of his hand before lighting it. "I think I'll make a fine old man, you know. I already have my boring memories to keep me company. Sometimes I just can't believe that Mac died trying to help hold on to that damn banana plantation of a country, and four years after Teddy declared the insurrection over."

Naomi could easily remember the sight of Michael staggering out toward the river after hearing of McEntyre's death and falling to his knees in the grass. It was early springtime, 1906, and the birds chirped in the cool breeze. Michael had been eighteen years old. Naomi had begun to follow him when their father came out of the house, took her by the hand, and led her back inside. She looked back at her brother, now hunched over on the bank, until her father shut the door on the scene. That summer, Jonathan Ward caught Michael bringing whiskey into the house for the first time. Michael had dropped a wink at his sister as their father poured the bottle down the kitchen sink and spoke in even, cold tones about never again and absolutely not. The following fall, Michael threw a Halloween party in the rathskeller without asking his parents' permission, a party that rose out of the basement, so that the skeletons and vampires who had been wooing pixies and witches on the four wooden thrones in slurred whispers then chased them through the halls with slurred laughter. Michael, dressed as Poe's Red Death in a scarlet cloak and red skull face paint, promised a pestilence on anyone who touched Naomi, thirteen at the time and the only other member of the family in the house that night. The revelers roared and booed but didn't disobey. Michael didn't declare the party a success and over until he slid down a banister on the main staircase, red cloak billowing behind him, and crashed into a statuette of Dante his father had bought on a trip to Tuscany. Michael lay amid the pieces, saying, "Virgil, where the hell are you now?" Naomi remembered his guests all vanishing soon after, fleeing like children, some of them advising her to leave Michael there and throw a blanket over him.

On the back porch, that Tuesday morning in 1914, Naomi said, "Mother was upset you missed your birthday here." Her voice was light and conversational, as if she'd seen an interesting piece in a magazine about it. She didn't look at her brother, but he felt her close attention. "She took to her bed after dinner and hardly ate a thing."

Their father's phrase, *took to her bed*. It stirred a departed childhood for both of them—all of the times their mother had vanished from the first floor and they'd heard those words. They sat and let the ripples settle.

Michael clucked his tongue. "She's been taking to her bed a lot these days, hasn't she?"

"It's been worse in the years since Father died."

He smoked and looked at the river. Naomi drank her coffee.

"The two of them," Michael said. "You'd think one of them would have been a little more cheery. Aren't opposites supposed to attract? They should have been married in a morgue."

Naomi looked at Michael and his smile faded.

"You'll be leaving again soon, I guess," Naomi said.

"You know me. Fancy-free."

"I had hoped you might stay for the summer. The children love you—they actually think a strange uncle is a wonderful thing."

Michael smoked and smiled out over the water.

"So many people gone," Naomi said. "It feels like an abandoned train station here sometimes."

He chuckled. "You've got two small kids and a fretting mother. I'll bet an abandoned train station sounds pretty good some days."

They shared the quiet a bit longer, not unhappily.

"He loved you, you know," Naomi said.

"I know, Naomi. I wish that made a difference more often than it does."

She remembered finding Michael asleep in the tea house once, almost a year after Mac's death, his feet up on the table, a mostly empty bottle on the floor beside him. Bits of earth clung to the bottle on parts of the label and in the molding under the cap. It gave off a deep, dank smell. She didn't know how long he'd been there and hadn't seen him go out to the tea house, though she had been sitting on the porch herself for some time and practicing on her flute, which her father thought she could play for her mother in the evenings. When Naomi began to slip the bottle into Michael's coat pocket, he stirred and an old iron key fell out of his pocket. It was long, made of wrought iron, and a pair of hands cradling a heart and a crown on its end drew her eye. Michael stirred, took the key and the bottle gently from her, and dropped them both in his pocket, his eyes open in slits. "Shhhhh," he said, "don't give up the underground, sweet girl," and closed his eyes again, as if he'd never awakened.

Jonathan Ward had converted the old garden house into a playhouse and given it to Naomi on her eighth birthday. Mary, Naomi's nanny, was the first one to call it the tea house and to suggest Naomi host her dolls there in a fancy party. Michael called it the clubhouse and taught Naomi to play cards there and how to make an oath of solidarity. They entwined pinkie fingers to make the bond eternal.

Michael stretched in his chair on the porch and pulled a watch from his breast pocket. "Well, I have to catch a train."

"Right now? You haven't even eaten."

"Soon. Less than a half hour. I'd better get moving—good thing I'm already packed." He picked up his suitcase and kissed Naomi on the cheek. "Hug those babies for me."

"They'd like to say good-bye, Michael, I'm sure."

"I'm only going to New York," he said. "Okay, and then maybe London. Depends on my friends' traveling plans. But I'll be sleeping it off out here before you know it." He squinted through the glass into the sunporch at Mary. "I'd better give the old girl a chance to warn me about being me before I go." When he opened the door, Mary looked up from her paper as if she already knew everything that was going to happen from then on.

Naomi stopped him on the front porch and took his hand. "I never know when it's the last time I'll see you for a while." She drew an envelope packed with bills from the pocket of her robe and tucked it into his palm. "Cable from wherever you end up."

"Of course," he said, and kissed her again, though the cable never came. The whiskey Naomi smelled on his breath was sharp, not stale like the whiff she'd caught on the back porch. Michael walked out into the morning sun and went down the drive in a quick step. He whistled "The Battle Hymn of the Republic" in the way he had often done to irritate Mac when he visited home from West Point. Naomi watched him go, not closing the door until he walked up the street out of sight.

When Naomi had given birth to the twins on June 23, 1912, Donald had not protested his wife's wish to name the infant boy Michael. "I suppose a name isn't a curse," Donald had said, and left it at that. If she had tried to explain her choice, Naomi might have told Donald about time spent with Michael during one of their father's long silences, about card games in the tea house, and about winter afternoons when she and Michael took sleds to a long, gently sloping hill a few blocks from the estate. She might have told about Michael's jokes and pratfalls in the snow, all for her amusement; of Michael turning somersaults, landing facedown in the snow, while she sat on her sled and laughed; of Michael's own laughter, muffled in the cold white, drifting across the strange winter stillness of an afternoon and shaking his body, lying prostrate in the sparkling snow.

PART FOUR

17.

That Which Is Done

On the first day of school, Mary drove Emily and Michael to St. Anne's Episcopal School for Boys and Girls, as she would most weekdays until late June. An expansive lawn swept up to the massive granite steps in front; impenetrable-looking woods lay just beyond the school. The building was long, low, and monastic, with thick columns stretching across the façade of the first floor, creating shadows and suggesting intrigue. St. Anne's was not a boarding school. Its two floors afforded ample space for classrooms, a modest student body, and a tiny faculty. St. Anne's Episcopal Church stood apart from the school, old and gothic. The fading date on the keystone read *1711*. At noon every day, the clangs of the old bell in the steeple quivered through the stone halls and the dust motes revealing themselves in the bars of sunlight falling through the windows.

As the car swept up the curving drive to St. Anne's, Emily looked out at the little school and reflected that this would be her last year there, that in the following autumn she would go to a prestigious private high school much closer to home. Emily watched a procession of nuns walking from a gray stone house that served as a convent, a hundred yards or so from the school and mostly concealed by trees. The nuns' habits fluttered like black wings.

Emily imagined the familiar halls and the black iron gate running through the center of the school, dividing the boys from the girls. Many young romances had been made more dangerous and enticing by this gate, and many nervous kisses had been exchanged between the cool bars when no black habits could be seen. Emily had not been involved in these adventures herself, but had heard of quite a few and even on occasion seen them take place. Once Emily had turned a corner to see a friend of hers, Laura Rosewell, hurry to the gate and kiss a thin, dark-eyed boy waiting there. Turning away, Emily felt a strange excitement and embarrassment. It had been a moment between Laura and the dark-eyed boy, and it had been her moment, one that would stay with her long after most of her St. Anne's memories had broken down into subconscious tatters. She never spoke of the incident to anyone, though she often thought of it afterward.

None of the children at school knew anything about spirit knocking. None of them would look at her and see anything but a young girl with no greater claim on the universe than any of the other children at St. Anne's. This realization gave Emily a sense of comfort and cast a veil over the tea house, spirit knocking, the five ladies, and their departed loved ones.

At the end of the first week of school, on a Friday afternoon, Emily sat by the Delaware with a Bible in her lap. Mary had just brought the twins home from St. Anne's. Without changing out of her gray-and-white school uniform, Emily had gone to sit by the river and read her assignment for second-period Bible Study. Her instructor, a soft-spoken, ancient man named Mr. Curruthers, had told the class to read Ecclesiastes over the weekend from the sturdy old King James Bibles he had given out on the morning of the first day of school. As Emily read, she recognized some of the words from Reverend Atkins's sermon on the Sunday morning Stan Loewry had appeared at Ravenwood. *All the rivers run into the sea,* she read. *Yet the sea is not full.*

Her mother came down from the house and crossed the grass to the place where Emily sat. "You'll get stains on that skirt," she said.

"Not if I sit still."

"That's the trick, isn't it?" her mother said, gathering her own skirt around her to sit down beside Emily in the grass. Her mother looked at the open book. "Ecclesiastes," she read aloud. She looked away across the water. *"The thing that hath been, it is that which shall be. And that which is done is that which shall be done: and there is no new thing under the sun."*

Emily looked up from her book. "You've memorized all this?"

"Not all. Parts. I don't want to distract you from your studies, Em," her mother said, making no effort to get up.

"It's all right, Mama."

A group of geese swam in circles on the river. From time to time, they ducked their black heads into the river and pulled them back out, shaking the cold water off in a small spray. Emily and her mother watched the geese until her mother said, "Did you know, Em, that your father wanted to be an archaeologist?"

Emily squinted at her. She studied her mother's face, and the way her mother's eyes moved over the surface of the river and the geese, as if looking at neither. "An archaeologist?"

"Yes. I was just thinking about it." Mrs. Stewart turned to Emily. "You do know what an archaeologist is?"

"Yes. They dig up old bones and things. Right?"

"They dig up lots of things. Arrowheads. Tombs. Cities."

"I've heard of them," Emily offered.

"Your father," her mother said, "would have liked to have done that. When the time came for him to go to school, his father—your grandfather—wouldn't hear of it. He would have said that archaeologists dig up old bones, too, but not the way you said it, if your grandfather ever said so much in one breath. He considered it to be nonsense and childishness." She watched the geese and rested her chin on one hand. "Your grandfather wasn't a bad man, but he was a stubborn man. He had his ideas of what people should be doing, and digging up the ground looking for old spear points was not one of them. He thought a doctor was a fine thing to be, and since your father was a very bright man, and was very interested in all kinds of things, and because it made his father happy, he became a doctor." She turned again to Emily. "He was a very *good* doctor," she said.

"I know, Mama."

"I remember your father explained to me once how an archaeologist sees a landscape. Look, over there." She raised her hand and gestured across the river at the leafy edge of New Jersey on the other side. "You see lots of trees, right? And bluffs? Your father once pointed across here and told me that an archaeologist would look at all that and imagine the things that might be *underneath.* He said that a person develops eyes to see what people have done to a landscape, or to recognize the kinds of places people are always drawn to. And the things underneath these places are what they're really looking for; the things buried by people, and by time."

Emily gazed across the Delaware at the dense trees. She imagined bones and old tools and arrowheads littered everywhere in the earth below. Of course, she thought, there would never be that many things there, but if there were only half as many, or a handful, or a single thing . . .

"Your father," her mother said, "was always interested in the things beneath things."

Emily nodded at this. "Isn't everyone?"

"Not so much as you might think."

The two of them watched the geese a minute and listened to the soft wind in the trees, not particularly waiting for the other to say anything. Finally, her mother said, "I received a letter from your father while he was in France. He told me how the fighting was going, and he wrote that he sometimes thought he couldn't sew another man back together. Sounds like Dr. Frankenstein, doesn't it? That's what your father wrote: *I feel like Frankenstein, Naomi. Except I don't make the dead ones come back to life, I sew up the live ones so that they can go become dead.*'"

Emily blinked at her mother, but Mrs. Stewart's face held the same remote friendliness. Emily touched her mother's hand. Mrs. Stewart squeezed back, then let go and folded her arms around herself. "The things we want to be," she said. "I thought I might be a writer, when I was young."

"A writer? Of books?"

"Sure."

Emily rarely saw her mother reading books, though she consumed newspapers and magazines.

"You didn't get all of your love of books from your father," Mrs. Stewart said with restrained amusement. "I used to live in novels—Charlotte Brontë, Jane Austen, Dickens. I thought I might be able to say something, too, about people's lives, about everything. Isn't that what you read novels for?"

Emily gazed at her mother, her mouth slightly ajar. She nodded. Yes, that was what she read novels for, though she had never thought about it in quite that way. It was as if her mother had put her finger on Emily's temple and said, *I know who you are.*

Mrs. Stewart patted Emily's knee and started to stand. "Mary is putting some tea on, and I thought you might want some. Where is your brother?"

"He got changed and went to see Albert," Emily said, beginning to get up herself.

"I wonder how that boy can stand it, the way Michael torments him."

"Michael's not so hard on him," Emily said, immediately wondering why she would say such a thing. "He and Albert are friends the way boys are friends."

"Yes, I guess that's right. It doesn't change much when they become men. But you'll find that out, the way you find everything out eventually." And her mother turned to walk toward the house. Before following her mother, Emily looked back across the water to New Jersey. For all she could see, the trees may as well have sprawled away from the Delaware in a vast and continuous forest out to the Atlantic Ocean, a forest full of all the stories told by the people leaving broken arrowheads along the river; living stories that clung to the trees in the same way things waited in the earth; stories upon stories falling backward in time to the sea.

18.

A Quality of Light

On a still morning in the third week of September, on the first day in many days of no rain or threat of rain, Emily lay in bed before dawn, unable to go back to sleep. Out her window, in the farthest reaches of the distant eastern horizon, she saw suggestions of pink and blue beginning to stretch out against the night sky and the dwindling stars. Emily slowly realized that an unmistakable smell came to her through the stirring curtains—a crisp smell, full of forgetfulness and memory. The scent struck some part of her that seemed somehow older than herself and said, *Summer is gone.*

A few hours later, walking with Michael from the car to the entrance at St. Anne's, Emily basked in the fading glow of her morning discovery. The grounds were still very summery to look at, and the trees had not begun to change, but the smell of autumn held sway over all. Emily knew that once the pull of the season set in, everything would rapidly change with it. Before they entered the building, Michael had said, "What the hell are you so happy about?"

Later that afternoon, Emily sat on a large old chair in the front hall at Ravenwood. The fading daylight fell over Emily and the book in her lap—*Frankenstein*. She realized she was falling effortlessly asleep when an apologetic knock came from the front door. All of her sleepy thoughts scattered; the book almost fell from her lap.

No, she thought in the instant before consciousness reclaimed her. *Not yet.* She found Mr. Holt standing on the porch with his ironic frown. "Hello, Emily. How are you?"

They had not seen each other since a week before school started, and Emily had not expected to see her tutor until the following summer, if at all. Mr. Holt carried a broad leather case in his hand. He hoisted it up for her to notice. "I came to show you the painting," he said. "I thought you might like to see it."

"Oh!" Emily said, gesturing for him to come in. "It was very nice of you to think of me, Mr. Holt."

"Not at all. You had something to do with it." He pulled a canvas from his case. After looking around the room for the best light available, he went over by the window where she had been reading. "Ah, building monsters," he said, noticing the book on the chair. He looked back at Emily, who still stood near the door. Mr. Holt placed the painting on the chair to catch the light.

Emily crossed the room and faced the canvas. There was the tea house and the cobblestone drive, the green lawn and trees, the azure sky—some features rendered starkly and others only suggestions described in soft touches. The light from the window did not so much hit the colored oils as float over them, making the brushstrokes in turn seem to hover above the canvas. A figure of a girl looked into one of the windows of the tea house, and in the windowpane a translucent reflection looked back. The girl was clearly Emily, in her form and size, in the shade of her hair; it was unmistakably Emily's reflection in the window, wearing a startled expression.

"It's wonderful," she said.

"Thank you. It's a good effort, I think."

"You painted me."

"Yes."

"You put me in your painting."

"As I said, you sort of gave me the idea. I realized that I didn't just want to paint this odd little house, but that it needed some . . . humanity. So there you are, looking for ghosts, and finding something else entirely."

Emily focused on the surprised face in the windowpane. "Finding what?"

"I don't know." Mr. Holt considered a moment. "Imagine whatever you want in there."

"What do you call it?" Emily asked.

"I don't have a title yet. Is *The Tea House* too obvious?"

She said, "How about *Spirit Knocking?*"

Mr. Holt turned to her with a curious look. "You are the strangest girl," he mused aloud. "*Spirit Knocking?*" He looked again at the painting, then back at Emily. "Very unusual . . . somehow appropriate."

"Of course, you should name it whatever you want," she said.

"No, maybe it's proper that you name it," he said.

"I'll get Mother," Emily said. "She'll love it." On her way up the stairs, she looked back across the front hall to where Mr. Holt stood considering his painting, hand on his chin, deep in thought. The large window, reaching up nearly to the ceiling, framed the man and the chair and the painting, and would make a nice painting itself, she thought. She continued up the stairs and heard Mr. Holt mutter something she could not quite catch, like a man talking in his sleep.

Albert Dunne found Emily reading under a tree. She pulled herself out of Mary Shelley's dream and turned her head to see him slouching before her, a slight flush on his cheeks. "Albert! I didn't hear you coming."

"I'm sorry if I scared you," Albert said, looking a little terrified himself.

"Did you want to ask me something?"

He cleared his throat. "I wanted to know, Emily, if you would visit my father."

Of the many things Emily might have guessed Albert was about to say, this would have been among the last. "Your father?"

"I told him, Emily. About spirit knocking."

Emily closed her book. "When?"

"I told him in August. But he didn't listen. And then he asked me about it. The other day."

She felt goose bumps spring up on her forearms. Her voice hardened. "Did somebody else tell him about it, since you did in August?"

"He asked me about it, and I, uh, told him. Everything."

Emily closed her eyes. "Does Michael know this?"

"Please don't tell him," he said. Albert took his hands out of his pockets and immediately stuffed them back in. His forehead wrinkled. "My father wants to see you. Not Michael. I didn't tell him anything about Michael."

She weighed the consequence of declining, saw Mr. Dunne striding up to the front doors of the mansion and pounding with his fist, ready to tell her mother everything—though her mother finding out was beginning to seem like the inevitable outcome to Emily. And in any case, Emily thought, *So be it.*

"*Please,* Emily," he said.

"We talked about this sort of thing."

"You're the only one who can help him." Emily followed his eyes and saw Michael descending the front steps.

While out in the neighborhood with Michael a year or so before, Emily had seen Albert looking out of a window of his family's house—a cluster of dark gables and windows veiled in heavy curtains. Albert's pale face and eyes peering out, barely catching the light, before he emerged to join them in the street. Albert's face in the window recurred to Emily as Michael reached the bottom of the stairs.

"All right," she said.

"When?"

"Saturday morning, ten o'clock. Meet me around the corner from your house."

Michael strolled up beside Albert.

"What's with you?" Michael asked him.

"Nothing."

"You look like you're about to ask Em to marry you."

Albert released a weak laugh.

Michael turned to his sister. "Well?"

"I'll need a few days to think about it," she said.

"Careful," Michael said. "She has strange powers."

"I have to go," Albert said, turning away.

Michael watched him hurry down the drive toward the gate. "What was all that about?"

"You know Albert. I think he's interested in more ghosts."

"Really? He is devoted, I'll give him that. Unfortunately for old Al, we were only working out the bugs on him."

"If I thought you actually had any sympathy for Albert, I'd be touched," Emily said, reopening her book.

"If I thought *you* had any sympathy for him," Michael said, "I'd be insulted." He stretched out on the grass, hands under his head, and began to whistle.

Emily turned her attention back to her book. On the page, Victor Frankenstein followed his creation across an icy landscape to a hut where the creature would tell his dismal tale and demand that the doctor use his arts again to relieve the monster's loneliness.

19.

BALANCE

On the way to meet Albert Dunne the following Saturday morning, Emily realized that she had never met Albert's mother. Of course, over the years, Emily had from time to time glimpsed, at a distance, a woman wrapped in a coat and known that in the barest sense she was looking at Mrs. Dunne. Emily had seen an automobile drive up or down the street with the shadowy shapes of people inside, and known that the car belonged to the Dunnes, and that one of the darkened shapes was Mrs. Dunne. Emily had certainly heard of Mrs. Dunne, and of what a strange woman she was, and of her dead son. It was well-known in the neighborhood that Mrs. Dunne had not come out of her house for three months after Patrick's death, and then not often in all the years since. Nerves, they all said. Doctors came to the house at odd hours of the day and night, and the neighbors watched and waited. Mr. Dunne, for his part, was not much more visible than his wife, though Emily had seen him many times: he was a portly bald man who resembled a photograph of Henry James she had seen in one of her father's books. Though James scowled in his portrait, Mr. Dunne had a quick and bright smile. When Emily did see Mr. Dunne, she always thought that he looked like a man capable of a frightening frown. But having no real sense of Mrs. Dunne's face—the eyes, the mouth, the nose, the chin—Emily realized she would not have been able to recognize the woman if she passed her at that moment on the street.

Emily found Albert standing on the corner, looking with concentration along the curb. "Your dress is very pretty," he said, glancing at her.

"Thank you."

He led her to his home, which really did have a looming, brooding quality, even without Albert's pale face in the window, even outside of Emily's painting memory. Albert moved with a purpose, keeping just ahead of Emily. He opened a gate in the short, wooden fence that surrounded the house and gestured for Emily to enter. He stepped past her to the front door and repeated the gesture, indicating a chair in the spacious living room. Albert went to the far side of the living room and a set of folding wooden doors, slipped through them, and Emily was alone. The curtains allowed a slit of sun to come through, creating a daylight-rimmed semi-darkness. She took the room in: a fireplace, some old-fashioned furniture, and a small clock, keeping the seconds noisily on the mantel, belying its size with its insistent voice. Photographs stood on either side of the clock. Rather than cross the room to look at them—she did not want Mr. Dunne to discover her wandering around the living room—Emily instead squinted to make out the figures in the frames. There were Mr. and Mrs. Dunne, perhaps a decade before, dressed as if for church. Emily understood that this picture was to be dignified, as the Dunnes looked almost indignant in it. In the other frame stood Albert, looking no more than two years younger, also dressed formally, also not smiling. Emily looked for a photograph of an older boy, of Patrick, and found none.

Albert emerged through the folding doors. "My father will be with you soon." He waited a moment and added, "I'm going to leave now."

"You don't have to—"

"My father would prefer it."

Albert slipped out of the living room, leaving her listening to the clock. She focused her will on feeling relaxed, closed her eyes, and reviewed the room in her mind: the low shades, the mantel, the photographs, the clock. She made a conscious effort to digest the Dunne house, reminding herself of how effective her trick had been on her friends (*who were after all only children*) and of the adoration of the ladies (*who were a bunch of silly old women, anyway*). Soon Mr. Dunne would enter the room, expecting her to reach his dead son (*who had died in the same war as her father*).

Unless he sees the truth, she thought. *Unless he already knows the game before it has begun.*

A few minutes passed, then several. She found herself watching the clock. Her confidence began to fade. Finally, the folding doors opened, and Mr. Dunne stepped into the room. His bright eyes fixed her where she sat. He closed the door behind him and gave Emily an appraising look. "Hello, Emily," he said.

She stood and answered without hesitation. "Hello, Mr. Dunne." In that moment, Emily knew she had been kept waiting intentionally, in an attempt to throw her off balance. This realization restored her confidence. "How are you, sir?"

"Fine, thank you," Mr. Dunne said. His intent eyes glittered. "You are Naomi Stewart's daughter."

This mention of her mother was also meant to unnerve her, Emily knew. "Yes, I am. Do you know my mother?"

"Of course." Mr. Dunne made his way around to an empty chair by the fireplace. "Please, have a seat." He sat, never removing his eyes from her. "Of course I know her to say hello. Does your mother know you're here, Emily?"

"No, sir. Mother puts no stock in these things."

"I don't have a history of seeing ghosts myself. My wife has strange fancies, sometimes."

Emily nodded.

"I am intrigued," Mr. Dunne continued, "as you may guess. Albert has been very impressed by your *talents*."

"Yes, sir."

"Emily, I am not in the habit of playing games, so let's get right to it."

"All right. How can I help you, Mr. Dunne?"

"I believe you can probably guess at that. But first: Is there some sort of payment involved?"

"No, sir."

"Your family has enough money, I suppose," he said, revealing his teeth for an instant. Another thrust, another attempt to unsettle her.

"Yes, sir," Emily parried, in a bright, pleasant tone.

"I want you to . . . contact someone for me. Albert tells me you can do that?"

Emily found herself trying to anchor the moment to her will, to claim control from Mr. Dunne of this small piece of everything. She was relieved and amazed to remind herself again that what she needed to do was let go.

"I can try, Mr. Dunne. These things are tricky; sometimes I succeed, sometimes I don't. I must ask you something very personal, Mr. Dunne."

His eyes narrowed. "Please do."

"How much are you interested in making contact?"

His mouth became a short, tight line. "Very much."

"Good. It is very important that you understand how much I need you to want to reach this person. I will need your help in that way, Mr. Dunne. Without your help, this can't work."

"Yes," he said, "all right."

"Is this a comfortable place for you?"

"This will be fine."

"Albert explained to you how it works? One knock, no, two knocks, yes?"

"Yes."

"Good." Emily closed her eyes and folded her hands in her lap. She had worried about fear in this moment, but felt none. She had held concerns about working alone, without Michael there to encourage her, provide some distraction and coordination with the audience, but felt at ease with this domineering man in his darkened living room. The darkness in the room would be hers, soon—she would inhabit it with something Mr. Dunne needed. She did not question her mood or motives then; that would come later. At that moment, Mr. Dunne was looking for a spirit, and she was the spirit knocker. "Now, Mr. Dunne, why don't you tell me about the person. The person's name."

"Albert hasn't told you?"

"It is important for me to hear you say the name." Emily began to feel she was floating out of her own body, listening to this voice—her voice—so clear and steady in the shadowy room.

"Patrick. My eldest son, Patrick Dunne. He died in the War. He was eighteen years old," he said, his voice desolate and feature-less. "He had been sent to France only a month before."

Thoughts of her father and the War stole into her concentration. How he had looked in his uniform, the day he left Ravenwood. Her mother's talk of him saving lives, not so much memories of specific talk as a running narrative of her father's absence. The strange and horrid day her mother had told her that he would never come home. And all the years since.

But the thing to do was to gain balance and keep it. She placed her father with all the make-believe ghosts that had crowded around her over the last few months—a place he seemed to belong at that moment, obscured in a crowd of blurred figures.

Mr. Dunne became silent, and Emily allowed the silence to hang around them, a silence made up of clock noises and stale, dark air. "Now," she said, "why don't you tell me about Patrick? Before the War?"

When he answered, Mr. Dunne spoke steadily, leaving little space between his words, as if afraid of being interrupted or mis-understood.

"Patrick was born on February 3, 1900. It was an easy labor for his mother—only took a few hours. He was bald, I remember. I was afraid to hold him, but my wife wouldn't stand that. He grew fast—got to be almost six feet tall by the time he was fourteen. He was an active boy, a very energetic boy—he liked to play sports. Liked baseball. He was better and faster than any of his teammates. I know what you think. But he was. I never much cared for the game, until I saw that boy swing a bat. He was fairly good at his studies. Not the best in his class, but he always tried. He had a great deal of energy. Not lazy. No one can say that. Patrick loved dogs. Had a dog named Alexander, a retriever he doted on. He would hug that dog as if it were his own child.

"Kind. He was too kind. The world devours that kindness, I told him, once. The world devours it and you with it. He was one of those people who laugh easily. And so people were drawn to him. So many people. So many girls. But he had this one friend, the one he got himself tangled up with. I had warned and warned him. This friend . . .

". . . this friend, he . . .

". . . this girl . . .

". . . this girl was no good for Patrick—the wrong kind altogether. And all those girls he could have been interested in. All the girls interested in him. Tall and strong, so handsome. Just the kind of man that women like, that women want to be seen with. But this friend . . . this girl. Patrick was just going through an immature phase at the time. Something weak in him, something I had feared for years. Something in his way of kindness.

"I warned him.

"Such a strong, handsome boy. I told him I didn't approve. And he knew that I wouldn't. He knew, and he tried to keep it all from me. He tried to hide it all, tried to . . . He knew it was wrong. I tried to tell him that these feelings would pass. Boys do things they regret as men, I told him. All boys. One day they become men and they regret. He knew I would not approve—could not approve. He knew. I told him to be a man, for God's sake, and he looked at me and said, 'You want me to be a man?', and enlisted. This was in March of 1918. What did he care about the Germans in France? Nothing. They may as well have been fighting that war on the moon. He enlisted to spite me, to show me. And he died there—before we knew it, he was dead. His mother never knew why Patrick ran off. I spared her all that."

Emily allowed the silence to settle again. She opened her eyes to see Mr. Dunne looking at the wall. His face hung in deep folds like the curtains around the windows. He felt Emily's gaze, and turned a steady look on her.

She swallowed. *Balance. Let go.* "All right," she said. "Are you ready, Mr. Dunne?"

"Yes."

Again she closed her eyes. "Now I want you to close your eyes and reach out for Patrick in your mind. I want you to want him here with us. I want you to think about him in any way you can that will bring him here."

Eyes closed, they sat in the dark together. Emily found herself thinking of Patrick Dunne running off to the War to die—of Patrick's mother and the things she did not know. So she concentrated on the darkness. She imagined it was the true darkness found beneath the earth—the true darkness of the universe without stars. If she could meet Mr. Dunne here, if she could go beyond herself and be fully released into this shared darkness, then perhaps, for a short while, Patrick could live again for both of them.

"All right, Mr. Dunne. Why don't you ask a question?"

"You've found him?"

"Yes. I believe I have. Patrick? Are you here?"

A short quiet spun out, then a soft knock rose above Emily, followed by another.

Mr. Dunne made a small, strange sound, like a sudden clog in a drainpipe.

"Please, Mr. Dunne. I don't know how long I can keep contact."

"Patrick?" he said in a strangled voice. "Patrick. You're here?"

Two more knocks, slow upon one another, as if with an effort. Mr. Dunne stood up. "Patrick? Patrick?"

Emily opened her eyes. "Mr. Dunne?"

He sat down, his hands flat beside him on the couch. "Patrick," he said, his eyes moving over Emily and not seeing her. His mouth twitched.

Emily felt her stomach contract. Her vision blurred for an instant. "Mr. Dunne," she said, her voice starting to crack. She had forgotten all her thoughts about remote and distant darkness. She could only feel the exhilarating and terrifying motion of the words she was saying, and hardly believe what she was about to say, how she suddenly wanted to explode the spell. "Mr. Dunne, listen—I have to tell you—"

His eyes locked on her and shone. He raised one finger to silence her. *No. Not now. Please.* "Patrick," he said, his eyes holding hers. "Patrick. You are home?"

Her breathing settled. She felt her body relax into the shape of her chair. Two knocks floated up between them.

Mr. Dunne's face closed up, and he lowered his chin to his chest. When he looked up at Emily, his eyes held a soft glow. "May I ask a few more?" he asked her.

"Yes, of course."

Emily and Mr. Dunne shut their eyes.

Patrick . . . are you at peace?

Yes.

Are you happy, Patrick?

Yes.

Have you . . . are you . . . do you understand, Patrick?

Yes.

I miss you.

Yes.

Do you . . . ?

Yes.

"Thank you, Emily," Mr. Dunne said.

She opened her eyes and found his holding that same soft glow.

"That's enough now," he said.

"I hope I haven't upset you, Mr. Du—"

"No. It's all right. I just would prefer to be alone right now." He made no effort to stand, while he seemed to be listening for something very far away. "You will come back to see me. Won't you?"

"Yes, Mr. Dunne. Of course I will."

When she went out into the blinding daylight, Emily found Albert sitting on a bench on the inside of the fence. He sat on the edge of the bench, his hands folded, his head down. Albert sprang up when he heard her come out. He caught her along the path to the gate. Emily had never seen him move so quickly.

"Did you find him?" he asked. "Patrick?"

"Yes—yes, I did, Albert."

He made a face she couldn't read for pleasure or unhappiness. His features got tight around his eyes; he tucked his lips together and nodded. "Good. Good. How was Father?"

"He's . . . happy," Emily said. "He's happy we found Patrick. Your father asked him—"

"No, no," Albert said, almost jumping away from her. "No, no, that's okay . . . uh, that's fine, Emily. Father was happy?"

She couldn't just turn to the gate. His eyes weren't flitting away now. "Yes. He was very happy, Albert."

"And you can do it again? If he asks me to come for you?"

"Yes," she said, as if she thought nothing of going back into that shadowy house and of coming out again to find him in an agony like this, hopping after her and wearing that face. "Yes, I can."

Albert took her hand. He changed again before her. Albert turned into someone she had never seen, an Albert Dunne who wasn't dreading the next thing a person might say or do. The tremble in his fingers as he held her hand didn't contradict the luster that had dropped over his features. And at that moment, Emily could see Albert as something more, one day, than the lonely boy who tagged along after Michael, the kid who spent so much time at Ravenwood but was never out of the shadow of his gloomy house.

"Thank you, thank you," he said to Emily.

She had to clear her throat to speak and blink to keep her vision clear. "You're welcome, Albert. You're very welcome."

He let go of her hand and turned back to the house, looking over his shoulder as an afterthought. "Well," he said, "see you later."

"Bye," Emily said, and let herself out through the gate onto the street. She still felt the imprint of the gentle squeeze he had given her hand when she told him she would come back to make his father happy again. In her fingers, the same lingering charge that she had felt coming off of Mr. Nerov's flute, off of Mr. Pomeroy's hat, empty now of the head it had sheltered. She stuffed her hands into the pockets of her skirt and hurried back to Ravenwood, to be with people who had never seen Albert as she had found him when she first came out of the house—people who wouldn't look at Mr. Dunne on the street and think of how his mouth had twitched when he heard the knocks that told him his son had come home.

20.

ASTONİSHED

Mrs. Pomeroy welcomed Emily and Michael into her house with a nervous and delighted grin. Her overabundant happiness made her seem ridiculous and enviable all at once. "This is a special visit, children," she said. "Very special."

The ladies sat in their familiar chairs. One unexpected addition sat among the ladies—a large man in a dark suit who observed the twins from a comfortable chair across Mrs. Pomeroy's parlor. He had an immense white beard with dark streaks in it, a bald head, and cool, reflective eyes set deep in his face. Emily buried her surprise quickly, given her practical training. She glanced at Michael and believed she caught a barely concealed and kindred look of recognition in his eyes.

"We have someone here to meet you," Mrs. Pomeroy said, giddy embarrassment reddening her full cheeks. "A colleague of yours, you might say."

Miss Sophia giggled, and Emily felt she was surrounded by the girls at school, always so excited about something but reluctant or unable to call it by name.

"Children, this is Mr. James Randall," Mrs. Pomeroy said.

"Pleasure to meet you," Emily said. Her mouth was drawn in a straight line.

"Hello," Michael said, his eyes hooded.

"How do you do?" the bearded man said in a deep baritone, perfect for a lecture hall or a chapel.

"Mr. Randall also has a gift," Mrs. Pomeroy said.

The children raised their eyebrows at Mr. Randall.

Mrs. Pomeroy said, "Mr. Randall is sensitive to spirits, as well."

Mr. Randall took a deep breath and said in his large voice, "Please, children—why don't you have a seat?" And then this familiar and improbable bear of a man did a remarkable thing: he winked at the twins without winking at them.

Emily and Michael sat.

Miss Rose leaned forward. "Mr. Randall has been doing this for some time," she said, "and he's very interested in your talent, Emily."

"We've told him not to underestimate you because of your age," Mrs. Lattimore said. She looked at Emily to let her know she had personally been quite vocal on this point.

Mr. Randall stood up with surprising grace for a man of his size. He crossed the room and stood before Emily and Michael. The children's experiences since late June—along with his strange familiarity—gave them a different perspective of this man than they might have had previously. The children imagined that in turn Mr. Randall's background allowed him a certain view of them seated before him. The three met in Mrs. Pomeroy's parlor as material beings in a desert of phantoms.

"These fine ladies have said some wonderful things about the two of you," Mr. Randall said. "I hold them in very high regard, and so I have no choice but to extend this regard to both of you." Mr. Randall's eyes surveyed both of their faces; he turned on his heel and paced in a circle. "As Miss Rose says, I have been at this a long time, and it is a rare and marvelous thing to meet another in this coarse world who understands something of the Great Beyond."

The ladies nodded, closed their eyes, or shifted their bodies to agree that this had also been their experience in the coarse world.

"Particularly," Mr. Randall said, "in someone so young. You are twins, I am told?"

"Yes, sir," Michael said.

Mr. Randall nodded and nodded at this. "And how old are you?"

"Thirteen, sir," Emily said.

"Thirteen-year-old twins," Mr. Randall mused, resuming his seat across from them. "How is it that you discovered this talent of yours?"

Emily began the explanation she had run through many times. Michael assisted in the usual places. The twins told it simply; Mr. Randall listened with reserve and concentration. Everyone waited for Mr. Randall to respond when the children had finished. The bearded man took another deep breath and said, "It's like listening to someone tell my own story."

The ladies showed their pleasure with polite and silent pride.

"Can there be any doubt of the validity of what you say?" Mr. Randall asked the group. He sat forward and folded his hands, his head bowed in thought. He lifted his eyes at Michael and Emily. "If you are both ready, and if the ladies are ready, I would like to begin."

"Shall we have a visit with Regina?" Miss Sophia suggested.

"We will need a moment of quiet, as always," Michael said.

Mr. Randall gave Michael a brief and appreciative look that melted into an expression of patriarchal concern.

The stillness of Mrs. Pomeroy's parlor before a spirit knocking was a comfort to the twins, even in such odd circumstances. The bearded man, with his own inscrutable past, sat in patient expectation.

Michael said, "Emily needs you all to concentrate on bringing Regina Ward here today. All of us must want it to be, so that Emily can make it so."

On their way home from Mrs. Pomeroy's house, Emily and Michael talked about Mr. Randall, who had struck them both immediately as the same unlikely man.

"He kept trying to figure out where the sounds came from," Emily said.

"He couldn't figure it out, though. You could see that."

"And I'm sure that frustrated him, though he would never show it."

In Mrs. Pomeroy's parlor, each of the ladies had questioned Regina in the overtones of an exhibition, the intentions of all gathered in the room bent on Mr. Randall.

Mr. Randall's turn came to ask a question. "No, thank you. My purpose is to observe this phenomenon. Please continue."

Emily considered this a good sign. If Mr. Randall wanted to debunk the proceedings, he certainly would have participated, she reasoned. If he wanted to make a bother of himself, he certainly appeared to be a man who could do a fine job of it.

The session ended with Michael explaining that Emily would need to rest, and the ladies commiserating and showing their appreciation, again as much for Mr. Randall's sake as for Emily's.

"I must say I'm very impressed," Mr. Randall said. "Such understanding in two so young. I would have thought that one would have to live much longer than yourselves to gain such a grasp of these matters."

"Thank you, sir," Emily said.

"Thank you very much," Michael said.

Mr. Randall again leaned forward in his chair. "These matters are of great importance to all of mankind, children. You understand that? All of the world should know about what we have witnessed here. And many of them would very much like to know. To be involved. Don't you think so, ladies?"

The ladies assured Mr. Randall that the world would like to know.

"I want the two of you to think carefully about what I have said," Mr. Randall urged. "History has been made today, in this room. History has been altered—forever. We are blessed to be here for such a thing. Something that would seem impossible to many, but not to us, who have seen history change before our eyes." Mr. Randall squinted at Emily and Michael. "I want the two of you to fully take my meaning."

The spirit-knocking session gave way to Mr. Randall's presentation, in which each of the ladies, one by one, sat before him.

Mr. Randall folded his hands and closed his eyes. His body settled into a relaxed and yet somehow firm posture. Each breath he took became more controlled, more serene, as if he were shedding a burdensome and contrived form to meet with a simpler, truer essence in a faraway place. When he spoke to each of the ladies, his brow furrowed. As she observed Mr. Randall, Emily was reminded of a person listening to a telephone message, from time to time pulling himself away from the receiver to share the importance of the message with another in the room who could only watch the listener's face and wait for the message to be given in fragments.

"Miss Rose, you had an aunt who lived in this area," Mr. Randall said. "Your mother's sister."

"Yes, our aunt Helen lived only a few miles from here—she was our father's sister," Miss Rose said, looking around the room to take in the reactions of the others. Whether her aunt had been her mother's sister or her father's sister did not seem to concern Miss Rose much, Emily noted.

Mr. Randall said, "Your aunt had a beloved pet."

"Yes, yes—her dog, Trooper—oh, she adored that dog. Aunt Helen was heartbroken."

"This dog," Mr. Randall said, listening hard for the far-off voice, "disappeared one summer."

"No."

Mr. Randall's brow became more furrowed. "I'm sensing grief over Trooper."

Miss Rose's eyes widened in recognition and wonder.

"Trooper died of an illness?"

"Yes, yes, a terrible illness—the poor creature wasted away to nothing."

"Your sympathy is much appreciated—know that Aunt Helen appreciates your kindness."

On their way back to Ravenwood, Michael said, "And he kept his questions general, just like we worked it out in our act. But he is so much better at it. I guess he *would* be. Glossing right over his misses, like they never happened—very nice."

Emily reflected on Miss Rose's reading. "I'll bet most everybody in that room had an aunt who lived nearby, and half of those aunts probably had pets," she said.

But of course Emily and Michael watched Mr. Randall with the special sight allowed guild members—even apprentices. His praise came from experience and pleased them both, despite their guarded reservations.

"What about all that 'the world should know' stuff?" Emily said as the twins made their way home.

"I wouldn't worry about that."

"You wouldn't?"

"No. That's just more talk for the ladies. It's all for the show—you know that."

Emily shrugged. "Yes, I suppose. He seemed sincere enough about that, though."

Michael grinned. "That's the trick, isn't it?"

In Mrs. Pomeroy's parlor, the rest of the ladies had taken their turns before Mr. Randall as they had before Emily and Michael.

"Miss Sophia, I'm seeing a pocket watch . . . an old watch . . . your father's watch?"

"Mrs. Lattimore, I'm sensing a boy who liked to make jokes—some young relative of yours?"

"Mrs. Nerova, your husband was a man of many regrets."

"Mrs. Pomeroy, your mother was a devoutly religious woman?"

And Miss Sophia saying, "Yes, I seem to recall my father had a beautiful watch. I don't know what became of it." And Mrs. Lattimore saying with a twinkle of admission, "My younger brother was a terrible prankster—he loved to play jokes on everyone in the house." And Mrs. Nerova shaking her head with a tear in her eye. "No, no, the one thing my husband never do is regret." And Mrs. Pomeroy, wearing her elaborate silver crucifix, her lower lip trembling, "Yes, my mother was very devout. She lived in Christ always."

The most amazing thing of all was that Emily and Michael had both recognized in Mr. Randall a man whom they had not seen in four years, and then only for one memorable hour. A man who had played a much more comic role than the professional and prophetic James Randall—the magician of their so-called Aunt Becky's birthday party, the Astonishing Antoine.

21.

FRAGMENTS

"OF COURSE, WE MIGHT BE WRONG," EMILY SAID TO Michael. They were sitting by the river in a lowering dusk.

"Of course, but I don't think we are. Both of us? Do you think we would both be so sure?"

"No."

Emily picked up a stone and tossed it out toward the middle of the Delaware. The stone broke the surface and disappeared. At the periphery of her vision, she saw a shadow waddle in the green leaves clustered down the bank to the river. She kept her head still, expecting the groundhog could sense even a sudden turn and a direct look. She said nothing to Michael about the groundhog, imagining that it might wander right up to them if it believed itself invisible. "Strange things certainly happen," she said softly, her thoughts shifting to Mr. Dunne's glittering, intense eyes.

A rustle in the leaves as the groundhog slipped away.

"Yes, they do," Michael said.

"How interested do you think Mr. Randall is in us?" The children had agreed to call him Mr. Randall in accordance with the magician's wishes, though they were sure this was no more his real name than the Astonishing Antoine had been.

"You heard him, Em."

"We were supposed to be finished with all this by now. Summer's over, Michael. This man is making fools of those ladies—"

"Those ladies make fools of themselves."

Emily squinted at him. "They and God knows how many other people—and for lots of money, I suppose." The twins had seen Mrs. Pomeroy slip an envelope into the magician's hand when she led him to the front door. Mr. Randall had taken the envelope with a nod, as if accepting a sacred duty.

"Of course it's about money. It always gets back to money," Michael said, as if he had lived for many years and seen the hand of greed exerting control over everything human in the world.

"If it's all about money, Michael, then why do we do it?"

Michael looked out over the river. He shrugged. "Because they want us to. Because we can. Why else?"

Without answering, Emily folded her arms across her knees and thought of Mr. Dunne. She thought of how close she had come to telling him, of his eyes holding hers and demanding her silence.

Late one afternoon in early October, Emily roamed the house. She was the only one home. Boredom drove her through the halls, the sort of restlessness that conceives both wonderful and terrible ideas. Emily felt a sense of urgency that she unconsciously associated with October, the first full month of autumn, the time when the ycar begins to collapse into a short procession of observances: Halloween, Thanksgiving, Christmas, and the coming of the new year. She would not actually recognize this collapse until late November or early December, when it was well under way; for the time being she drifted through the halls, restless, bored, and strangely unsatisfied.

Emily stopped at the top of the stairs. Her mother's bedroom door stood at the end of the hall. The locked drawer in her mother's dresser waited inside. She walked to the door—only another door to walk through into another room; a room to be exited, a door to close behind. Emily entered the room and stood before her mother's dresser. She tugged on the drawer's knob, finding it as resistant as before. On her way out, Emily stopped again within the doorway. She was reminded of a distant day when she was seven years old and had stood under this doorway, gazing up at the white frame far above her head. Her mother had come over to ask Emily what she was staring at, and her mother's head appeared to almost brush the lintel from Emily's point of view. This illusion had given Emily a quiet feeling of awe.

Looking up at the lintel at that moment, in October of her fourteenth year, it did not seem so far away, though Emily was a small girl. She reached up her hand, stood on her toes, and judged the distance between her outstretched fingers and the frame. She dropped to a half-crouch and jumped straight up in one motion, feeling the joy that comes from being in a body that can jump or run or climb. Emily smacked the lintel with more force than intended. The door frame trembled; the walls absorbed the soft shockwaves. Emily regained her feet and looked up at the lintel.

Something small and dark extended over the lip of the narrow ledge. She jumped with all of her might and for a moment touched the cool, leading end of the concealed thing—just long enough to feel that it was a key—and a moment later she was on her feet again and catching the toppled little key in her palm, small and made of brass, almost featureless, the sort of key often used to lock jewelry boxes, china closets, and dresser drawers.

Brassieres, girdles, underwear. A small box of hatpins, barrettes, loose buttons. A wooden box with a pattern of roses and vines on the top, containing thick bunches of letters bound together with string, greeting cards, postcards from San Francisco, Chicago, Munich, Rome, Paris. A large photograph album in thick, brown leather. There were no photographs on the first page of the album, only words written in Naomi Stewart's careful hand, written in white ink against the heavy black stock of the page. The words formed a narrative: *Ravenwood mansion was built beside the Delaware River in 1867, just outside of Philadelphia. Robert Ward, master of the house, was the son of a wealthy Virginia landowner. Robert named the house and the estate around it for the old family estate in Scotland, which had been named for a relation in England. This house, he expected, was a place where his family would be happy.*

A large old picture of Robert and Elaine Ward on their wedding day dominated the second page. Robert, a man in his early middle age in a dark frock coat, a large mustache, and a relaxed expression that denied any discomfort, stood with his young bride. Elaine stood beside her new husband in an elaborately embroidered white dress, like a girl on Easter Sunday. Mrs. Stewart's handwriting across the bottom of the page read, *Robert and Elaine Ward, May 4, 1863.*

Another photograph revealed Robert standing in a dark suit on an unfamiliar porch, smoke trailing from the cigar in his mouth. Robert squinted through the smoke at the camera, and in this aspect seemed to be winking at the photographer. The tidy white script said, *March 13, 1864: Robert at the Virginia plantation, three days after the birth of his son, Jonathan. Robert's firstborn son had been dead nearly 25 years by then.*

The middle photograph on this page showed a slumped old man standing beside a river, his white hair windblown and his beard unruly. The old man seemed to be smiling in spite of himself. *Robert standing beside his beloved Delaware, a month before his death, September 1884.*

And at the bottom of this page, a picture of a black woman in a white bonnet and a thick cotton dress standing on the porch of the house in Virginia. The woman stood with a firm posture, her arms crossed before her chest. She looked at the camera with a level and impatient gaze. *Addie Ward at the old mansion in Virginia, 1861. Addie was the mother of Robert Ward's first child (rest his innocent soul) and the true love of Robert's life.*

Two more photographs on page six: *Elaine and Robert on their 15th wedding anniversary, May 4, 1878. In less than two years she would die of tuberculosis.*

And there were more pictures of babies, children, and adults— in christening gowns, by the river, in photographers' studios, in fine chairs. Sons and daughters, brothers and sisters. Wives and husbands. Amid the photographs, the graceful handwriting provided fragments, small and large, of many characters in a long story. *In his favorite chair . . . the spot where the cherry blossom tree would be planted . . . with her old dog Scout . . . on Easter Sunday, dressed for church . . .* Some parts of the album opened on blank spots apparently intended for misplaced photographs. Half of one page had been left empty with the expectation, as the writing told, of placing a *Portrait of Regina Ward, age sixteen, four months before she would fall down the riverbank and pass away.*

A few pages were full of Emily's grandfather Jonathan Ward— as an infant, a child, a young man. *1864—In his father's arms, both of them so dour. Dressed for riding on a windy day, April 1875. On the day of his sister Regina's funeral, 1883.* Under a picture of Jonathan standing with slumped shoulders in the shadow of the house, hands in his pockets, Mrs. Stewart's script asked, *What is it about unhappiness and rich men's sons?*

A page and a half of blank space followed these photographs and details. A packet of more pictures and some handwritten notes, bound together with string, rested here like a stack of bricks between unfinished walls. In the picture on top, Jonathan's face was almost lost beneath the knotted string. This was an older Jonathan—grandfather Jonathan, if he had lived to see his grandchildren. He stood on the riverbank at Ravenwood, the sun creating deep crevasses where the wrinkles on his face gathered.

Emily heard footsteps and voices in the sunporch. She replaced the album, closed the drawer, and locked it. Standing on the chair from her mother's desk, she placed the key on top of the door frame and tried not to topple off the chair when she heard Mary's voice in the house below: "Hello? Anybody home?"

October 25, 1911

WEDNESDAY MORNING

Naomi was sitting on the front porch when Stan Loewry came up the cobblestone drive in the new silver Rolls-Royce touring car he'd written her about. Gleaming, all chrome and hard lines, leather burgundy seats, it shone like a dream of money. Naomi had been thinking about meeting both Stan and Donald only six months before at one of her father's regattas—the last one her father would ever hold, the last time she saw him laugh or even smile in public. Naomi's brother Michael had been there on that April afternoon, a rare exception for one of her father's parties, and he had been drunk and harassing some of the guests up until he introduced Naomi to Donald and Stan. She remembered feeling like a girl in front of these men in their early thirties, trying to appear poised in her brown dress that moved gently around her long, slender figure, only a few weeks past her eighteenth birthday. Stan had been well-dressed, even for one of her father's parties. He had taken her hand and smiled without reservation. She saw Stan take in her hair, her chin, her neck, her eyes, and her form in one light roving motion of his eyes. Donald, lanky and blond, could hardly hold her look and took her hand in his own, one that made Naomi think of the oversized paws of retriever puppies.

Michael said something scornful about rich boys and told Naomi, *These two are* men *meant for high service. Men of dignity. I've been grilling them for information, picking at their hearts.* His words, drunk and grand, teasing but dissatisfied. *This one,* his hand on Stan's shoulder, *has more money than any of the great leaders of industry here today. And he's* uncertain *about his feelings for his father's money. Imagine it, Naomi. He's practically an anarchist!*

This one, Michael had said, taking Donald's arm, *is a doctor. Look at him—it's perfect. Oaths and all of that. Marry this one for his money,* Michael said, nodding at Stan, *but put your trust in this one for his just and mild nature.*

Sounds about right, Stan had said.

Donald had spoken up and politely shrugged off Michael's hand. *Stan's a knight at heart.*

Stan drove the silver Rolls smoothly around the turnout at the foot of the steps and glided to a halt before Naomi, her paper now folded in her lap. The headlamps of the car shimmered even in the shadow; the flying lady mounted on top of the front grill, an angel cast in silver, soared in stillness; the top down; Stan's smile, without a ghost of doubt.

"Not getting enough attention, Stan?" Naomi asked, standing to greet him.

Stan turned off the car and stepped out. "Look at it!" he said, beaming over the hood. "Everything is going to change so fast now. Come on—let me give you a tour of the neighborhood in it. You have to see the trees blur past in this thing."

"No, thanks, Stan. I can't."

Stan ascended the porch and stood before her. "I drove out here to show this machine off and you say, 'No, thanks'?" he said, holding a sense of fun in his voice. He had the face of a man who had never been disappointed in his life. But Naomi knew where to look in his eyes. "Expecting company?"

"You could say that." Naomi wanted to share in the banter, to be clever and ironic and invincible. She heard the failure of it in her own voice. "I'm pregnant," she said, abandoning safety.

Stan's eyes shot up toward the closed front door nearby.

"Don't worry," Naomi said. "Mary is out visiting a friend. Mother is in her room; the nurse is with her. She's been in her room a lot since Dad died."

He took the seat beside her. His eyes had changed. Naomi saw a terror of hope there.

"The baby is Donald's, Stan," she said. She felt a soft shudder in her chest and enclosed her body around it, squeezed its tremors out along her arms and down her spine.

"You're sure?"

She nodded. "I had my cycle since you and I were together."

Two months before, that single time Stan and Naomi were together, the late August evening thrum of insects and the silhouettes of bats flapping between the trees against the soft blue twilight. Stan and Naomi in the trees near the stream leading from the river and away from Ravenwood, away from the house. Naomi's fear of being seen from the house, of Mary simply knowing in that way she had, of being alone with Stan, of the excitement. The confused unhappiness and expectation and longing to forget in those months following her father's death in April—her ache for Donald's adoration and for Stan's impulse to be hers. She had thought to get the old iron hands-heart-and-crown key she wasn't supposed to know about as a child, the one that had dropped out of her brother Michael's pocket in the tea house, to lead Stan the old secret underground way from the house—but instead she had thought of Donald, who knew the secret way, and taken Stan out the door like any guest and led him on a stroll to the stream behind the house. Stan's hands on her in the trees, his mouth, the soft grass, his fingers undressing her. His question after, if he was her first. *No. Once before, with Donald.* His stricken silence at her honesty, his fingers no longer stirring her dark hair.

"Does Donald know?" Stan asked Naomi on the porch.

"Yes, I told him after I spoke with the doctor. He's asked me to marry him."

"Does he know about us?"

Naomi sat up straight and held Stan's eyes with hers. "No. He doesn't know about that one time." Her mouth felt chalky at the finality in her voice.

Stan stood up and went to the edge of the porch. "I can't figure who's at a disadvantage here: him or me."

"Would you really like me to tell him now?" Naomi asked.

"Does it matter what I would like right now?" Stan gazed out over the silver Rolls.

"It always matters." The shudder arose in Naomi's chest again—a trace of it emerged in her throat.

"But it doesn't change anything. You're going to marry him."

"Yes."

"You love him."

"Yes."

"You love me."

"Yes." A hitch in her voice caught the word. She released a breath. She held her hands in her lap. She could not touch him, could not lift her hand and have it shake in the air. "I do love him, Stan. Very much. He's a good man."

"*I know he's a good man*. I know that, Naomi. And I know how you feel about him." Stan turned and looked at her, his eyes bright and hard. "I want you to know I don't care. You remember that. I haven't changed my mind about anything." He strode down the front steps and went to the front of the car. He took the crank at the base of the grill in his hand and looked up at Naomi. He was Stan behind the wheel of the Rolls again—before even getting back in—coming up the drive in his fast silver machine. "It's amazing. You just wind this up," he said, turning the crank until the engine kicked into a low growl, "and a team of horses at full gallop can't catch you. You can outrun a train. Imagine it." So much friendliness in his voice.

Naomi blinked. Her eyes stung from his smile. She would not look away as he climbed behind the wheel. "Don't try to outrun any trains," she said.

Stan put the car in gear and the engine leveled out to a purr. "Not when you're in the car, Naomi. You'll give my best?"

"I will."

"Then I'll be seeing you," he said, and pulled the car around the turnout, down the drive, and out onto the road.

On the day Naomi had met Donald and Stan, at her father's regatta—which her brother Michael liked to point out was more of a boat parade than a boat race—sounds from the boats on the water had distracted her from the two men before her and

Michael's obnoxious remarks. Rows of bright sails waved in the sun, and people stood at the rails on the decks and called to the shore. A cheer went up from the crowd around the tables. They held their drinks up toward the approaching sails.

Naomi's father, Jonathan Ward, hurried to the riverside. There was a desperate quality in his delight at seeing the boats and hearing the voices. Naomi felt sure everyone sensed it, that they all wanted to fulfill something this wealthy man alone on the bank seemed to need, the reason he had gone to such expense and trouble to bring them here, mostly business acquaintances who'd never had a private conversation with him.

On the boats, a great whistling and shouting began. Some of the men started to stomp around on the decks, calling to their friends on other boats across the water. Soon a chaotic, flat, thunderous rhythm of feet drifted to the riverbank, and the crowd around the tables cheered again. The men on the decks of the sailboats broke into a jig and reel, beginning with only a few dancers and spreading from boat to boat like a fever.

"The revenge of the Irish!" Michael had called out to the men on the boats, and those who heard laughed. They danced arm in arm, their heavy bouncing tread gaining a kind of order and sounding deeply in the Delaware beneath them. Someone had begun to sing an old Irish drinking song, and the other men on the boats picked it up and carried it across the water: *"And it's no, nay, never—no-nay-never-no-more—will I play the wild rover, no never, no more!"*

Michael laughed and applauded. He raised his glass and finished his drink. He whistled loudly between two fingers at the singing dancers on the boats.

Naomi heard Donald whistle the tune of the song growing on the river and spawning scattered voices on the bank. Donald's whistle had a sad, pretty lilt that the voices in unison did not. Naomi turned to look at Donald and saw Stan Loewry smiling and watching the boats on the Delaware. Before Naomi could look away, Stan caught her eye and smiled at her, then turned back toward the river and joined the joyful, resigned voices.

PART FIVE

22.

Dorothy Allen's Wisdom
and an Agreement

EMILY AND MARY STROLLED TOGETHER ALONG THE PATH
by the river in a cool October breeze.

"Mary? I wonder if you'll tell me another story."

The carriage house came into view around a bend in the path,
beyond the trees. It was composed of the same bricks as the tea
house, but it hulked against the tree line at this farthest end of
the estate from the house, the creek just beyond the trees. It
looked solid, impregnable—only a few narrow windows across the
second-floor façade, two great sets of doors on the first, heavily
padlocked. An ornate and watchful-looking stone relief of a horse
head above the doors, eyes directed out over the grounds. The
darkness inside the carriage house like the unthinkable dreams in
the horse's head if it could dream.

Mary thought a moment and asked, "Is there a story you have
in mind, Emily?"

"How did you know there was?"

"Sometimes you just know."

"I want to know about my mother and father," Emily said. "I want to know about when they met, and how it was, and all of that."

"And you would prefer not to ask your mother about these things?"

"I'm not sure she would want to tell me. She talks about Daddy, once in a while, but not very much about the two of them together."

"That has been her way for some time. But it wasn't always so." Mary took a breath. "Your mother met your father when she was eighteen, at one of her father's parties. Your grandfather used to get all of his clients and business acquaintances together and throw regattas—sort of like boat races. Your grandfather would stand out there on the bank and call to the people on the boats like a child, so happy, in front of all his fancy friends. Anyway, your father and mother met at one of these regattas. He was thirty-one, I think. They fell for each other. They started seeing one another all the time, and she was crazy about him. She had never really been courted—your grandfather wouldn't allow it before she turned eighteen—and your grandfather wasn't so happy about this older man coming around after his daughter. But they were going to be together one way or the other, you could see that. I asked your mother, 'Do you love him?' And she said, 'Yes, Mary—please tell me what to do.' I told her what I tell everybody, 'Be patient and see what happens. And be careful.' But that's not what your mother wanted to hear at the time. And before very long they were married. In December of that year, it was." Mary walked on, holding her hands behind her back as if they held her unsaid words.

When she spoke, her tone was in answer to a question Emily had not asked. "Your mother and father were very much in love, Emily. There are people who try to tell you that life is simple. But life is not simple. You are a young woman and it's time you started to understand that. Your mother always said she didn't care a thing what people thought, but she withdrew into this house to get away from it. And when your father died, she tried to forget the world. We may as well have bricked the front door up."

Mary and Emily walked on in quiet for a moment.

Mary said, "But she has begun to remember. And she wants to remember." She cleared her throat. "Tell me, Em—are you becoming very interested in your family history?"

"Yes, very much."

"I think you should talk to your mother about it. I think your mother has wanted to talk to someone besides me about this family and this place for a long time now."

At the next opportunity, when the house was quiet and Emily felt she could sense every movement, she retrieved the key from the lintel over her mother's door and curled up on the floor with the inscribed photograph album. Her discovery of the album was only a few days old. The bound packet of photographs and notes had gone missing. For a moment this gave her a jolt. Emily took this as a sign that her mother sensed the violation of her privacy. The pages the packet had been placed between remained blank.

Emily turned to the pages devoted to her mother and father.

Naomi Sarah Ward, 1893– . . .

Emily's mother as an infant, as a little girl, as a young woman.

In one picture, her mother stood in front of the tea house on a bright day, dressed as if for an important luncheon or church service. She appeared on the verge of laughter. Beside the picture, Emily's mother had written, *Donald Stewart took this picture on September 20, 1911. He told me silly jokes to make me smile, this man I had known less than two months, who would be my husband.*

Emily turned to her parents' wedding picture (*Donald and Naomi Stewart, December 12, 1911*) and looked at their faces. Her father looked like an overgrown boy in his tuxedo, even though he was thirteen years older than his young bride. The cuffs of his jacket were cut as they should be, but they would have matched his expression better if they had been too short. Her mother's beautiful happiness filled Emily with wonder. She tried to imagine that these two people in the image before her had talked secretly together, rushed to meet each other in their passion, spent lonely hours apart thinking of one another, and existed together in the living, breathing world apart from the colorless fraction of a second captured on the page. Her mother had written no commentary beside her wedding picture.

Emily turned the page and found pictures of her father, from infancy to manhood. In one of these he stood beside a very young Stan Loewry—both of them smiling—in front of a grand old gray building. Her father smiled as if he thought nothing of it; Stan as if he already knew how the photograph would turn out. *The freshmen at their leisure—Stan and Donald at Princeton, March 1898.*

There was a picture of Donald Stewart holding two infants on the opposite page. Her father beamed through his glasses at the camera, shocks of his blond hair falling over his forehead. *Donald, Emily, and Michael, three days after the children's birth—June 26,*

1912. Donald loved the twins from the time he knew that a birth was on its way (not knowing that it would be a birth of twins) and became the children's father in the instant that I told him.

Emily imagined this man in the picture waiting for his child to be born. Did he want a son or a daughter? Emily wondered. Nine months seemed like a long time to wait for something like a baby.

She remembered when she had first learned about babies from a girl at school named Dorothy Allen, four years before. Dorothy had told her about how men and women got together and what body parts they used. *The man takes his thing, and puts it in the woman's place . . . her place down there . . . he puts his thing in her there and nine months later, a baby comes.* On the evening following these revelations, Emily had lain in bed and remembered this description of men and women together and gotten a strange feeling in her abdomen, a feeling that demanded she press her palm over her stomach and roll the ball of her hand in slow circles that had made her confused and happy all at once, something she would often do when feeling lonely or frightened in the night. As the years passed, Emily had begun to press her hand on her stomach when alone and feeling particularly—almost alarmingly—alive. The night after her conversation with Stan in the tea house, Emily had imagined he stood in her bedroom doorway, speaking softly, and she had rubbed slow circles across her stomach.

Nine months to consider names. To pretend that your child was in your arms. Nine months on the calendar of her parents' lives. She and her brother born in June 1912. October to June. Her parents' wedding photograph: *December 12, 1911.*

Your mother and father were very much in love, Mary had said. *There are people who try to tell you that life is simple.*

But only whores let men put their things there, my sister says, Dorothy Allen had told Emily.

But what about moms and dads . . . ? Emily asked Dorothy.

That's different . . . moms and dads are married *. . . nobody marries a whore . . .*

But life is not simple, Mary had told her.

Emily turned to the photograph from her parents' wedding day. Her mother and father, so well dressed and handsome together, had felt the dizziness that made her press on her own lower belly, they had felt the crazy compulsion and found a place to perform the secret that everyone knew. Everyone but little children, who would know soon enough. How strangely dishonest it all seemed, the whole world trying to keep this secret from itself.

Noises in the house below crept up through the floorboards, telling her that the time had come to put the album away and replace the key in its place above the door.

And on this afternoon in October, Cat Pomeroy knocked at the front door. Michael answered. They went behind the house along the path that circled around to the cottage beside the tiny creek, winding away from the Delaware into the trees. Cat talked; Michael nodded, and nodded. They stopped and faced each other in the shade—Michael's back to the house, Cat in a half-turn.

"All right?" she asked.

"Yes, tell them all right."

"Have you told your mother about any of this?" Cat searched his face and turned fully toward him, her eyebrows raised to show her indifferent power.

"No, of course not. She would be . . . impatient about the whole thing," he said.

"Impatient. I guess she would be."

Michael leaned forward and kissed Cat on the lips. She did not return his kiss—she did not pull away. She teetered just a bit on her heels.

He stepped back. "Is that all right?"

"Yes."

"So you'll tell them?"

"Yes. Yes."

"Good. And let's keep this between us for the moment. Emily has a lot on her mind. As for my mother, it's better that my mother be left out of all this. And I'll be coming alone—please tell them that."

Michael lingered on the path after she had disappeared around the house. He crossed the lawn to his customary tree, sat down in its disjointed and spidery shade, and looked out over the river.

23.

HELLO,
UNSUSPECTING STRANGER

MICHAEL PASSED THROUGH THE WOODS ALONG THE DELA-ware on the Saturday morning following his meeting with Cat, searching the path winding off through the mostly bare trees. He approached a bend in the path and caught a wisp of smoke from the man's pipe before he saw the man himself.

"Good morning, Mr. Randall," Michael called ahead, as the large man's figure came fully into his view.

"Good morning, Michael," Mr. Randall said in his deep, reso-nating voice through a veil of smoke. Mr. Randall held his pipe in his white teeth. "This is a perfect morning to stroll through the woods, don't you agree?"

"Yes, sir."

The bearded man extended his hand and swallowed up Michael's thin fingers.

"Now," Mr. Randall said, releasing Michael's hand, "shall we?" He turned and gestured ahead at the tree-lined path.

They moved on in silence. The woods stirred around them in a drowsy prelude to the stillness of winter. The sparse shade from the canopy of tree limbs above and the tattered carpet of leaves on the ground appeared on the path before them as shadows piled on shadows. Mr. Randall tapped the stem of his pipe against his forehead, as if he were stroking his beard. "Michael, I wonder if you realize how special your sister's talent is. If you see her for the amazing young woman that she is."

Michael said he did. "Emily is gifted in a way that most people wouldn't understand."

The bearded man nodded, his hands folded behind his back. "Yes, gifted. Most people could not conceive of such a thing. Could not, eh, understand it? Yes."

Mr. Randall determined the speed of their progress in his methodical way; Michael remained in step.

"I also wonder if you realize how special your abilities are, Michael. Very important, what you do. I've watched you: I know. And I know that you know. I would even say that Emily's talent would be considerably less effective without your assistance. I don't have to tell you that, of course. You are something of a sensitive yourself, Michael."

Michael watched the patches of leaves lying scattered in advance of their slow, easy gait.

"I want you to understand what a remarkable lad you are. Far, far beyond your years. Most people wouldn't appreciate that, either, but there are those who would—like myself. I've watched you: I see it. And Emily—for a girl so young to be given such a powerful gift . . . It staggers the mind to think of it. There is a world of people who could never understand it, you're right to say, but there are many, many others who would understand it only too well. There are many, many other people in places you've never even thought of who would be as excited as I am about your sister's talent—perhaps even more so. There is no question about it. I have seen it. Look at our ladies."

Michael could see the ladies on the leaf-strewn path ahead for an instant, less substantial than the shadows.

"Exactly the sort of people I'm thinking of, who understand the meaning of such a gift. You and your sister aren't merely children to those ladies. Before the two of you, in the face of such wonders, they feel like children. And there are many, many more like them—in places you couldn't imagine, my boy." Mr. Randall's pipe trailed blue smoke that disintegrated into a gray exhausted haze behind him. "Now, I'm sure that an intelligent, inquisitive young man like yourself cannot help but wonder why I have asked to speak with you," he said. "I'm sure you would like an explanation of some kind."

Michael adopted some of Mr. Randall's meticulous manner. "You would be right to think so."

"Of course. I like to be plain when I can, Michael. I have asked to speak with you and your sister—a wise choice of yours to come alone, so that we can talk like this—I asked to speak with you so that I could present you with a story and a proposition. Are you interested as far as that goes?"

Michael nodded.

"Good. As you know, it helps when people are of one mind in this sort of thing. The story is about a young man I once knew, quite a good friend of mine, actually. The only person I have ever trusted in regard to my best interests. This young man was born in poverty, some years ago. Fortunately for yourself, Michael, this has never been your trouble, if you don't mind me remarking."

Clear-eyed, undaunted, Michael looked at Mr. Randall's searching eyes and shook his head. *Not that easy.* "Why would I mind?"

"Of course not, of course not," Mr. Randall said, flicking the topic away. "As I was saying . . . This young man, unlucky in birth, was nevertheless a clever sort, and patient. Born with certain abilities, certain skills. With no formal education, he decided to make himself into something of a gentleman, and he decided he would go about this work in any way that seemed fit or necessary. He took stock of his origins, and decided that he would learn everything he could about the ways of the world and make the best of his situation. So he took his studies from whatever teachers he could find and learned them well, took to books and read them aloud in his solitude—read them several times, if one book was all he could get ahold of for any period of time. And he grew, and learned things about the world and about other people—as you are learning—and he learned things about himself. One of the things he learned about himself—the same thing you and your sister have learned about yourselves just recently—was that he was a sensitive type, sensitive to the feelings of others around him, sensitive to things that most people perhaps miss. Even performed as a magician, for a time."

Michael, his head bent in attentive courtesy, never missed a step.

"This gift of Emily's, that you have been instrumental in helping to develop, this gift is combined with a sensitivity and a style uncanny in one so young. This young friend of mine, he discovered such things in himself. Not precisely the same, understand, but of the same sort, of a similar beauty and style. He discovered in himself a knack for tricks and feats of all kinds. And so this poor young man, who had learned as much as he could from as many books and teachers as he could find, and had learned to turn a word or two to his advantage, he went out into the world and prospered. Prospered? He did more than that: he conquered. He gained entry into the homes and clubs of those who would have ignored his body in the gutter not many years before. This young friend of mine found himself being warmly welcomed—pursued!—by all sorts of influential, well-bred people. A young man with a background like yours must have seen many of the kind. Old money, new money, *royal* money. Can you imagine that this young friend of mine, who had once picked crumbs from beneath his mother's table, found himself before some of the royalty of Europe, before lords, ladies, *emperors*? Yes." Mr. Randall gestured before them, as if these lords and ladies could be cast there for Michael's consideration and recalled up the magician's sleeve. "And he has been to more parties at more mayors', senators', governors' homes— grand balls, they were. Poets, painters, playwrights—of the finest stripe—stage actors, steel barons, oil barons, literati, *et cetera, et cetera, et cetera.* He saw the world, and everything he earned he earned through tenacity, cleverness, courage, and good sense. And everything he earned was his own. And these new friends of his that I've been telling you about? These wonderful new friends? They adored him. He gave them the things that they needed— gave them in a way that he knew they needed. This clever, sensitive young friend of mine made these fine people so very happy, they relied on him to come to their aid again and again, to ease their sadness, relieve their loneliness, soothe their aching hearts with messages of comfort and hope. And they adored him for it. Why not? Such happiness as he brought them is nothing for any of us to sneeze at, my boy."

Michael looked along the path ahead of him, his ear cocked slightly toward the words that poured from the large man beside him.

"This young friend of mine made his mistakes, of course. He lost out in some of his ventures, trusted one or two other ambitious young men more than was prudent—more than his deepest nature should have allowed—and ran into a few obstacles. Ups and downs, Michael, that is our lot in this world. He suffered false starts, bad decisions. He himself with no allies, no well-wishers. He had to rely from time to time on his old wits and abilities, had to make his living in ways he thought he was long past; in ways not nearly so fine or beautiful—so meaningful—as he had come to know. He was still a master of people's needs, still quite skilled and capable, but he had to regain his footing, start again. The men of this world—the men who master the world—suffer such setbacks. It is all part of a life of courage, Michael. Each one of us is given the choice to be courageous or not—to rise to adventure or not. He found his footing again, and has done quite well for himself. He found new friends, allies, and well-wishers. The world is full of people of influence and means with needs to be met. Passionate people, who appreciate the sort of things men like you and I can offer them—who appreciate these wonderful gifts and are eager to repay such gifts in kind. Don't be deceived for one moment that only old women and children appreciate such things." Mr. Randall upended his pipe's bowl and shook out bits of crumbling ash with two quick snaps of his wrist; his free hand dropped a fresh clump of tobacco into the bowl, having hardly stopped at his pocket.

In another passing motion, a match sprang up in his fingers. He struck the match along his pipe and relit it, the crackle and sigh of his pleasure sharp in the crisp air. "And everything this young man achieved he achieved by his own wits and courage. And everything he earned was his own."

The two of them came toward the end of the woods.

"Now, Michael, for my proposition. I would like to have you and Emily join me in my travels around the world—to Europe, to Asia, to Africa—I would like you both to come with me and meet some of these friends of mine. People who would appreciate the two of you. Appreciate? They would adore you. Naturally, I would need your mother's permission. Perhaps she could join us."

The notion of his mother packing her bags to join the twins and Mr. Randall in a spirit-knocking tour of the world gave Michael a laugh to tamp down into his chest—almost as fantastic an idea as Emily contacting the dead. But then Mr. Randall must have built a life in chasing impossible things, in pulling things out of the air that others wouldn't dare dream of.

"My mother is not one of those who would appreciate such things," Michael said, his voice flat.

Mr. Randall clucked his tongue. "I see, I see. I suspected as much. But perhaps she could be persuaded. Sometimes a person just needs a small push."

"My mother is not easy to push."

"Of course, of course. I wouldn't suggest anything else. Still, you are a persuasive young man. Perhaps you could talk with your Negro servant—she has great influence over your mother, I think? I understand the woman even sits down to table with the family? Such admirable liberality."

"Mary is even less friendly to this sort of thing than my mother," Michael said.

"I've no doubt that you know best about these matters. I'm merely saying that such things aren't widely accepted. Never mind the ladies and their Mrs. Lattimore. They are an odd lot, our ladies—eh, exceptional—and do you think Mrs. Lattimore's cultivated British manners don't allow certain privileges with some in this country? And their *countess*? Do not be deceived, Michael. But then, after all, what is more important—whether or not Mrs. Nerova's blood is old Russian blue, or whether or not she and the other ladies believe it is so? I leave that to you."

Michael imagined the ladies all sitting together, waiting for them in that faded parlor, certain of a world without death. How many more like them? In places he had only dreamed of, far from Ravenwood and its long, quiet days. Grand houses that dwarfed his family's home. Distant coasts, ancient cities. Theaters and footlights and so many eager eyes. "I assume you will need an answer soon," he said.

"Again your perceptiveness amazes me. You understand these matters very well. Yes, I will be going to Europe to visit with some good friends in the Rhine Valley, then on to France and Italy. I'll be gone for nearly two months. My ship sails the day after tomorrow. I wonder if I could have some sort of answer from you by then—please forgive the short notice, but sometimes we must make the most important decisions in the least time."

"And in two months you'll be back here?" Michael asked.

"In two months or so I *could* be back here, if I were made to believe that important business would be done."

"All right. Two months, then. In that time I can talk to my sister, I can talk to my mother. I will think of something."

The bearded man's eyes glowed. "I have no doubt of that, Michael. Perhaps I should meet with your mother before boarding that ship? Just so that she will be familiar with me. To move things along."

"No. That's not a good idea, sir. We will talk again when you return."

"And I can be sure that you are of a serious mind on this business, Michael?"

"Yes, sir. You can be sure."

"Wonderful, my boy. I will be happy to come see you again. I'm sure I'll have a story or two to tell. I look forward to seeing Emily again, and to talking with your mother. We should be moving on. The ladies are expecting us."

"Please apologize to the ladies for me," Michael said. "I'll be heading home now." He turned away with a purpose back along the path in the direction they had come.

"I will see you in two months, Michael," Mr. Randall called after him, his oversized voice full of his pleasure at how the conversation had gone, full of encouragement and an offering of solidarity. Mr. Randall's voice showed no surprise that Michael should turn back home now; it sent him on his way with blessings of safe travel and happy outcomes. "Give my regards to your sister."

Michael trudged through the dry leaves, head bent. In the woods behind him, Mr. Randall started to sing in a grand baritone about faraway places and ship horns, about the wide sea and the stars and the distant northern lights.

24.

PATRICK

On a mild evening in the second week of October, Albert appeared at the door. He glanced toward the empty stairs when Emily let him in.

"My father would like to meet with you again."

"He was very upset," Emily said, sitting down in a nearby chair. "Last time."

"Would you please come see him? It's been bad lately." Albert stuffed his hands in his pockets.

Michael could be heard at the top of the staircase, whistling. He would find her undisclosed visit to Mr. Dunne a betrayal, made even more galling by Albert's involvement. Or he might find it funny, more than anything—Mr. Dunne calling on her to search for his son, playing games with Emily in his house and ultimately almost begging for more. Michael might laugh.

"All right," she said. "When?"

"Soon," he said, and Michael came down the staircase behind him.

"Starting a little secret club, are we?" Michael said.

"Don't worry, Michael. No one would dare start such a thing around here without letting you run it," Emily said.

"See that you don't."

Emily stood, wished Albert a good night, and headed for the stairs with her book tucked under her arm. The tune she hummed as she reached the stairs gave them leave to exclude her from whatever they liked.

Albert met Emily the following Saturday morning along the way to his house, and led her to the living room, where this time Mr. Dunne awaited her. Albert's father sat in the same chair he had occupied on the morning he had first met Emily. His eyes were glassy, though no less penetrating than she remembered them. His mouth, which she recalled as hard and thin, seemed somehow loose and uncertain.

"You can go, Albert," Mr. Dunne said.

Without a word, Albert was gone. The front door shut behind him. It occurred to Emily to wonder where Mrs. Dunne was; somewhere nearby, she imagined, resting her nerves.

"Please have a seat," Mr. Dunne said.

Emily sat and watched him. He looked steadily back, his moist eyes catching the light that crept into the room around the drawn shades. She made no effort at small talk; she offered no pleasantries of any kind. This was not a social call, and she knew it. After a moment of quiet, she said, "Are you ready to begin?"

· · ·

Again Emily faced Mr. Dunne in his darkened living room, during the third week in October. Each time his features seemed more pinched, his eyes older and more detached.

"Hello, Emily," he said. "Have a seat."

"Mr. Du—"

"Things have been bad, Emily. I tell you that in confidence."

"Of course. I understand."

"Well then," he said. "I am ready now."

He asked his questions, exhaling after each answering knock. Patrick was free of pain and loneliness; he dwelled in happiness; there was peace at the end, yes. Emily answered each question with carefully spaced knocks, always maintaining the idea that her connection with Patrick was tenuous, and that with every moment his presence became more difficult to feel. When she opened her eyes, she found Mr. Dunne looking through the wall over her head, forgetful of time. When the knocks told him of peace, she saw him feel it in this room, before her. It wasn't an absence of weariness; it was an acceptance of it, for a moment, if only what had been was not all that could be. She sometimes wondered what this expression would look like on her mother's face—imagined what might happen if she led her mother to the tea house and said, *Mama, I need you to help me bring him here.*

"Will you visit again?" Mr. Dunne asked.

"Yes," she said, her stomach seeming to expand and contract within her at once. She waited for him to say that this peace belonged to him now, that she had given it to him and could go out into the sun. That she need not come back. "Yes," she said. "Yes, I will."

. . .

In late October, Mr. Dunne again sent his son to Ravenwood. Emily had given her last session with Mr. Dunne a great deal of thought, and considered telling Michael about these secret meetings more than once. But somehow the darkened living room and Mr. Dunne's remote peace and Michael could not occupy the same space in her head.

Emily considered Mr. Randall's methods—the tactics of inference, of waiting for cues, of playing within reasonable limits of probability and taking chances in the knowledge that most slips would be first forgiven and then forgotten. When her thoughts had drifted toward emulating his technique, Emily pulled herself up short. The risk—amid all the risks she had taken—seemed too great. *She might as well try to reenact Mr. Randall's magic act,* she thought. But after the last session with Mr. Dunne, she was not so sure. In her mind she could see him sitting there before her, listening to her fears about this new risk. And in this place of her imagining, Mr. Dunne silenced her with one raised hand and said, "Patrick, can you speak to us?"

When Albert brought Emily into his home on her next visit, he led her past the living room, through the front hall, and stopped at the bottom of the staircase. The stairs climbed up into a dark, narrow corridor.

"My father is in his study," he said.

"Should I wait in the other room?"

"No. He would like to talk upstairs. He's waiting. Just knock on the second door on the right."

Emily stood at the foot of the stairs, looking up into the gloom. She took a long, even breath, and placed her foot on the first riser.

The second door on the right sat at an angle, so that it faced her fully, flat and resolute, as she crossed the landing toward it. She knocked twice. Mr. Dunne's voice came to her through the deep-stained panels: "Yes, Emily. Please come in."

The room was filled with tall, glass-paned cases packed to bursting with books. Mr. Dunne sat in a chair by a fireplace, where a low fire burned. His face was deeply shadowed in the weak, nervous glow.

"Please. Sit." His hand flapped toward an empty chair near his own.

Emily took her seat and met Mr. Dunne's look. She felt the rise and fall of her breath, felt the gentle expansion and collapse of her lungs. She had come to the Dunne house this time determined to try Mr. Randall's method, despite her fears. There were things that needed to be said, things Mr. Dunne was not and maybe could not say, things he didn't quite know how to ask for. It was one thing for knocks in the air to echo back what Mr. Dunne needed to hear, but if she could make Patrick speak to Mr. Dunne, break the silence in the house with words, the right words, maybe . . . Maybe. She couldn't simply turn from this place, having come this far, and leave it worse than she'd found it. But she would have to turn from it soon; although she couldn't accept how much of it was out of her hands, she spent no time in her mind denying that she could not keep returning for long.

"Mr. Dunne," she said, "I have something to tell you."

He slowly focused on her. "Yes?"

"Mr. Dunne, I've been having strange dreams."

His eyelids lowered, as if he had expected this. "Yes."

"Dreams about Patrick. Actually the same dream. It's not very clear—I can't really see him—and it doesn't last long." Emily closed her eyes. "He's in the distance, coming toward me—out of a sort of fog—and he is talking to me."

"Talking," he said.

"Yes, talking. I can't quite hear what he is saying, but it's the same thing, something he needs me to hear, and he comes in closer out of the fog—and I know that it's him, even though I still can't really make him out—and he keeps talking. I follow him out to the tea house—"

"Tea house?"

"Our playhouse, near the rose garden. That's where I've first met all of the spirits. It's easier to make contact in the tea house. So in my dream, Patrick leads me there."

"Ah." A flicker of understanding and suggestion in Mr. Dunne's tone. "Yes."

"Then I stop trying to see him and try very hard to hear him. And finally, something like a voice comes to me, very faint, in broken words." She opened her eyes.

Mr. Dunne sat rigid in his chair. "What about your *noise?*"

"No other spirit has ever tried to reach me this way. It frightened me very much at first."

He made a snorting noise, half listening to Emily's words. "And you can make this happen anytime?" he asked.

"I'm not sure. It's only happened in my dreams. But I think I can, with your help. I would like to try."

"What do you need me to do?"

Emily had prepared for this moment while lying in bed. She

would meet Mr. Dunne and Patrick in the darkness as she never had before—she would release herself to it and become the instrument. She would feel it and make the man slumped in the chair before her feel it. She would open herself to a place in the dark Michael hadn't even imagined, and more than even the ladies, Mr. Dunne would believe. Mr. Dunne would believe because she would go there with him wearing believing eyes and ears herself—something she could never explain to her brother, something he could never do while laughing behind a closed face. "I need you to help bring him here. Concentrate on bringing him here to us." She closed her eyes and let go.

"Mr. Dunne?"

"Yes?"

"I need you to tell me about Patrick again. As you remember him."

"But I've already told you—"

"Please, Mr. Dunne. Secrets can't help us here."

"Secrets," he said, as if the word seemed absurd to him.

"Give me as much as you feel you can."

Mr. Dunne sat in silence. The dark place devoured the quiet.

He took a hesitant breath.

"Patrick was born in February of 1900. He was bald, I remember. I've told you he was an athlete . . . well liked . . . had lots of friends. A good-looking young man; unusually good-looking. All of the girls noticed, some of these girls not to my liking. But he wanted my approval, I thought. At one time my approval meant something. At one time he wanted his father to be proud of him—and I was. Easy to be proud of a boy like Patrick. At one time he understood that I worried *about him. He understood that I had to be the father. Had to be careful to keep things in order, keep things from going wrong. Because you really have to choose one or the other. Always. Always the choice. And he took things hard—always took everything so hard. I worried about that, too. I worried he would be weak. That is the other choice: weak or strong. I tried to explain that. I did not make this world. I did not make it so."*

Emily stopped looking for Patrick in Mr. Dunne's words and opened herself up to seeing him before her. Eyes closed, Emily watched a young soldier step out of their shared darkness, over Mr. Dunne's shoulder. He wore a formal uniform, like the one she had seen her father wear, like the one they would have buried his broken body in, if her mother had not buried it in old coats in an attic closet. The soldier was tall, well-built; he had fair hair, like Albert's, and his face was sturdy but still boyish. His hands were folded behind his back. He looked at Emily with a polite awkwardness—a wish to be recognized and a reticence to interrupt.

"He was always the best behaved of any of the children, of any I've ever known. A careful child. You should have seen him arranging his blocks; such an eye for straight lines. He would build a tower straight and tall and grin at me.

"He could see the need for order—I knew that. I knew it was in him to see it. Patrick could have made the right choice. And he was respectful. Adults loved to talk with him. Said it wasn't like talking to a boy at all. So serious. And thoughtful. He was respectful and thoughtful and could see the need for things to be . . . just so. At one time he saw."

The soldier shifted his gaze to Mr. Dunne. The soldier's face filled up with shadows. His eyes vanished in dark pools.

"He didn't understand how I worried about him. I wanted him to *be popular, to have friends. He couldn't help having friends. But those people, they get their hooks in you, too. That's another thing. Those people, they get close and get hold of you. Waiting for a chance. 'Smile,' I told him, 'but not too much in your heart. Don't make yourself blind.' All those friends of his, all of those girls. Chasing him. And why did he need a friend like that? This new friend, I knew there was something wrong with that man the moment I saw him. Funny-looking. Fussing over Patrick like a damned, silly girl."*

Emily searched the soldier's face. The girl Mr. Dunne mentioned before? The friend?

The soldier looked steadily at Mr. Dunne.

"So many girls. And Patrick spending so much time with this—" Mr. Dunne made a choked, disgusted sound. The words clogged up in his throat.

"Go ahead," Emily said in the dark place. "Say everything you need to say. I'm beginning to feel Patrick nearby."

The soldier shifted his gaze back to Emily, looking at her out of the shadows around his eyes. A glittering there—an accusation.

"This friend of his from New York City . . . I told Patrick how God damns such a thing. Some things are unnatural. Patrick's mother—so blind. A damned fool. 'Don't you think God is watching all of this?' I said to him. 'God sees you, Patrick. You have no idea how a man like this can twist you,' I told him. 'Be a man, for Christ's sake.' And this wonderful friend who led him around by the nose, when the fun had been had, he left. Because that's what happens. Because Patrick had made his choice."

The soldier stiffened and looked prepared to pull away, back into the greater shadow.

"'But that's what these friends do,' I warned him. Went looking for

the next bit of fun. I knew this man for what he was the moment I saw him. 'Patrick, my God, let him go. In your mind, let him go. In your heart. Be a man.' I tried to tell him it was just a phase. 'You're just a boy.' Sickening. 'Patrick, this sort of thing is no good,' I told him. Tried to tell him. Wrong. Twisted. You have another chance, Patrick. God forgives. Forgiveness is right here—you only have to see that you need forgiveness and ask for it.' And he went to that shitty War over this man. 'Men fight wars,' he told me."

"All right, Mr. Dunne," Emily said.

"Went and got killed so that I would know . . ."

"Mr. Dunne? Patrick is here."

The soldier watched Emily over Mr. Dunne's shoulder.

"I can hear him," she said. "I hear him talking, but the words aren't clear yet."

Mr. Dunne waited. Emily was sure she felt a faint tremble emanating from him. The hairs on her arms raised themselves.

"Patrick," Emily said, "is saying that he can't stay long. He can't tell me why, but he wants us to understand that he will stay as long as he can."

The soldier began to move his lips, forming silent, methodical words.

"He wishes he could speak with you himself."

Mr. Dunne made a small noise.

"He wishes he could see this house again. He is talking about an old neighbor, someone who was very kind to Patrick when he was a child."

"Mr. Williams," Mr. Dunne said, "a man who lived around the corner. He always told Patrick these corny jokes, just to get a laugh out of him. Mr. Williams passed on some time ago."

"Yes, Patrick knows. Patrick recalls that you liked Mr. Williams very much."

"Mr. Williams was a bothersome old gossip. But he liked Patrick."

"Mr. Williams's jokes are dear memories to Patrick, even now."

Beneath it all she always knew Patrick was not there, yet the soldier, watching Emily, formed his silent words. She had to see him, had to see his lips moving, hear the voice she could not hear, fill in the tiny pieces she could not know. But it was difficult to hold on, in a strangely similar and very different way than all the times Emily or Michael had told the ladies she was losing her grip on contact with a person gone from this world.

"Patrick had a favorite toy as a child, a wooden dog?"

Mr. Dunne sat in silence.

"A wooden horse?"

Mr. Dunne cleared his throat. "Yes, I brought a wooden horse home for Patrick from a business trip. It had a bright red saddle. Patrick was only two or three at the time, and he broke it before he was five. I'm amazed he would remember that."

"Patrick has remembered many things he'd forgotten since he's been gone."

Mr. Dunne drew in a short breath.

The soldier's mouth, stilled, tightened.

"Patrick is talking about his dog, the one he loved so much. He seems to be focusing on things about this house, about this place. Because he misses it all so much. But there is more he wants to say. Patrick is saying there isn't much time left."

The soldier took one step backward and disappeared into the empty blackness all around Emily and Mr. Dunne.

"He is saying he is sorry, that he misses you. He is sorry he didn't come home from France."

Mr. Dunne choked out a breath.

"He understands how much you loved him—how much you worried about him. He wants you to know that everything is all right."

Mr. Dunne covered his face with his hands—she heard the muffled sound of his cupped breath. Emily felt her words begin to pile up in her own throat. She breathed in the air of the dark place and steadied herself.

"He wants you to know he understands, that he has come to tell you he forgives you. He understands everything and he forgives you."

Mr. Dunne breathed hard through his fingers. *"All right,"* he said in a strangled voice.

Emily opened her eyes. Mr. Dunne sat before her, his face in his hands, his body shaking. Emily waited—she thought to reach for him, to jump up and go to him, but remained in her chair. The dark was gone, and here he was. She looked at her own folded hands until Mr. Dunne sat back in his chair and raised his eyes.

"He is gone?" he asked.

"Yes."

"Will he be back?"

"I don't know."

"But we will try again. You will come see me again."

"Yes, Mr. Dunne, if you would like that. We can try again."

"All right. I would like to be alone now. Thank you, Emily. I need to rest. Good afternoon." He did not rise from his chair.

She went to the door, looking back at the man watching her with red eyes. "Everything will be all right," Emily said, and went out of the study, through the dark hall, down the stairs, and out the front door, squinting, suddenly drunk on sunlight, trying to imagine how she could ever bring herself to come back.

25.

BURÏED HÏSTORY

NEARLY A MONTH HAD PASSED SINCE EMILY HAD VENTURED
into her mother's bedroom alone. She had been picking over the
details of her birth and her parents' wedding day, placing it all
among the rules she had received from Dorothy Allen, from the
pastor at church, and from just about every adult in every way,
even when they didn't know they were leveling rules. Adult poses,
adult talk. She considered what Mr. Randall must think of the
things people said and did and the distance between. She saw Mr.
Randall wink at her without winking.

Emily thought of what the people who delivered the rules
would think of her visits to Mr. Dunne, of everything that had
happened around spirit knocking since June. She thought of her
parents' young love, of their faces in that photograph album.

What did they know? What did any of them know? The rules.
She felt, to her mild astonishment, beyond it all. There was an
orphaned feeling in this, but a thrilling one, too. Her parents had

apparently been beyond it all. She longed to see their young faces in the album again, as the days went by, to see a few instants from their lives together.

One Sunday afternoon in early November, an opportunity finally presented itself—the opportunity was not ideal, complete with an empty house, but seemed sufficient. Her mother was away for the afternoon in downtown Philadelphia with Stan Loewry, to stroll through the art museum and eat lunch at an exclusive restaurant. Michael was somewhere burning daylight with Albert Dunne. Mary sat in the sunporch bent over a ledger, marking with a pencil, turning pages backward, making more pencil marks, turning pages forward again. She would be at this for some time, Emily knew. In these circumstances, the song of the key above her mother's door floated through the halls of the house and found Emily, idle and restless in her bedroom. She crept to her mother's bedroom and then up to the attic, the album clutched to her.

She paged through the pictures and story fragments, some familiar, some recent additions. There was a picture of her lost uncle Michael as a boy—Emily immediately recognized the resigned eyes. In the photograph, he stood on the porch at Raven-wood, looking thin against the hard daylight pouring in from the left. *Michael Ward, 14 years old. He was already a worry to his parents. Especially sensitive in a sensitive house, Michael kept people at a distance, even when being friendly. Michael's sadness created a ring around him, but his joy, so bright and pure, could be even more frightening than his despair.* Her great-grandfather Robert Ward on the gallery, looking out over the river. *The lord of Ravenwood surveys his dominion, early 1880s.* Her great-grandmother, mouth small and tight, holding an infant in a sprawling lace gown that spilled onto the floor. *Elaine Ward and Regina, summer 1867.* The births; the deaths; the marriages. And all of the eyes so full of the unknown.

Emily turned to a set of pages that had been blank and now featured five photos: of her great-grandfather Robert Ward, of her great-aunt Regina, of her grandfather Jonathan, of her uncle Michael, and of her mother. Beside each picture, her mother's handwriting scratched out in white, careful and tidy. The page was arranged somehow unlike all the others; she looked at the photos and the white words and felt her mouth go dry.

The picture of Robert showed him standing in front of the mansion in his middle age. His eyes, even in the old, dim image, shone hard. The vitality of his happiness at that moment caught in Emily's throat. *Robert dreamed the place and made it real. It was a place for the family to continue long and prosperous into the misty future. And when his dream of all it would be fell away, he went up onto the gallery with a bottle and looked out over the river. His soul remained up there, and then the place truly was his ancestral home. One afternoon, while Robert nodded off there, Regina fell down the riverbank.*

Regina, sitting on the front steps in a dark dress with a ruffled collar, holding a calico kitten in her lap, wearing a brighter and happier face than Emily had seen in other photographs. *Regina, aged 15, the one nobody talks about, the doomed daughter. Did she fall down the riverbank in an accident or throw herself down into the rocks? Only one fragment from Jonathan Ward, before forbidding the topic in his house. No one was watching the riverbank that day the way they watched Regina near the staircase, which she had also tumbled down.*

Jonathan, outside the tea house, squinting in the harsh daylight.

When the picture was taken, he was already turning gray. *Jonathan, his father's son. He tried to make the place into a playground for his children and then fled from their appetite for living. He tried to teach them hope and went up to the gallery to escape it. He never turned to the bottle, as his father had toward the end, as if that made any difference.*

Uncle Michael, standing with a cigarette on a small balcony overlooking a narrow, cobbled street. He smirked at the camera, his features in a pleased disorder, as if he had just been laughing. *Michael Ward in Valencia, Spain, 1912. Always happiest away from home. Only really happy at Ravenwood while making his niece and nephew laugh, on the odd occasion he came home. Like his grandfather Robert, he tried to drink away unhappiness, which hovered ever outside of everything. He tried to lose himself in crowds of fast friends, in travel. And then one day he did lose himself. One day in May of 1914 he gave me a kiss, boarded a train on his way to New York, and disappeared from the world.*

And her mother, a laughing young woman in a light party dress. Over her shoulder, sails arrayed on the river, lost in the light and shadow. *And there I am, Naomi Ward, happy on the day I would meet my husband. As the years went by, I found it harder to be the encouraging daughter, the hopeful sister. The bouts of contentment grew shorter, the uneasiness and retreat stayed longer, insinuated deeper. By and by, it was as familiar as my father's chair. And one day I realized that I had stood on the platform waiting for a train, a train I had boarded some ways back. Suddenly I felt the world slipping away below me, the terrifying rattle of speed.*

Emily's hand recoiled from the page and into her lap. Her heartbeat thudded in her ears, yet she could not hear it. The photograph of her mother on the riverbank seemed to be dwindling before her, resolving itself to nothing.

Wait, she thought. *Wait a moment.*

She turned to the next page before she had fully thought of it. She realized dimly that this was the place where the bound packet of photos had been. Her mind latched on to this thought. There was the photograph of her grandfather from the top of the packet, his wearily content eyes, his heavily wrinkled face. *Jonathan Ward in March of 1911, only a few months before his death.* She leaned in toward the photograph, squinting at the face of a man she had never known. The thoughts behind that face were closed to her, closed to the person on the other side of the camera, and closed for all time. *Jonathan was a man of extreme feelings, who could entertain friends for hours and yet not speak more than a few words at a time to his wife or family for weeks. He told me, "Life is not a simple thing." Two days later, Jonathan Ward hanged himself in the carriage house at the far end of the Ravenwood estate, away from the main house. On one of the front doors, which he had locked, he nailed a note to the groundskeeper:*

Jim,

You'll find me in the backroom upstairs. Come in alone— don't let anyone else in with you. For God's sake, don't let the children anywhere near. I'm sorry, Jim, for this. Tell everyone that I'm sorry. Tell my wife I'm sorry.

Emily closed the album, her hands shaking. She experienced the sensation of standing up too quickly in harsh sunlight. The dust in the soft beams of light falling through the small window danced and danced in the air. She rose, almost dropping the photograph album. She caught the album against her knees and sat back down. Suddenly there seemed too much dust in the attic, too much light in the soft beams from the window, and too many shadows all around the room.

"Goddamn it," Emily said to herself, as she had heard her father do years before when faced with something that defied words. "Goddamn it, goddamn it." She dropped the album on the floor at her feet with a dull thud, followed by inexcusable silence. She picked the album up and hurried through the halls of the house, shuffled in hurried steps down staircases, strode through the dining hall, carrying the album held away from her like an explosive, and arrived in the sunporch, where Mary sat at the table bent over the ledger book, making marks with her pencil. Mary looked up at Emily's face and registered some surprise; this surprise changed as Mary caught sight of the photograph album.

Emily stepped to the table and slammed the full weight of the album down.

"Your grandfather was not a bad man," Mary said. She and Emily walked along the riverbank, following one of the paths that led around the estate. "He was like his father—I told you about Robert Ward—more or less a good man, with good intentions, but . . . sad. Your grandfather was a very sad man, a lot of the time. Given to changes of mood. I saw your grandfather go from laughing and happy to sullen in a few minutes—and then stay like that for a day, or a week, or longer. He was always kind to me, but he was cruel sometimes to your grandmother. He would shut her out for long stretches of time—shut everybody out. Your mother always suffered over it. She wanted his approval, naturally. And she had it; he was devoted to her. But he kept her out, too.

"And he went out to the carriage house, after all those years. I remember the morning Jim found him. I believe that was the beginning of the longest day of my life, and there had been some long days before. Your grandfather was sick by then. Sick in his soul. Such a thing casts a long shadow on a place; your mother has never really gotten past it. She was eighteen at the time. And your grandfather had told her all the things he couldn't bring himself to tell his wife. Then he went out to the carriage house. He told your mother because he knew she was the strong one and that she would forgive him. That's all a lot of people want, to be forgiven."

Emily saw Mr. Dunne, his moist eyes; she heard him asking her to come back. Mrs. Nerova, almost collapsing, her fire gone.

"These things aren't easy. Your mother has spent a lot of years thinking about all of this. I think your mother is tired of not talking about things. That's why she's putting that album together, you know. For you and Michael. She doesn't want to keep this all locked away forever. Your mother is afraid to talk about all of this. And she is afraid to not talk about it." Mary turned to Emily and watched her until Emily met her eyes and held them. Then Mary looked away and resumed her easy manner, in keeping with their strolling pace.

Emily kept seeing her mother sitting in the sunporch, over the years, her eyes forgetful, wandering suddenly toward the river beyond the windows.

"All those years before I came here," Mary said. "All that time. Your great-grandfather, Regina . . . Well, I've heard stories but I can't really say much about all of that. I've told you everything I've heard on that already. But I saw how hard it was for your grand-mother, who tried harder even than your mother to make your grandfather happy. All of this business about happiness," Mary said, shaking her head. "As if you might find a box of it under the stairs and be all set. Your uncle Michael left this place to find it. Nobody knows what he found. Peace, I hope. That stays with your mother. She has never really grieved him, buried him in her heart. I believe she thought she could save Michael, which is why she named your brother after him, and why your father let her do it, though he never thought much of your uncle."

Emily watched her feet carry her forward. "Are Michael and I . . . like them?"

Mary stopped and waited for Emily to be still and again meet her eyes. "You and your brother are unlike any people I have ever known. Do you understand?"

"Yes, Mary."

Mary picked up her stride again as if they had never stopped. Emily followed after, thinking of the bright eyes of Robert Ward, of her mother's laughing face.

"And that is all I want to say about this," Mary said. "Your mother will have to tell you more when she is ready to talk. People decide at some point that they want to talk. You take your sum-mer tutor, Mr. Holt. What do you know about Mr. Holt, Emily?"

"I know that he loves books, that he paints, he whistles."

"Did you know that 'Holt' is short for 'Holtzenberg'?"

"Um, no." Emily's summer tutor, the man who had painted the tea house and her beside it, had also chopped off more than half of his name. How strange.

"Mr. Holt is Jewish. Not that he talks about it very much. Not everybody likes Jews—I guess you've found that."

Emily had heard it said that the Jews had killed Christ, that they were crafty, selfish, and greedy; that they banded together against outsiders and could not be trusted. "Yes," Emily said.

"He is also very aware of this, so he goes by the name of 'Holt,' and folks let him tutor their children. One day I was chatting with him on the porch and he told me all of this—because all of a sudden he was ready to talk. He had seen me at the breakfast table with you, your mother, and Michael, and decided that maybe he needn't worry about such things in this house."

Emily saw the carriage house ahead, between the trees.

Mary took Emily's hand and led her toward another intersecting path leading back toward the house. "A person leads a secret life in many ways, Emily—every person you could meet."

"Mary?"

"Yes, Em?"

"What is your secret story?"

"That," Mary said, "is for another day."

As they approached the house, Mary stopped. "Em," she said, "I can't condone you going into your mother's things. You know that. Under the circumstances, I'm inclined to be lenient. But you know that I can only be so lenient."

"Yes, Mary."

"I want you to promise me that you will tell your mother about this, in time. I don't expect you to tell her when she gets home from the museum, or tomorrow, or the next day. But soon. It is not my place to approach your mother about this—unless you won't do it. And I'll know that you didn't. I want you to promise me that you won't go into your mother's drawer to look at that album until you've spoken to her." Mary had taken the album back to its usual place before they had left the house, and returned the key to its lintel. "I need you to promise me that."

"I promise, Mary," Emily said. She knew as she said the words that the promise was one of convenience only; she knew this, but brushed the thought away. The matters at hand were far beyond the limits of such promises.

Coming home to a house even quieter than usual, Michael found himself going to the attic in search of something to add to the act once he and Emily renewed it, something old and new, something from Ravenwood, or from the place it had once been. He started with the boxes, his hands passing over the things they'd passed over months before. He stood away from the stacks of boxes, hands on his hips, scanning them. Their shapes and labels were familiar—only old things in there, nothing new. Michael's eyes fell on the closet door. Nothing new in there. Not even worth opening.

He crossed the attic and opened the closet door. Deeper shadows, more boxes. The pale garment bag, which he took in his fingers, feeling the material beneath, the buttons at the cuff. Michael took the hanger in hand and pulled the garment bag from the rod, holding it before him, its excess length piling at his feet. He closed the closet door with his free hand and draped the bag over his arm, the bulk of the uniform within shifting, some smaller, denser weight coming free and bouncing inside. Michael held the garment bag at full length before him, stretching his arms over his head. A thud on the wooden floor that reminded him of the taste of coins.

A long iron key, old and tarnished, with a tiny pair of hands holding a heart beneath a crown. Michael had seen this arrangement of heart, hands, and crown before, on one of the benches in the rathskeller, the one at the end of the room farthest from the staircase. Instead of birds or roses in the carved ivy, a pair of graceful hands presenting and protecting a heart wearing a crown, more ornate than the one on the key, with detailed edges and the hollow impressions of gemstones.

Michael draped the garment bag over his arm again, dropped the key into his pocket, and switched off the lights in the attic on the way to the stairs.

June 30, 1918

SATURDAY MORNİNG

Naomi sat in the sunporch reading the newspaper when she heard Donald come in through the front door. He went straight to the main stairs. She didn't see him, only heard his footsteps. It wasn't until she heard the front door open that Naomi realized she had been waiting for him to return, half paying attention to the news bunched up in black type on the page.

Outside on the back lawn, Emily and Michael tossed paper airplanes into the air. The angled bits of white took to the soft morning air and either soared for a moment or went to the ground in zigzag courses. Mary sat on the back porch, and every so often called out for Michael to watch out for the riverbank, or for Emily to toss the plane, not throw it. The twins had turned six a week before. Sometimes Naomi marveled at how much they seemed to know, how their chatter and play landed nearly or square on adult matters of love and loneliness and disappointment and joy and regret. It sometimes seemed that they came to these things with clearer eyes than adults, who talked themselves out of so much.

And then these moments would fall away and the twins were innocent immortals again, unmoved by the countless days and nights that had gone before. Naomi had begun to think that the end of childhood came with the consistency of memory. For now, the paper airplanes flew or crashed with no great consequence, and Naomi could lose herself in stories of war and disease and local celebrities.

Donald moved through the hallway above, and Naomi heard one of the heavy library doors thud closed. He went there in retreat, more and more. Donald had gone up to the library the other day, after a conversation they'd gotten into after dinner, when the children went out to catch lightning bugs on the back lawn. Mary had vanished, also; she had made the observation weeks before that Naomi and Donald didn't spend enough time talking on their own. Mary of course knew that they hardly spent any time talking at all, but stopped short of saying so. Naomi and Donald talked of the children, of things that needed to be done, of his practice. They were consummately adult and responsible, far from the children they had become again together in 1911, when their secret lives took possession of their days and they poured themselves out to one another, when they had recklessly put themselves at risk and felt the exhilarating absence of doubt, the joy of willing self-destruction. Naomi remembered the first night they made love, the fascination of his mouth as he talked, how he seemed to be confessing even when joking, his desire to give himself as he was to her, making himself—all his faults and regrets, his guarded memories—an offering to her. Her longing for him felt like dying, like being freed from fear of death or anything else but for this need to go unanswered—a salmon held downstream, a hummingbird locked in winter. For Stan Loewry she had felt a passion that made her drunk and reckless, but that never extinguished her doubts of Stan's nature—so charming, but injured and unsteady, genuine but never done searching himself and the world for a reason to hope and a reason to give up. In Donald, Naomi saw a beauty and a sadness without self-pity. He wasn't naïve about people's lives, but he held it against no one, least of all himself.

On the night Naomi led Donald out to the tea house the old secret way—the way Donald would call Grandpa Robert's garden path to get a smile from her—she couldn't imagine a time when she wouldn't simply fall into this feeling for him, carried down into the depths of it with the promise and inevitability of gravity. When she took him to the little redbrick house for their first time together, it seemed to her that the struggles and griefs of the past had all led to this, that she could see the shore. His hands on her in the dark, the moonlight on the rose trellises outside the window. His heart pounding in the warm, breathing well of his abdomen, his lips on hers, on her nose, her eyelids. His hesitations and polite deference gone. The smell and urgency of his tongue in her mouth, the taste of sweat along his jaw. His sigh when she unfastened his pants and reached inside to feel his pulse.

But two nights before, at the dinner table, they had not talked through most of the meal and left the expanse of table between them when the twins and Mary abandoned their chairs. Donald sat at the table reading the newspaper, his unfinished dinner getting cold before him. Naomi had been sitting back at her place with another part of the paper, the metropolitan and arts sections, when Donald commented, without looking up from the newsprint, that the War would test many people, that the world was being tested for the future. He'd been reading again about the recently ended battle in the Belleau Wood, near the Marne. The engagement of U.S. Marines there with Germans in a position to crash through those woods and farther into the Western Front had caused a sensation. Almost two thousand Marines dead after the battle ended. There was talk of the end of the war, a blow to tyranny in Europe. There was actual hope glimmering and more than glimmering in all of the flag waving and speech-making.

After several minutes of quiet, with no real conversation following Donald's remarks, he had set the paper down and said, "Naomi, I have to ask you something."

She looked up, knowing this couldn't be pleasant but trying to look interested and attentive. His face told her she was right. Not angry, but resigned, exhausted, and certain of something.

"Did anything ever happen between you and Stan?"

He had never come out and asked before. The shadow of Stan, an abstract thing in their relationship, unnamed, unimportant for years, and somehow appropriate then, in this time when they hardly confided in one another, when their defenses softly enveloped them as the other entered a room. The question had been a flitting ghost in the years when it mattered most, so insubstantial she didn't know if it existed in Donald's mind at all or if only she nursed it in secret. And there were children to raise and Stan left the United States and the years went by. Donald and Naomi began to lose each other in the days, slowly at first, so easily, particles carried away on the tide. When Donald asked this unexpected question, Naomi realized that the ghost had never gone at all.

"Where the hell did that come from?" she had said, after

looking at him, at the puzzle of his expression. All she could read was exhaustion. "Have you been up nights thinking about this?"

"I don't want to attack you, I don't want to argue," he had said, and she had no doubt he meant both. "I just want to know. I've never known for sure. I just want to know." The appeal in his voice shocked her, struck through her numb surprise and the silence that had built up between them. She wanted to go to him; she wanted to run from the room.

"No," she had said. The word was hollow in her mouth. "Nothing ever happened between Stan and me."

Donald had watched her a full moment longer, then nodded. He laid his paper down on the table and stood up. "All right," he had said, and walked away from the table. Naomi had remained at the table and listened to his footsteps go up the stairs and on to the library, still feeling the hollow word on her tongue. A scatter of lightning bugs caught her eye beyond the window, and she heard a cry of joyful discovery from Emily to Michael, saw the twins raise up their glass jars in the lowering twilight, the shaggy tree line on the other side of the river, the bats in the blue strip of sky. Summer night.

Now Naomi heard Donald's footsteps come down the hall from the library, turn at the stairs, and walk with a purpose to the sunporch. He stepped into the room, a tall man, his thatch of blond hair just a bit too unkempt for a doctor, youth still glowing on him as he approached middle age, even with his tired and severe gaze, which found hers waiting for him. He stopped and stood in the doorway. Naomi thought he looked like a man who'd been gone much longer than a little over an hour. They watched each other, then Donald walked to the window. As she had on the night he'd said Stan's name for the first time in years, Naomi set her paper down, this time before he spoke.

"I've enlisted," Donald said, watching the children's thrown paper airplanes soar and twist from the heights down to the earth.

Naomi steadied herself with a hand on the table. "You've . . . *what?*"

"I've enlisted. I went down to the recruiting office and filled out the paperwork. I've already committed. I'm to leave for training in a week." Still he watched the airplanes, his silhouette hard against the light from outside. His eyes didn't follow the twins, but floated over them.

"Donald . . . How could you?" Naomi hardly had breath to speak. She felt as if a knot that had held everything she was and knew in her middle had given way.

"You don't need me here right now, Naomi," Donald said, turning away from the window. "But those boys need doctors. I wasn't the only one at that recruiting office. You should have seen them— babies. All fresh and young. They are going to face a horror they couldn't imagine and they do it willingly. Joyfully, Naomi."

She remained seated. She could not stand. "Those boys have been listening to parade music, Donald. They have no idea about many things. As if any of that had anything to do with this."

"I can't stay here pretending the rest of the world doesn't exist, Naomi."

"And what about the twins? What about your practice?" She could not ask him what about her. She would not ask it.

"The practice will wait. We're at war. Everyone understands that."

Anger flushed up from Naomi's chest. The slipping knot was

gone, forgotten. "Is that what you're going to tell Emily and Michael? *We're at war?*"

"Yes," he said. The frustration he would usually let loose when she engaged him like this never appeared. He had abandoned his anger. He stood there only with what he had done, with the unchangeable fact of it. "I'll tell them people need help far away. That Daddy is going to help them." These words, prepared for children, came from him without guile. Somehow in all of this he had told them to himself and heard.

Naomi felt tears close by. She gathered herself along her spine and looked fully into his eyes. "There is nothing heroic about running away, Donald."

"Heroic," he said, as if the word were new to him. He looked back out the window. Naomi suddenly imagined him dropping the word into the river like a stone. "We need some time apart, Naomi," he said, still turned toward the window. "For years, I thought I knew who we are—husband and wife. It's gotten so hard to know these things."

Naomi had been finding it harder to know these things herself, as the years went by. "Donald . . ."

"The twins are young, they will hardly remember it. The War isn't going to go on much longer. Even the Germans know that now. I will help those boys as best I can and come home. Maybe we'll be able to better talk then. How many years do you think we can keep our troubles from Emily and Michael? Soon they will know. Sooner than you think."

Naomi did stand up then. She walked on numb feet to the window and stood beside Donald. She did not reach for him. Her arms hung at her sides, as his did. "Is this about Stan Loewry, Donald?" Naomi said.

"Is it?"

Their voices lacked heat. The dust was already settling, for the moment.

"And what if I told you that something had happened?" she said. "What would that matter now? What would you say?"

Donald put his hands in his pockets. It seemed an almost contented gesture of resignation to Naomi, losing herself at that instant in their calm tone on all of this, which could not last. "I'd say let's talk about it after the War," he said, and walked away from the window, out of the sunporch, and upstairs to the library.

Outside Michael took a running jump and tossed his airplane into a breeze that proved true—the airplane swept up over the back lawn and out toward the river, no longer just a piece of folded paper, but a thing with wings, airborne. The twins ran after it, exulting, and Mary stepped from the porch calling for caution from both of them, something of the children's excited amazement in her own voice.

PART SIX

26.

SWIMMING WITH THE DEAD

ONE AFTERNOON IN THE SECOND WEEK OF NOVEMBER, Cat Pomeroy came to Ravenwood with a letter for Michael, postmarked in London.

"Grandmama asked me to give you this," she said, handing Michael the letter and watching his eyes as he took the envelope in his fingers.

Michael tore the letter open in the privacy of his room.

Michael,

I hope you and yours are well. My absence has been longer than anticipated. You understand. Perhaps this has given you a chance to better consider things.

I am not one to write long letters, so I'll keep this brief.

*I can't say for certain when I'll be traveling your way again,
but I plan to see you soon and I will be anxious to pick
up our conversation. I trust you have been attending to
matters.*

*Best regards,
J. L. R.*

Michael focused on the mysterious middle initial "L." An
impulse sprang up in him to crumple the letter into a tight ball
and throw it in the kitchen garbage. Instead he folded the note
and tucked it into the top drawer of his dresser.

Three days later, Albert Dunne, again dispatched to Ravenwood,
found Emily reading in the library.

"Father would like to see you, Em. He told me to tell you that
he must see you."

She sighed. The darkened study, Mr. Dunne's eyes. "All right,
Albert. Once more."

Emily mused over making this her last visit to the Dunne house
and the man with moist, penetrating eyes. Her efforts had not
seemed to banish a single shadow from Mr. Dunne's study. She
would have to use the right words, words of regret and resignation. *It has been getting very hard lately, Mr. Dunne. I find myself
unable to keep hold for long. I often can't reach through at all anymore.
Something has changed. Things have become very difficult lately. Very
strange and difficult.*

. . .

Michael found Emily in the library, reading. In his hand he carried a torn envelope, which he set down in front of himself as he took a chair across the table from her.

Her eyes flitted from the envelope to Michael's face.

"I was wondering if you had considered picking up the old game again," he said.

"Michael." Some impatience crept into her voice. "I would have thought that you would have grown bored of it long ago."

"Em, you have to think of this as a developing thing. First we perform for a bunch of kids, then we entertain a group of old ladies. Things develop, from one phase to another."

Emily closed her book. "Maybe Mama could sell tickets. We could get a big circus tent."

Michael picked up the envelope and began turning it in his hands.

"What's that?" Emily asked.

"A letter from Mr. Randall."

"A letter from the Astonishing Antoine?"

"I spoke with him once, weeks ago. I haven't told him anything. He doesn't know how you make those sounds. He knows that ghosts have nothing to do with it, but not because I told him."

"Does Mr. Randall want to be part of the game? Is that what all of this is about, Michael?"

He raised his eyes from the turning envelope. "More or less."

Emily pushed her book away and stood up. "Absolutely out of the question. Let me guess: Mr. Randall wants to put us on Broadway."

Michael set the envelope on the table again. His eyes and voice became cold, appraising. The appeasing posture he'd entered with was gone. "Do you want to sit around here growing old like Mama? Is that what you want? To just become a piece of furniture in this house?"

"Mi—"

"You are so full of *shit*, Em."

Emily jerked, her eyes wide.

He leaned forward, looking hard at her. "You act concerned about how these people *feel*. About playing tricks on them. The truth is, you love being the magical girl."

"Michael—"

"You have the nerve to imply that I don't care about how they feel. Then you let those damn silly old women treat you like a queen. And the only reason you want to stop there is because you're afraid. You're afraid to go further, that's it; not that you're so concerned with the *feelings* of these people. They want us to trick them, and you know it—we couldn't very well do it if they didn't want us to, and you know that, too." Michael picked up the envelope, stood up, and began to turn from the table.

"Michael, don't just turn your back—"

He whirled on her, his eyes bright and hateful. "Or what, Great One? You'll run and tell Mama?"

"We will talk about this later, Michael. When you've calmed down." She opened the door and went out into the hall, the words in the library still ringing in her head. She had reached the main staircase before she heard Michael's footsteps following her down the stairs, out the front door, across the porch, and down onto the cobblestone drive. The mid-November air braced her. She closed her eyes and felt it surround her.

"Em."

"Not now, Michael."

He ran ahead of her, stopping her, and spitting his words in her face. "Can't stand tricking anyone anymore, is that it? Do you think the truth matters to these people?"

"Get out of my way, Michael. I don't want to see you right now."

"Are you worried about these fools' feelings? Because if you are, then give them the lies they want."

Emily looked at her brother's wild eyes, so much more exposed than his usual considering gaze. A touch of sympathy rose up at this, a sensation she was just beginning to feel when Michael said with withering scorn: "Do you think their feelings matter because they matter to *you?*"

"Because they matter to anyone!"

Michael stepped back. "Em," he said, his mouth sounding dry. "Em, listen . . . we can fix this. Work it out. Just listen."

"No," she said, with little breath. The look of control beginning to settle over Michael's features made her stomach clench. "That's it. It's finished."

She stopped at the gate a moment, then hurried away from the estate. Emily made her way through the streets in a reverie of anger and sadness, arriving on the Dunne porch in the long shadows of dusk, and knocked on the front door. Stirring movements reached Emily from inside the house. Mr. Dunne opened the front door. "Emily?" he said, as if he had not seen the girl in many years and believed her dead.

"Mr. Dunne, I have to talk with you."

She hurried past him into the living room and stopped in the center. Mr. Dunne followed her. "What is it?"

She had tried to ease his pain. He would understand. Tears of relief seeped into the corners of her eyes. "Mr. Dunne, I'm sorry, I can't visit you anymore. I'm very sorry."

"What is it? What is this?"

"Mr. Dunne, it's not true, about Patrick."

"What is not true about Patrick?"

"I can't contact Patrick, or anyone. It's just a sound I make with my ankle—" she blurted.

Mr. Dunne's nostrils quivered. *"What is this about?"*

"I wasn't trying to play tricks on you, Mr. Dunne. I was only trying to help. It's just a sound I can make." Emily found herself putting her right foot forward, placing it under Mr. Dunne's wide eyes. She produced one clear knock, followed by another. "I can make as many as I like," she said. "It was just a game, and then I wanted to help."

Mr. Dunne lifted his stare from Emily's foot. His face fell slack and ashen; his eyes squeezed to hard, dark points. "No. I was there. It was real."

"Mr. Dunne—"

"You are a damned liar," he said.

"Mr. Dunne," she said, *"please.* I'm telling you the truth." A single tear ran down her face.

Mr. Dunne recoiled as if Emily had laughed out loud.

"How can you try to keep my son from me? Don't tell me what's true—I know what's true. You're lying. You think you can keep him from me?"

Emily took a step backward. "Mr. Dunne . . ."

"Get out of my house," he hissed. *"You get out of my house, you lying little bitch. Get out of here right now."*

Emily rushed out the front door into the lowering dusk. She could hardly believe she was the girl Mr. Dunne had cursed, moments ago—that she was the girl who had fled from home and come here for this. She didn't want to believe it. She hurried along the street back from where she had come, holding herself around the waist, huddled and only seeing the looming shadows around her as blurs of light-tinged dark.

Albert found his father sitting in the living room with his head in his hands. "Was someone here?" he asked.

His father did not answer. A low sound emerged from behind his fingers.

"Father?"

Mr. Dunne lowered his hands and looked at Albert. Salty streaks spread down his face in glittering arrays.

"What is it?" Albert asked.

"I can't stand to have you look at me with your stupid, empty eyes. Get out. Get out of here."

Albert stepped back from his father, eyes wide, looking as if he'd nearly swallowed the lower part of his face.

Mr. Dunne turned away, already not seeing Albert. The boy had vanished for him.

Albert fled the house, as Emily had, though with a good deal more confusion. The shadows of evening had deepened since Emily had returned to the street. Albert followed his feet away from the house, gasping through his pain. The cold night air barely touched him as he made his way off the streets and into the woods along the river. He hurried through the trees and stood on the riverbank. His breath strangled him; small noises came from his mouth that fell flat amid the shadowy trees. The stars hung shining over the river. A shudder ran through Albert's body. Under the stars he felt shame and disgust transform his hurt into a poison that rushed into his abdomen—he vomited in the grass by the glimmering river.

When he straightened up, nothing had changed. Only the stars that he saw with his stupid, empty eyes and the river he was too cowardly to swim in. Albert wiped his mouth with his hand, then looked numbly at the poison shame he had smeared across his palm. He thought of dipping his hand in the river and feeling the cold, dark water carry his pain away. He went to the edge of the high bank and looked down. The last tendrils of dusk still rode some of the rushing water and the night air rushed around him. He scuttled down the bank through the few brittle weeds. He thought of the old swimming ghosts and felt sure they understood shame and fear and disgust. Albert had seen people swim in this river by day, had watched Michael dive from the grassy side out toward the deeper part of the water. Michael was a strong swimmer and not afraid of ghosts. Albert imagined how easy it would be for him to dive into the water as Michael had, how the cold water would swallow him whole. And the old ghosts would swim around him and the faraway stars would shine down.

27.

The Valley of the Shadow

Cat Pomeroy, walking along the river, saw some-thing bump against the riverbank, something caught in the reeds and still subject to the ebb and flow of the Delaware. The spot was part of a lonely stretch of river, perfect for a lonely child to walk along. She approached the floating thing slowly (*a bundle, a large bundle of cloth*) and saw pale fingers sticking out of the water among the reeds. A bloated face with tightly closed eyes and a limp mouth rippled beneath the water. "Oh," Cat said to herself, sitting down hard in the faded grass. She knew the bloated face, could recognize in its distorted features a person she had known from early childhood, a person whose face she had never studied, but that rose before her through the water—and the effects of the water—as clearly as if this person had arrived on the bank to consider the floating thing beside her. Though she would not have put it quite this way at the time, it occurred to Cat, who had been

humming as she walked along the riverbank, that ultimate things
are at stake even on the sleepiest afternoon.

The news of Cat's discovery traveled fast. The story came to
Ravenwood first. The estate was only a short way up the riverbank
from where the floating body had reached out of the water at Cat.
She had hurried to the house in a dreamy, staggering run, fleeing to a place where she believed magic could be found. Michael
answered the front door. She could not speak for a moment—she
could not cry, she could barely breathe. "Michael," she finally said,
"the river . . . the reeds . . ."

The story moved through the neighborhood in a way that good
news could never travel. Everyone who heard the story felt some
morbid awe, however faint, at the thought that it could have been
his or her body floating in the reeds, or the body of his or her
child; some thrill, however fleeting, that it had not been. A black
pall, visible to every adult and child, settled over the Dunne house.
A small coffin would come out of the front door, they knew, followed by a shuffling dark-clothed procession.

Two numb days passed at Ravenwood in anticipation of the
funeral. The twins' mother kept them home from school. Emily
found herself standing lightheaded on the gathered heap of everything that had happened, astounded at the dizzying height these
simple things amounted to. This perspective removed her from
everyday experience, it seemed; for the first time she truly felt like
the Queen of the Underworld, having more to do with the dead
than the living. Of all the monuments around her in the graveyard
on the day of the funeral, the angels and obelisks, there were no

grinning skeletons, no due given as she had seen in the pictures of old carvings she'd found in her father's books to the biggest player. Death—the cosmic joke, the great necessity. Looking at the closed coffin, she felt surrounded by ghosts in somber dress. The reverend's frock hung about him in gleaming white, a bright and material fact in a shadow world. His words were a benediction for the dead. It seemed only appropriate to her that a band of spirits would gather from the graves that stretched out in all directions under the gray November sky—spirits that bowed their heads and said in dull tones of old regret, *Amen*. Her brother looked blankly at the coffin, his mouth pinched. Her mother stood beside her and spoke words of comfort for the living: "It's all right to cry, children. We respect the dead with our grief." Mary reached for Michael in his black suit. Michael's eyes never moved from the small coffin. "I am the resurrection and the life," the reverend said, his own sorrow-settled eyes cast down at the coffin rather than toward the gray sky. "He that believeth in me, though he were dead, yet shall he live."

Emily felt a sick, insulted feeling on behalf of herself, her mother, Mr. Dunne, her father, the boy in the coffin (*Albert, his name was Albert*), and for every creature that had been born into the world to die. Humanity seemed to her one long, ghostly procession, flitting and vanishing from an indifferent world, lost briefly between the dark before and the dark to come.

Albert's parents stood close to the grave. Mrs. Dunne leaned against her husband's arm and looked at the hole before her. Mr. Dunne's face hung around his eyes, directed vaguely at the intersection of the sky and the horizon. He never glanced at Emily—not at the viewing, not at the church, and not in the graveyard. Mrs. Dunne looked once at Emily, her eyes flat and unreadable. In the instant their eyes met, Emily saw inside the darkened master bedroom of the Dunne house. She imagined Mr. Dunne lying rigid and grim in bed.

The reverend said, "So when this corruptible shall have put on incorruption, and this mortal shall have put on immortality, then shall be brought to pass the saying that is written, 'Death is swallowed up in victory.'"

On the night of the funeral, Emily found herself on the front porch in a dream, sitting in the swing on a summer afternoon. The sky was the color of dull bronze, not the softer hue of most summer sunsets. Night approached. She awaited someone on the swing, someone who had come a great distance to see her. She watched the cobblestone drive for her visitor, but the drive remained empty and the front gates stood closed. She would have to get off the swing and meet him; she must open the gate and allow him in, for he had come a long way and over great obstacles. Emily stood up and walked down the porch steps and onto the drive, hurrying to beat the dusk. She had only gone a short distance when she turned her head toward the river and saw Albert Dunne standing at the top of the bank, watching her. Pale and bruised-looking, hair plastered to his forehead, he stood in wet clothes hanging heavy on his slight frame. His face was the color of white lilies and leaves floating in a puddle of rain. His eyes had a clear glow she had never seen him wear in life. He said, in a damp voice, "Go to Mother." The words came to her on the odor of pond moss.

Emily amazed herself by finding her own voice. "Albert, I can't. She . . . I—"

"Go to Mother," Albert said.

"But, Albert, please—"

"You've already waited too long," Albert said.

"*I can't!*" she screamed at the drowned boy on the riverbank, and found herself alone in bed. No dead boy waited for her on the riverbank outside her window. But she feared that he waited for her in that bronze-colored sunset with night close behind. Almost an hour after she had awakened, Emily drifted into a fitful sleep without dreams.

Thanksgiving passed. The twins' mother, not one to arrange large dinners, found the table strangely underpopulated, despite the fact that they were not short a single person from the year before. Mary offered a prayer. Plates heaped with turkey and potatoes shuttled along. A boat filled with thick gravy made its way around, clinking against the plates and the surface of the table. The last week of November brought a desolate, wintry look to Ravenwood. Emily waited for Mr. Dunne to come to the house. She imagined him striding up the cobblestone drive, his eyes bright and hard. She sometimes imagined that Mrs. Dunne followed behind her husband in the black dress and veil she had worn to the funeral. But the Dunnes never marched up the cobblestone drive, and the house at the end of the road remained quiet.

Emily and Michael did not speak to each other of Albert Dunne during these weeks. They hardly spoke to each other at all. On their way to school, at the dinner table, in the halls, the twins approached each other like two killers who had buried a body deep in the woods, far from prying eyes, and did not trust one another— and barely trusted themselves—with such a secret.

. . .

Emily went down to the tea house on the first Saturday afternoon in December. She stood at the door and imagined that Regina waited inside. Placing her hand on the knob, she felt a tingle in her fingers that reminded her of the late Mr. Nerov's old flute. The door creaked on its hinges—a soft, acquiescent sound in the cold air. A thin dust had settled over the surfaces within. She ran her finger across the tabletop, considering the narrow swath she cut in the dust. A few spiderwebs hung abandoned in the corners. Emily went around the table and sat in her appointed place. She looked out the front door of the tea house, which she had left open, and imagined a great procession of guests lined up through the doorway and down toward the gate, each one having come a long way to sit at this table with her and feel her power. *Necromancy*— that was the word the book of make-believe in the library used for communication with the dead. They would come from far away, though the old laws forbade such practices, and the line of visitors would wind out the gate and down the street. She closed her eyes and produced one knock, then a second, slow and deliberate. The sounds reverberated with the same wintry resonance as the door hinges. When she opened her eyes, she saw an empty doorway, the cobblestone drive, and the bare trees beyond.

Emily stood on a chair and reached up onto the lintel to find the key waiting in the dust. Mary had kept to her word. Emily had often caught Mary watching her and wondered how long it would be before Mary approached her again about the key, the locked dresser drawer, and the photograph album. For the moment Emily was content to let circumstances spin out as they might, to allow time for Mary to approach her, or to approach her mother, or for other things to happen.

She unlocked the drawer. Three envelopes, stacked together and bound in string like the photographs, sat on top of the familiar photograph album. On top of the stack, Emily could see that the envelope had been addressed to her mother and bore a Rhode Island return address, mailed less than a month before. Emily believed she knew whose hand had made out the envelope before she began to clear the stack of its string binding. Emily pulled the first envelope away from the other two, opened it, and drew the folded paper from within. Her fingers were quick, steady, and assured.

Nov. 16, 1925

Naomi—

I am writing to you from my father's place in Newport. I love to be here after the season has long been over, with the whole staff at home and the family in New York. I also love the gray sky over the gray sea (I know—it's the melodrama of it that I love). But it seems the sea shows a truer face on an afternoon in November. Even more majestic, more ominous, and more unforgiving. You see? I can attach my Catholic guilt to anything.

Naomi, I am not writing this to talk about the sea. I suppose you figured that already. I haven't forgotten my proposal of years ago. I stand by every word I said then, I still feel the things I felt then. I know, I know. You loved Donald, and he was a good man—at one time I loved Donald more than I had ever loved another person. But in the past few months I have only become more certain of what we have now, of what we had then. My fear of frightening you away has kept me from pressing the issue. It is always so much easier for me to write what is in my heart; banter (a gutless craft) seems much handier in person. The last thing in the world I want to be is clever.

I let so many things go while I was away. I thought for a time that this had happened to my feelings for you, along with the rest. These feelings held on longer—much longer—than all the others, but I hoped that they too had floated away. Then I came to Ravenwood in June. I went only as a friend, I told myself. And I believed it! The moment the car pulled up and I saw your face, I knew I had tricked myself onto that porch. Of course, I couldn't let on then, but I felt like falling over when you stepped out of the car.

I have given everything up, time and again. I have renounced everything, only to slink back in necessity. I have never renounced you. I tried. When I found out through friends that Donald had died in France, I nearly ran straight to the port to book passage—and I felt like a ghoul. I was ashamed of myself then, I am ashamed now, but I would be even more ashamed if I were not honest with you about all of this.

You have been lonely too, a long time. I know, though you won't say. And you have some feeling for me, wretched as I am—I see that, too. You have the most expressive eyes in the world, Naomi, when you let your guard down.

Please think about what I have said. I will come to see you in December, if you'll have me. I will be in Newport until the end of the month. You are always close to my thoughts.

Stan

Emily opened the second envelope, her fingers still steady as she drew out the folded note. The summoner of the dead must be as impartial as death, sure-handed and blind in pure sight.

Dec. 18, 1913

Naomi—

I will be leaving for Europe in a few days; I don't know for how long. I would stop at the house, but things are bad between Donald and me, as you know. He must see the way I look at you. Donald must hate me now—there was hate in his eyes when he threw me out. And I can't blame him. I'm not on the best terms with myself right now.

I hope this won't seem a sickening attempt at being noble, but please talk with Donald. Go and talk to him. The two of you aren't as close or as open with one another as you once were. I know; I watched the change and saw selfish hope in it. Desperate and selfish hope. I watched for it and I saw it, and so I'm certain it is a threat to you both. So much for noble attempts.

The States don't feel like home to me just now, and I think some time away might do me some good, if anything can. I felt I should give you some sort of good-bye, as you are the only reason

*for me to hesitate in leaving, and the only thing really driving
me away.*

Stan

The third envelope came away faster and with even less bus-
tling than the first two, so that the letter inside seemed to spring
into Emily's fingers.

Oct. 28, 1911

Naomi—

   *I can't begin this letter in any dignified way, as I write to
you in desperation. I am sick over all of this. I'm not a schoolboy
who's had his first kiss. I have forgotten the names of women I
spent days with (this is not a boast—I offer it only in dismay).
You are the intended of the dearest friend I have ever had, you are
carrying his child, but I can't get you out of my thoughts. I am in
torment, Naomi. My feelings have taken me beyond the pale—
beyond friendship, beyond custom, beyond reputation. I have
given things away easily before; I will give it all away now.
This is madness, I know, but I want you to be my wife, Naomi.
   Please forgive me.*

Stan

Emily rushed through the hall in the direction of Michael's
room. She knocked at his door. "Michael?"

· 286 ·

She opened the door on an unmade bed, a clutter of books on shelves, and a few old toys here and there, kept out of some touch of nostalgia and charity in Michael. On the shelf, a small glass-fronted display case containing a large green moth pinned to a bed of black fabric caught her eye. She had not seen this case or the moth for some time. Michael had found the moth dying two years before and, once the wings completely stilled, he and Emily brought it into the house, into the sunporch, where their mother sat over a cup of coffee, paging through the paper. Mrs. Stewart said, "Just like your father," and gazed approvingly at the dead moth. "It must have been beautiful in flight," she said. She went to the attic and returned with the wood-framed display box, the kind people use to show off antique jewelry, the kind that decorations and emblems of high esteem are placed in to occupy wall space and make passersby consider everything that has been sacrificed since time out of mind. "This belonged to your father," she said. "It would make him very happy to see you place your moth in it."

"It's Michael's moth," Emily said. "He found it."

"Then this is yours," Mrs. Stewart said, handing him the box.

"What was it for?" Michael asked.

"It's for putting your moth in," she said.

In the library, Mrs. Stewart found a book on North American insects. On a small card that shared the frame, she typed *Luna moth (Actias luna)* and a short description of the moth's life cycle as a creature with wings.

Alone in Michael's room, Emily went around his bed to look at the moth, which had turned a darker shade. When its feeble wings had tired for good, the moth had glowed a pale leafy green. Camouflaging, twig-shaped strokes of brown across the front of its forewings—complete with perfectly symmetrical spots parading as small leaves on each wing—had been its hope against hunters during its first week with wings and last week of life, bent on flight and reproduction and death. Long, brushy antennae hung in a dry wilt above its head. A blue band, freckled in white stars, hung around the corner of the display case. The band betrayed something hanging behind the case—something that would have been perfectly at home under the glass. She was about to reach for the band, when she heard a creak in the hallway. In the same instant, Michael said from behind her, "Something interesting?"

She turned and faced her brother, standing in the doorway. He looked tired, much more tired than a thirteen-year-old boy should look.

"No. Just the moth." She stepped away from the shelf.

Michael circled around her and stood near the shelf, the moth still showing a dim green over his shoulder. "What do you think?" he said. "Time to hang the old moon moth up somewhere?"

The fist she had carried in her stomach down the hall to his room relaxed. She threw herself into the distraction. "Yes, definitely. But we'll need to hang up other things to go with it. A moose head, for one."

"Or a rhino's head. That might be more dramatic."

"But then we'll have to wear pith helmets."

"Okay—forget the rhino head. But the moose head is asking for trouble, too. That's still a big jump—from moth to moose." He considered the moth, then turned to her. "What about the groundhog?"

"The groundhog is out of the question. And besides, no hunter could catch him."

"Right. I guess we'd better just leave the moth on the shelf, then. Save ourselves a lot of trouble."

"We could hang it in the tea house—"

An inaudible but profound thud—the moment collapsing to the floor—stopped her. She had hurried here with revelations to share and found herself even unable to enjoy her happy memories with Michael.

"No," Michael said, looking again at the moth. "Better leave it on the shelf."

Emily stepped away from the moth before she realized it. "Yes. Better leave it."

Michael moved toward the door.

Turning to follow, she said, "For now." And, "Michael," but he had already gone.

28.

THE TEA HOUSE

CHRISTMAS APPROACHED. SUNSETS DISSOLVED INTO BRIEF December twilights. The greater cold of approaching winter began to take root. Mary brought up the subject of getting a Christmas tree one morning at breakfast. There were shimmering crystal icicles to hang on the tree, bought in 1912 as a gift from Donald Stewart to his wife. There would be popcorn to string on long threads and wind around the tree. A fresh smell of pine would be in the air and on their fingers. Mary would light a fire; there would be hot chocolate. And the year would draw down.

During the last week of school before Christmas vacation, some of the instructors, even those inclined to be stern during much of the school year, allowed the children to play games. Some even led their classes in contests of word puzzles, important historical dates, and mathematical riddles. The younger students made decorations out of green and red paper, which the instructors hung over blackboards and windows. At one assembly, the pastor of St.

Anne's gave a lecture on the birth of Christ. "We must remember, children," he said, in a not-unfriendly tone, "amid all the fun, that the one who was born on Christmas Day also died on the cross for our sins. Remember, as you enjoy your holiday, that God so loved the world, he gave his only son."

Long after sunset that Friday, under a sky of bright and clear stars, a figure in flowing white moved through the streets of the neighborhood, trailed by its own billowing shadow. Light padding sounds followed the figure along the street, soft on the night wind. In one hand, the hurrying white form held something that could be mistaken for a walking stick at some distance, held away from its body, balanced forward like a kind of dowsing rod. The figure did not wander—it moved without doubt in the clear, small hours of the morning.

Emily awoke in the darkness of her bedroom, thinking that a muffled cracking sound—like the distant report of a rifle—still faded from her hearing. She held her breath and looked into the dark, convincing herself of the quiet. From outside the house, another loud report, coming through the closed windows of her bedroom in flattened tones. Though the cold night air outside scattered the sound, she thought that it reached the house from the cobblestone drive. Her skin pulled tight over her. She sat up in bed.

Another crack from outside, echoing off the house and spreading out over the river.

Emily jumped up from her bed and went out into the hallway. Stirring sounds came to her from Michael's room down the hall. Michael appeared in his doorway, eyes half closed, and blinked at Emily.

From the direction of Mary's room, Emily heard shuffling

footsteps approaching the door. Outside, another loud crack reverberated in the December night.

No, Emily thought. *No, no, no.*

She ran down the stairs and through the front hall. She pulled
back the latches on the door and threw it open on the clear cold
night outside. Down the cobblestone drive, at the threshold of the
tea house, a figure in white lurched backward and lunged forward.
The cracking noise—with some splintering in it—came to her
through the open door, loud, echoing, and ragged.

Light from the hallway upstairs spilled down the staircase.
Slippered feet hustled around the landing above. Emily could hear
voices—Mary's, her mother's.

No, she thought. *Go back to bed. This is for me.*

Emily ran across the porch and onto the cobblestone drive,
hardly aware of the cold stone beneath her bare feet. "Emily!" she
heard her mother call from the doorway.

The figure in white moved away from the tea house at the
sound and stepped out from under the portico over the door. In
the moonlight, less than ten yards away, Emily saw Mr. Dunne
in his nightshirt and boots. His breath tore out of him. His eyes
stood hard in a red, shaking face. In Mr. Dunne's right hand hung
a sledgehammer, which he raised and held before him, between
himself and Emily. Bloody streaks ran along Mr. Dunne's hands
and the shaft of the hammer. The pale fabric of his nightshirt—
tattered in places—bloomed with dark stains.

"Emily!" her mother called from behind, her voice moving closer,
down the cobblestone drive.

Mr. Dunne looked at Emily, then over her shoulder, then back
at Emily again, his eyes rolling and slow to focus.

"Mr. Dunne," Emily said, trying to steady her voice. "Please." She extended her hand, which shook before her.

He recoiled, his loose eyes glaring at her. *"No,"* he croaked. "You can't keep him from me. You won't bury my son." His eyes looked at her but did not see her. "So help me God, you will not put my boy in the ground." Stepping forward to the door of the tea house again, Mr. Dunne swung the sledgehammer with all of his force. The door, already splitting into jagged cracks, splintered down the center in a gaping hole. The two small windowpanes set in the top of the door shattered inward, tinkling on the floor within.

Her mother reached Emily and put her hands on the girl's shoulders to pull her back from the tea house. From behind her mother, Emily could hear Mary saying something, the commanding quality of her voice still detectable, though somewhat shaken.

Mr. Dunne stepped back from the broken door, bent over in his labored breathing, and looked into the dark interior of the tea house. He stood there for one long, floating moment, then his face contorted and he fumbled backward.

"Mr. Dunne," Emily heard Mary say, in a voice intended to soothe.

He slumped forward, barely keeping his feet, still looking into the darkened tea house, his eyes wide. The sledgehammer dropped from his right hand and clanged on the surface of the cobblestone drive. Mr. Dunne took another lurching step backward.

"Mr. Dunne," Mary said again.

On the street outside the estate, some of the neighbors had started to come out of their houses. A few robed figures had begun to cross the street to the closed front gate to get a better look at what the matter was.

"Please," Emily said.

His eyes rolled toward Emily, her mother, and Mary. He stepped back from them and turned his head toward the gate.

"Mrs. Stewart?" a man's voice called from the street.

Emily shook her mother's hands off her shoulders and stepped forward, holding her hand out to Mr. Dunne. In the dark beyond the shattered tea house door, a pale and slight form appeared, resolving as if out of nothing.

Emily, struck with a disorientation much more profound than the fright of confronting Mr. Dunne and his sledgehammer, lost all breath.

A head and shoulders in the dark, a hand on the splintered wood, a face streaked in dirt, dark eyes fixed on Mr. Dunne.

Mr. Dunne turned back toward the tea house and his face pulled up in a horrid grimace. Emily heard his breath hitch in his chest. The sound was as remote and unforgettable to her as the numb disconnect between her feet and the ground at that instant, as the cold air all around her and in her lungs.

Michael's face emerged from the dark, and Emily felt herself stiffen to the soles of her feet.

Mr. Dunne screamed then, a fractured sound like the splintering door. The scream settled over the tea house, the house behind them, and the river. Mr. Dunne turned to run toward the trees along the bank.

Mary and Mrs. Stewart followed. *"Mr. Dunne!"* Mrs. Stewart called. *"Mr. Dunne, listen to me!"*

Emily stood looking at Michael, who opened the broken door and stepped out in his dirty pajamas, as if he had crawled out from under the tea house. He looked at his sister like someone with nothing more to say.

Emily tore her eyes from Michael and turned to follow after Mary and her mother.

Mr. Dunne crashed through the bare shrubs, a ragged groan trailing behind him.

"Mary!—" Emily's mother called, rushing forward after Mr. Dunne when his groan became another short scream, followed by a sound like the riverbank sliding into the cold Delaware, busily making its way by under the moon.

September 3, 1939

The war has finally come. Hitler invaded Poland two days ago, and his panzers swept over the Polish army. The radio has been buzzing with it. This morning Chamberlain threw England's hat in. So it begins. A letter arrived yesterday from Mama in London, and she wrote some about the growing threat from Germany. I wonder what her next letter will say about Chamberlain's speech. I think she's afraid the U.S. will get tied up in all of this, like last time, and that Michael will run off and volunteer, as Daddy did. Maybe I should point out in reply that Michael's not the volunteering type, but I wonder if that would help. She doesn't know what to wish for in regard to her son.

Roosevelt was on the radio today. I sat in the sunporch alone, drinking tea and listening. He assured us of our neutrality. But, he said, he doesn't expect the American people to remain neutral in mind and body. A nudge?

So I sat and drank my tea and listened. I thought I would suffocate in this house alone, but it's been over two months since Mama and Mary left for Europe and I'm getting along fine. Becoming almost spinsterly, with my radio programs and my books and my tea. Mama said they'll be heading home soon, so my cloistered period is coming to a close. I sit on the gallery in the evenings sometimes, sipping my tea, and watching the river roll past. This journal business is all part of it—I haven't kept one since before college, before I was buried under papers and discourse and grades. And me putting my lot in with the dissectors. All that interpretation of neurosis and dementia. Four years of dreams and tics, of behavioral reasoning and clinical interest. In every portrait of Dr. Freud, in every probing look captured and deified for the ages, I saw James Randall, winking without actually winking. They will have me in grad school yet, though the years keep rolling by. I find myself taking those old doorstop textbooks down from the shelf and paging through them like the Sunday paper. I guess I will go when I am done with my radio programs and my books and my tea.

Michael calls every so often, and we talk about things. Another refugee from the university. He doesn't sound any more satisfied than he did a few months ago, but the cold mountain air suits him, it seems. Mama would have preferred he'd finished law school before disappearing into his hermitage, but she needn't worry. He could never stay out of the action too long. I think Mama has feared for some time that Michael would disappear in his wandering, like her brother did. I have imagined it myself: Michael, with a shaggy beard, turning his back on the world to lose himself in pursuit of that Sasquatch he's heard about in the Indians' stories. But I think that soon enough he will need assurance that the world is still here. I wonder myself what he'll have to say about the news. Maybe I'll call him before he can call me.

So all of this has gotten me thinking about old things. About Daddy, about the summer of 1925, about the tea house and everything else. So strange—I walk by that little redbrick house every day. Somehow I've gotten to the point that I only think about it if I stop and look at the place. I seldom think of the brick-lined tunnel running from the rathskeller to the tea house, though I walk over the tunnel several times a week. The entrances to the tunnel are bricked over now, but all that empty dank darkness is still there beneath the grass. My past floats around in my head, waiting to be noticed. It's amazing how willfully forgetful a person can be, and how much one can remember if one only concentrates.

For instance: I was going by the tea house this afternoon, and I looked out over the lawn in search of the groundhog. The groundhog—or I should say *this* groundhog; God knows how many this place has known—the groundhog has been very active this summer. Or perhaps not sly enough. Anyway, I've seen a lot of him. So when I go out, I take a look around. I very often find him. I went by the tea house and looked for the groundhog, but no luck. I found myself looking at the little house instead, at the replaced door that has hung in the doorway for almost fourteen years. And the memories of the place, dissolved down to old, unpleasant feelings, came together and were real for me again. And I found myself wanting to go over them, despite everything, because the old things need to be gone over sometimes.

The first person to spring to mind wasn't Albert or his father or Regina or even Michael, but Mr. Randall. That elusive old bear whom we met less than two months before Albert's death, the one who finished everything in trying to start it all anew. (I surprise myself at still insisting on putting it that way—"Albert's death.")

And Mr. Randall finished things and then finished them again. In late January, after Mama knew most of what had happened since the June before, a letter arrived, addressed to my mother, with the return address of a hotel in Hydesville, New York. I was reading in the sunporch when Mama walked in holding the opened envelope. She'd recently grown accustomed to severe shocks and mysterious claims. "Who is 'J. Randall,' Emily?" she asked in a casual way.

In all of our confessions that past December, neither Michael nor I had ever breathed the name of James Randall, only one of the man's many names. So I made my explanations, and Michael made his—telling me the details of his walk in the woods with Mr. Randall for the first time. When we told Mama that Mr. Randall had first appeared as the Astonishing Antoine at Aunt Becky's party, she had only shaken her head and said, "Of course. Of course he was."

Mama showed us the letter, typed up in neat lines, except for the lowercase *r*'s, which hung slightly below the other letters. The letter went something like this:

```
Mrs. Stewart,


    I haven't had the pleasure of making
your acquaintance yet, but I am a concerned
friend of your twins. Emily and Michael, as
you well know, are possessed of remarkable
talents, unlike any pair of children I
have met before. I would be pleased to
come by your beautiful home and discuss
```

these talents further with you in person, if
you'll have me. Your twins have gifts that
are of great interest to many—many, many
more than you might imagine. Please let me
know when such a visit would be appropriate.
I am prepared to travel on your answer.

Very best regards,
J. Randall

Mama prepared her response with Michael and me, allowing us to read it before she sealed it in an envelope and instructed us to take it down to the mailbox. When she handed us the sealed envelope—well, she handed it to Michael, but we both went down to the mailbox together—she said, "There. I think that does it." Her letter was very short.

Dear Mr. Randall,

Thank you for your kind offer, but I have discussed this matter with Emily and Michael, and we have come to our own conclusions. A visit, though generously offered, isn't necessary—and I would have to make places at the table for my attorney and, perhaps, one or two other officers of the court, in any case.

Best of luck,
Naomi Stewart

This letter raised questions in my mind—then and now—about other letters my mother may or may not have written at that time. I couldn't help but think of Stan Loewry when Mama took a week-long trip to Newport, even though years and years had passed by then; and when Mama booked passage to Europe, a similar shadow moved in my mind, even though Mary had gone along as Mama's companion. I have never asked Mama about Stan, his letters, or any of that. I thought for some time that I would, as the years went by. But as the years went by, I acquired the habit of not asking, and found myself not wanting an answer, despite my occasional curiosity.

While I'm on the subject of stirring shadows, the letter above was not James Randall's last one to Ravenwood. One more short note, addressed to Michael, arrived a few months later, bearing no return address, and stuck in the keys of an old typewriter cast in wrought iron, with silvery patterns of wild growing things on its sides. The toothy guts of it showed beneath its roller and knobs, which stood on struts like columns in an altar. The keys were pearly white and beaten to a burnished glow. When I found the typewriter holding the envelope like a faithful dog at the end of the drive, a billowing, purple-lined cape may as well have been pulled away to reveal it there. Michael still has the old, heavy thing, somewhere. He wrote his school papers on it until his professors complained of the *r*'s, hanging out of step and calling every sentence into question. The note inside was very brief.

```
Best of luck to you, young man. There is
a place for you in the larger world, if you
will only rise to take it.
```

It was the last note Michael received from the Astonishing Mr. Randall, as far as I know, and the old magician has moved on to other things in the larger world.

And, of course, in all these tea house thoughts, there is Mr. Dunne. I remember how he looked at me that night outside the tea house. His eyes, his torn clothes, the hammer—and the blood. Michael emerging from inside the tea house—how I fully saw him there, brother of my childhood, a moment before knowing him from the ghost Mr. Dunne thought he saw. And the fall. I was sure that when we reached the bank, Mr. Dunne would be dead at the bottom. But there he was, straightening himself up on one arm, sitting in the freezing river water, making a low moaning sound in his throat. I remember going down the bank with Mary and Mama in a sort of dream. Mary was saying, "It's all right. Be still now. We're here to help you." Mr. Dunne let the three of us hoist him out of the water and place him on the bank. He allowed it, I imagine, because his mind had not moved at all from the cold river water, except when his broken bones seared through the haze. He made a gurgling noise then that turned to a scream, then the scream dropped off into the same low, droning moan. Mary took my shoulder and looked in my eyes. "Run and get blankets, Em," she said. I scrambled up the bank, glad to get away from his pain. Michael stood at the top of the bank and watched. His face looked very small and pale in the moonlight. I will never forget that, either. And on the street I heard the ambulance arriving, and the dream that had begun the previous June was over.

Mr. Dunne convalesced a long time after. The nurse that cared for him would pass me on the street from time to time, and I swore she looked at me with cold accusation. Invariably I would drop my eyes from hers. My mother paid that nurse's wages, along with many of Mr. Dunne's other medical expenses—an arrangement she made with Mrs. Dunne only two days after that night in December. Mrs. Dunne, who had been allegedly hiding from the neighborhood all those years to protect her spun-glass nerves, sat in the sunporch with Mama and worked out all of the particulars with a very self-possessed demeanor for a woman whose husband had attacked the tea house with a hammer, then nearly killed himself out by the river. Mama's arrangement with Mrs. Dunne alleviated my guilt a bit—very slightly, almost imperceptibly—but I have heard it said that beggars can't be choosers.

Mr. Dunne died less than a year ago of a stroke. Mama offered to pay for the funeral, but Mrs. Dunne told her she had done enough. She would bury her own husband, I believe she told my mother. I could not bring myself to attend the funeral, though Mama and Mary went. I thought of writing an apologetic letter to Mrs. Dunne, but couldn't bring myself to do that, either.

I have often remembered the expression on Mr. Dunne's face when he looked through the broken door of the tea house and saw Michael there in the dark. That expression has been a part of my night thoughts for years. I know Michael seemed a ghost to him, but whether of Albert or Patrick or some combination of the two I can't say. But when Michael stood in that doorway, streaked in mud from the old tunnel under the tea house, whatever Mr. Dunne had come prepared to do he could no longer bear.

Of course he came to the tea house that night to get his boys. Albert was the first to tell him about the tea house, about its ghosts. I gave him Patrick back and took him away again. And in that rescinding moment, a sort of Passion Play in reverse was performed, which pulled Christ out of his ascent to heaven and dropped him back into his crude, discarded mold to walk the world again, only to die and be packed into a tomb (and from here to wander a weary while in hell); to be carried from this dusty tomb and crucified into renewed, pained breath; to be taken down from the cross—beaten, scorned, but full of hope—and hauled backward through thirty-three years to a miraculous womb that closed up behind and forgot the infant, leaving for the world a certain end.

Somehow the information reached us—as neighborhood information can, even to a household of recluses—that Mr. Dunne had skipped a few dosages of the medication he had been taking since before Albert's death. I have never known whether or not this is true, but it has been assembled in my mind with other fragments and notions into a story that I have gone over and over while lying in bed. In this story, Mr. Dunne puts some sort of pill in his mouth, a pill Mrs. Dunne brought to him, along with the obligatory cup of water, and Mr. Dunne takes the cup of water and docilely sips from it. As soon as Mrs. Dunne turns her back—perhaps on her way out of the room with the empty glass—Mr. Dunne removes the pill from under his tongue and tosses it into the wastebasket beside the bed. The pill is one of many he has recently disposed of; something buried in his deep-down, private darkness made the peace of the pills seem an intolerable insult. And now the dreams had returned—slow at first, but steady. That very afternoon he had awakened from a dream of his boys, locked away from him. And he couldn't let the little pills wash the dream out of his mind, because the dream is more important than anything he has felt in quite some time.

Lying in the dark beside his wife, Mr. Dunne looks up at the ceiling and holds on to the dream. He waits. Waits for his wife's sleep to settle into deep, steady breathing. Until the moment to climb out of bed has come, when the dream burned in his mind, the moment to slip downstairs, take the sledgehammer from the basement, and steal out onto the street. Outside: the dark street, the gate, the drive, and the door—all making up a vast space between Mr. Dunne and his sons. And when he shatters the barrier and looks through the broken door, there is the pale, slight boy, emerged from the ground, reaching out to him. Michael had discovered the key to the door built into one of the benches in the rathskeller, the secret door that covered the tunnel leading out to the tea house. The tunnel Mama and Mary later explained our great-grandfather Robert Ward had included in the original plans for the mansion and garden house; that two people close together could walk through, side by side; the tunnel Robert had drawn into his dream of Ravenwood as a way for him and Addie to escape the house unseen.

Michael had explored the mystery of the tunnel alone with an old gas lantern, finding the exit hidden in the hearth in the tea house. He still hadn't decided whether or not to share his newfound secret with me when Mr. Dunne had brought his sledgehammer to the tea house. When he realized the trouble was there that night, Michael had gone on impulse to the rathskeller and scrambled through the dark tunnel, fumbling his way with his hands. I asked Michael once why he had done it, if he had thought he could get out there first that way, what he would have done if Mr. Dunne had gone to him instead of running. Michael shrugged and said, "I had to do it." I have never asked him for more of an answer, though it has occurred to me that Michael knew nothing of my visits to Mr. Dunne then, and couldn't have known Mr. Dunne was out there, or what he was after. I suppose that Michael, like me, felt that whatever was happening out there was for him, and that he had to get there alone.

This old story was stirred when I stood outside the tea house today, and another along with it. I can tell the second one with a little more accuracy, having been there for all of it. It happened on an afternoon in December, ten years after Mr. Dunne's fall. I was opening one of the curtains at the front of the house to let some sun in and saw two ladies down the drive, standing in front of the tea house. Even from the window, after all those years, I was pretty sure I knew one of them. Normally I would have been inclined to simply watch them from there until they moved on. Instead I put on my coat and walked down the cobblestone drive to meet my visitors, feeling a little outraged all of a sudden.

I heard Mrs. Nerova's voice before I saw her face. She and her friend were both swaddled up in woolen scarves and hats, their faces obscured even when they turned to me at the sound of my boots on the cobblestones.

"Hello, ladies," I said, making an effort to be pleasant. "Mrs. Nerova, it has been a very long time."

Mrs. Nerova looked at me with searching eyes. She must have been in her early sixties by then—a decade of lines around her eyes and nose marked the time between.

"Right, a long time," she said. "I've only seen this," meaning the tea house, "from outside the gate. But today I walk by with Rosa," at the sound of her name, the other lady nodded at me, "and the gate was open—it is never open—and I had to show her. Which is all right?"

"It's fine, Mrs. Nerova." I was beginning to feel ashamed at my irritation. It seemed to me then—and seems to me now—that she was one of a very select group of people who owned a piece of the tea house, even though she had never been inside it. And this partial ownership gave her all the rights I had to it and perhaps more. "I'm glad to see you."

"Right, right. You too. So, Rosa, this is girl I told you about."

Mrs. Nerova's friend Rosa nodded again.

Then Mrs. Nerova, never a one for small talk, said, "I told Rosa all about this house, and you—she has heard it before, but today, the gate was open, and I thought . . ." She shrugged and cleared her throat. "Do you still practice?" she asked.

My utter discomfort regarding the subject must have been very strong and clear, because Mrs. Nerova waved the answer away before I could give it and said, "I understand. You want to be left alone."

"Mrs. Nerova—"

"No, no. Don't be ashamed. You can never be ashamed—none of that was your fault, Emily," she said, as if she'd been meaning to for many years.

Mrs. Nerova and I looked at each other; Rosa pretended to not understand the remark, and looked off at the trees.

"Come on," Mrs. Nerova said to Rosa, and they turned to walk down the drive to the gate. I watched them go, letting them reach the gate at the foot of the drive before calling after them. Mrs. Nerova and Rosa turned back with expectant faces. "Mrs. Nerova, I have to tell you something. It's about spirit knocking." I had the frantic feeling they would both begin laughing, which brought on a feeling of hot despair that almost got the better of me. An indiscriminate and unjust anger was close behind.

"It's a trick, Mrs. Nerova. It's a trick I did with my ankle—I can still do it."

Exchanging a look with her friend, Mrs. Nerova turned a smile on me. "We won't bother you," she said. "I understand you want peace and quiet. I understand."

"Mrs. Nerova," I said, a desperate child again, "I'm telling you the truth." I started to put my right foot forward, and felt transported back to Mr. Dunne's living room, putting my foot before his disbelieving eyes. This memory did not help matters. I made a crisp knocking sound in the December air, and the two ladies looked at my foot and then at me. Rosa, expressionless, like a person witnessing a family quarrel, unable to feign ignorance any further.

Mrs. Nerova shook her head, a generous and indulgent gesture, a saint receiving an afflicted fool.

"But—it's a trick! I can do it as many times as I want." To prove this, I made a series of sounds, varying them a bit in tempo.

She reached out and took my hand. "We're going, we won't bother you. But you come see me, whenever you like." And she squeezed my hand to let me know she meant it. She leaned in close and winked at me. "You know—they don't burn witches anymore." Then the two ladies went again on their way down the street. I stood alone on the drive, a bit out of breath. And I suddenly wished for Michael's company. I went back up the drive feeling like the only living thing for miles, and a very small living thing at that, while the groundhog slept in the earth somewhere nearby, dreaming his old collected dreams.

ACKNOWLEDGMENTS

Many thanks to my agent, Dan Lazar, and my editor, Amy Einhorn—two exceptional people from a world larger than my own who believed in this book. Their guidance and dedication made all of the difference. Very special thanks also to M. J. Rose, who fished me out of obscurity. For her talents, my admiration; for her enthusiasm and support, my everlasting gratitude.

ABOUT THE AUTHOR

Paul Elwork graduated from Temple University with a bachelor's degree in anthropology and Arcadia University with a master's degree in English. His stories have appeared in a variety of literary journals. *The Girl Who Would Speak for the Dead* is his first novel.